The Macmillan Students' Hardy
Advisory Editor: James Gibson

Under the Greenwood Tree

Other titles in the series

The Macmillan Students' Hardy

Under the Greenwood Tree

or The Mellstock Quire
A Rural Painting of the Dutch School

by Thomas Hardy

Edited with introduction and notes by
Anna Winchcombe

Macmillan Education

First published 1975

Published by
Macmillan Education Ltd
London and Basingstoke

Associated companies and representatives
throughout the world

Printed in Great Britain by
Richard Clay (The Chaucer Press), Ltd,
Bungay, Suffolk

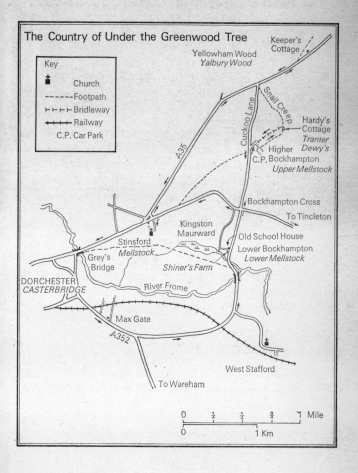

The Country of Under the Greenwood Tree

Keeper's Cottage

Yellowham Wood
Yalbury Wood

Key

✝ Church
---- Footpath
+-+- Bridleway
+++ Railway
C.P. Car Park

Snail Creep

Cuckoo Lane

A35

Hardy's Cottage
Tranter Dewy's
Higher Bockhampton
C.P.
Upper Mellstock

Bockhampton Cross

To Tincleton

Kingston Maurward

Old School House

Lower Bockhampton
Lower Mellstock

Stinsford
Mellstock

Grey's Bridge

Shiner's Farm

DORCHESTER
CASTERBRIDGE

River Frome

Max Gate

A352

West Stafford

To Wareham

0   ¼   ½   ¾   1 Mile

0   1 Km

List of Illustrations

Acknowledgements

The author and publishers wish to thank the following, who have kindly given permission for the illustrations to be reproduced:

The Trustees of the Thomas Hardy Memorial Collection: Plates 1, 2, 3, and 7
The National Trust: Plates 4 and 5
James and Gregory Stevens Cox, editors of The Thomas Hardy Year Book, copyright owners of the works of the late Hermann Lea: Plate 9.

The Life of Thomas Hardy, 1840–1928

1840   Born on 2 June at Higher Bockhampton, three miles from Dorchester. Began reading at an early age.

1848   Entered the new school at Lower Bockhampton. Transferred the following year to a private school at Dorchester.

1856   Became articled to John Hicks, a Dorchester architect. He described his life at this time as made up of three strands – the professional life, the scholar's life, and the rustic life.

1862   Began more advanced architectural work with a London firm. Took great interest in the cultural life of the capital, became enthusiastic about poetry, wrote many poems but failed to get any published.

1867   Returned home, assisted Hicks in church restoration, and finished the first draft of a novel by January 1868. It was never published.

1870   Visited St Juliot in Cornwall to plan the restoration of the parish church, and fell in love with Emma Gifford.

1871   *Desperate Remedies* was published. It was followed by *Under the Greenwood Tree* (1872), *A Pair of Blue Eyes* (1873), and *Far from the Madding Crowd* (1874).

1874   His growing success as a novelist encouraged Hardy and Emma Gifford to marry. During the next few years they lived in London, at Yeovil, and at Sturminster Newton, where *The Return of the Native* was written.

1878   Before this novel was published, they returned to

London, where Hardy worked on *The Trumpet-Major* (1880). In 1881 they moved to Wimborne. He had written a number of short stories and was to write many more, eventually collected into four volumes.

1883 When the Hardys moved to Dorchester, two more novels had been completed. Here *The Mayor of Casterbridge* was written.

1885 They moved into Max Gate, the house on the outskirts of Dorchester which Hardy had designed for himself. Here he wrote *The Woodlanders* (1887), *Tess of the d'Urbervilles* (1891), and *Jude the Obscure* (1895).

1896 The unkind reception *Jude* received from the critics, together with a growing financial independence and perhaps the feeling that he had achieved all that he could hope to do in the novel, meant that he could now turn to his first love – poetry.

1898 *Wessex Poems*, his first book of verse, published.

1902 Began, after planning it for years, *The Dynasts*, an epic drama on the Napoleonic War. It was published in three parts from 1904 to 1908.

1910 He received the Order of Merit and the freedom of Dorchester.

1912 His wife died suddenly. Hardy, smitten with remorse for their differences and the coldness of the latter years of their marriage, wrote many poems (over a long period) about his recollections of her.

1914 Married Florence Dugdale. The outbreak of the First World War made him regret having ended *The Dynasts* optimistically for the future of mankind.

1928 He died on 11 January. His last volume of verse, his eighth, appeared posthumously. Although his first books of verse had been indifferently received, he was by now regarded not only as a great novelist but as a great poet.

Hardy was born when Queen Victoria, who became Queen in 1837, was twenty-one. His life covers most of her long reign, that of Edward VII, and most of the reign of George V. He lived through nearly a century of increasingly rapid change. When he was born the railway had not yet reached Dorset, and public hangings were common. His grandmother talked to him about her memories of the French Revolution and the Napoleonic War, and he grew up in a small, closely-knit rural community which had seen little change for centuries. Hardy himself was to see that community radically altered by the impact of new ideas and inventions. Modern methods of travel and communication destroyed the traditions and the isolation and unity of the old village life, and brought about big changes in outlook and behaviour.

Scientific discoveries had led to a questioning of religious beliefs seldom doubted before. The simple faith of Hardy's parents, who took him as a boy to Stinsford church, was not possible for Hardy, who, like other distinguished Victorian writers, found himself torn between a desire to believe and an intellectual inability to do so. His wide reading and great intelligence made him aware of these changes; his honesty would not allow him to dodge their implications.

His loss of faith was one of the reasons for the sadness which permeates a great deal of his writing. Yet he consistently believed that the maintenance of Christian virtues was the only hope for mankind in the modern scientific age. He had a sensitive awareness of history and of the transience of human life, and much of his best poetry springs from this. It deals with events as remote as the Roman occupation of Britain and as recent for him as the sinking of the *Titanic* and the holocaust of the First World War. His novels were all written in the nineteenth century and deal with many aspects of the immediate past of that part of England, centred in Dorset, which for historical reasons he chose to call 'Wessex'. To appreciate Hardy's work fully it is necessary to share his

sense of history, his awareness of man's place in a universe
which seems indifferent to him, and his conviction that what
he liked to call 'loving-kindness' must govern our behaviour
if there is to be any hope for the human race.

Introduction

Publication

Under the Greenwood Tree was published in June 1872 but when we read the account in Hardy's *Life* of the path the manuscript followed up to the time of publication it is surprising that it ever got into print. Hardy had already written two novels. The first, entitled *The Poor Man and the Lady*, was turned down by two publishing firms, Macmillan and Chapman and Hall, the reader for the latter firm being the well-known novelist and poet George Meredith, who saw the young Hardy personally and advised him to put such a satirical and even revolutionary work aside because 'the press would be about his ears like hornets' if he published. Meredith also told him to try his hand at a 'purely artistic' novel with a strong plot. Hardy obediently followed this advice, abandoned the first story, and produced a second which he called *Desperate Remedies*, with a complicated and melodramatic plot, which was brought out partly at his own expense by yet a third firm, that of Tinsley Brothers, in March 1871. This novel appeared anonymously, a common practice in those days, and received mixed notices from the critics including a particularly bad one in *The Spectator* which stated that it was a 'desperate remedy for an emaciated purse'. This affected Hardy deeply at the time but he soon recovered his belief in himself sufficiently to begin work, in the summer of 1871 while in lodgings at Weymouth, on a third book which he describes in the *Life* as a 'short and quite rustic story'.

Its first title was *The Mellstock Quire* but this was later changed to *Under the Greenwood Tree*, 'as titles from poetry were in fashion just then'. The quotation is from Shakespeare's *As You Like It* and is the first line of the song Amiens sings in Act 2, Scene 5:

> Under the greenwood tree
> Who loves to lie with me,
> And turn his merry note
> Unto the sweet bird's throat.

He sent the manuscript this time to Macmillan and received a letter from them which he understood to be a refusal to publish it. Only later did he discover that they would have been willing to bring it out 'a little later on'. Being sensitive about rejections now, he got the manuscript back from them, threw it into a box along with some old poems, and began to think about his architectural career again, in spite of the fact that the young woman he wanted to marry, Emma Gifford, asked him to continue with writing as it was his true vocation. In the spring of 1872 he met Tinsley, the publisher of his first novel, who asked him when he was going to let him have another book. 'Never,' answered Hardy, thinking of the poor financial return from *Desperate Remedies*, over which he had lost £15 of his own money. 'Wot, now!' said Tinsley. 'Haven't you anything written?' Hardy told him that he had finished a short novel some time before but he did not know where the manuscript was and did not care. But he did ask his parents to search for it and when they found it he forwarded it to Tinsley without looking at it, merely saying that he did not want to have anything to do with the publishing accounts. Tinsley offered him £30 for the copyright and later added £10 for the Continental rights. Early in May 1872 Hardy corrected the proofs of his 'rustic story' in his London lodgings and at last, in the following month, *Under the Greenwood Tree* appeared and met with a 'very kindly and gentle reception'.

The story

In July 1871 Hardy had placed a marginal mark against two lines of *Macbeth* in his volume of Shakespeare's plays:

> Things at their worst will cease, or else climb upward
> To what they were before.

This was a guardedly optimistic statement and one that expressed his mood at the time. Later that summer, when he was writing *Under the Greenwood Tree*, he must surely have felt that the 'climb upward' had begun, for the novel seems to have been produced by a relatively happy man, one who was trying his hand at something he was best suited to do. He forgot about melodramatic plots and characters that were then outside the range of his experience and concentrated effortlessly, it seems, on the district around his home and the people who lived there. The action takes place in what are in real life the two hamlets of Higher and Lower Bockhampton, three miles from Dorchester, and in the church of Stinsford in the same parish, to all of which he gave the sweet-sounding name of Mellstock. The members of the Dewy family, tranters or carriers of Upper Mellstock in the novel, bear a strong likeness to the Hardy family, though the author's father and grandfather were builders and stonemasons and Hardy once stated that there was no resemblance between the Dewys and the Hardys. This was typical of his constant desire to avoid identifying any of his characters too definitely with real people, a feeling that probably arose from the closeness of the community in which he lived for most of his life. Other characters in the novel are remembered from his childhood and youth and even from stories of people who died before he was born, and they take part in activities familiar to him and speak the language he knew well.

The first page of the manuscript of the novel, in Hardy's clear, very modern handwriting, bears the original title of

The Mellstock Quire crossed out and *Under the Greenwood Tree* put in its place , with the subtitle of *A Rural Painting of the Dutch School* under it, an indication of how the author saw his work as a placid picture of rustic life, though this is not a strictly true description even of this novel. The opening passage about the different voices of the trees is a piece of Hardy's poetic style at its best and sets the tone of the background to this country drama. Hardy was not a trained naturalist but an inspired writer about Nature and all through the book there are revealing descriptions of scenes through all the seasons of the year.

The story starts like a simple theme in music, with the tale of the tranter's son falling in love with the village schoolmistress. There is a second theme, of no less importance, that deals with the fate of the village choir, whose string orchestra has played at the church service for many years but is finally replaced by the new organ which the heroine herself plays, a fact that adds a certain complication to the plot, for young Dick Dewy is a member of the outgoing choir and yet is devoted to the intruder. Throughout the novel there are deeper notes to be heard and the contest between Dick and his two rivals for Fancy's affections and between the choir and the organ can be seen to be symbolic of greater issues, of the contest between the old ways and the new that so often creates tensions in Hardy's writings. The machine that replaces human labour is in this case the mechanical music-maker, while the civilized manners that disrupt the old village communities are embodied in Fancy Day, with her training-college education. Like several of Hardy's other heroines she has to choose between the countryman and the more sophisticated man from outside the community, and the fact that she makes, in this instance, the right choice for her future husband allows the story to end happily. But the choir loses its battle with the enemy and a feeling of sadness creeps even into this light-hearted book.

Hardy could not have heard the little orchestra of violins and bass-viols playing in his village church of Stinsford as it had been disbanded when he was about a year old, but he had heard many tales about it from his parents and grandmother and he describes the individual members of his Mellstock Choir with sympathy and love. Later on, however, he felt that he had rather burlesqued them, 'the story not so adequately reflecting as he could have wished in later years the poetry and romance that coloured their time-honoured observances'. The men are introduced in the first chapter when Dick Dewy meets them on Christmas Eve at Mellstock Cross as they are on their way to the tranter's house to choose the tunes for the carol singing. Their outlines appear to Dick against the sky like black silhouette portraits and it is at first only in outline they are described. There is Michael Mail who seems to be 'engaged in studying some object connected with the surface of the road' and Robert Penny, the little, bespectacled shoemaker who was drawn from the real-life Robert Reason, who had a shop in Lower Bockhampton before Hardy's time. Following him are Elias Spinks, 'who walked perpendicularly and dramatically' and Joseph Bowman 'of no distinctive appearance' and Thomas Leaf, a weak young man who shambled along, 'his arms dangling nervelessly in the wind as if they were empty sleeves'. Up at the tranter's house, Reuben Dewy, his wife and four younger children and the two grandfathers, William and old James, are added to the cast of this rural drama and it is worth noting with what ease the young novelist manipulates his characters and sets his scene. The Dewys' 'long, low cottage with a hipped roof of thatch' is described lovingly since it is really the Hardys' house that he is talking about, where most of the novel was written and which was Thomas Hardy's home for about thirty-four years. Here the real choir would meet in the early years of the last century to practise their hymns and to prepare for the Christmas Eve carols. 'The rule was,' writes Hardy, 'to go to the northern part of the parish and play at every house before supper; then to return to Bockhampton and sit over the meal till twelve o'clock, during which interval a good deal was consumed at the Hardys' expense, the choir being mainly poor men and hungry.' In one of the poems that he writes about the cottage, *The House of Hospitalities*, Hardy remembers the Christmas festivities of the old days and regrets their passing:

> Yet at midnight if here walking
>   When the moon sheets wall and tree,
> I see forms of old time talking,
>   Who smile on me.

Much of the action in *Under the Greenwood Tree* is carried on in dialogue and Hardy's countrymen express themselves in his version of Dorset speech, skilfully modified to give the actual tones of these people without being unintelligible to an outsider. The heroine is introduced during a conversation about her pretty boot which the shoemaker has mended and he speaks of her as 'as neat a little figure of fun as ever I see, and just husband-high' which rouses Dick's interest and ours, so that when the choir, joined by the singing-boys in white smocks, goes the round of the parish and tunes up with 'Remember Adam's fall, O thou Man' outside the schoolhouse, we are as eager as Dick to see if the young lady will appear. But it is not until two more hymns are sung that a light comes on from an upstairs window and Fancy Day, wrapped in a white robe and with her 'marvellously rich hair' falling about her, looks out to thank them. From that dramatic moment Dick's heart is lost to the young woman and the story of his pursuit of her is started, and, as the review in the *Athenaeum* said in 1872, it is a book which could make people 'give up valuable time to see a marriage accomplished in its pages'. Dick's two rivals are humorously introduced in the next chapter in an unfavourable light, the crude Farmer Shiner roaring at the singers, 'Don't make your blaring row here!' and the tactful vicar calling, 'Thanks, villagers!' from the depths of the bedclothes. With these slight touches Hardy assembles his cast of players and sets the drama going. Although in later life he liked to say that he only wrote his novels in order to make a living and that poetry was his first and greater love, it is clear from *Under the Greenwood Tree* that, even at this early stage in his career, he shows in his characterisation, descriptive power, and ability to construct a good story that he has the makings of a great novelist.

One of the most entertaining scenes in the novel now follows, the party in the tranter's cottage. Hardy always loved music and the excitement of country dances. From the age of twelve onwards he had played the fiddle at village weddings, at parties in neighbouring farmhouses, and once at a homestead to 'twelve tireless couples in the favourite country-dance of "The New-Rigged Ship" ' when the hostess had to stop him after three-quarters of an hour of non-stop playing lest he should 'burst a blood-vessel'. There is frequently a description of a dance in his work and those who like to find patterns in his writings may feel that his heroes and heroines perform a kind of symbolic dance in their relationships with one another, first approaching and then withdrawing, as Dick and Fancy do here, while the other characters join in the movements also.

But there are many patterns in Hardy's work and his use of symbols is always interesting. For instance, in *Under the Greenwood Tree*, shoes and boots seem to have some symbolic meaning for Hardy and to be used as indications of people's characters and ways of life, so that Fancy Day appears at first, as we have seen, only as 'a small, light, and prettily shaped boot', her grandfather's boots show that he had had a hard life, with his large bunions and his foot damaged by being trodden on by a horse, the growing up of a family is indicated by the time when 'the oldest daughter's boots be only a size less than her mother's, and the rest of the flock close behind her'. Bees are another symbol used here and elsewhere by Hardy with romantic connotations, with ideas of courtship, love, and procreation connected with the taking of the honey from the bees and the swarming of the hives.

The dance at the tranter's is a beautifully observed, comic occasion where the heroine flits from Dick to Farmer Shiner and back to Dick again and where the other characters form a lively background. The dance tune with its title – 'Triumph, or Follow my Lover' – is symbolic and Dick is totally involved in pursuing the beautiful girl whose dark eyes were 'arched by brows of so keen, slender, and soft a curve that they resembled nothing so much as two slurs in music'. The Dewys and the Pennys whirl around with them and the large Mrs Crumpler, 'moved so smoothly through the figure that her feet were never seen: conveying to imaginative minds the idea that she rolled on castors'. The sitting-room at the cottage at Higher Bockhampton still has the stone floor that was sanded to make it slippery and the 'beam bisecting the ceiling' where the mistletoe hung. 'Imaginative minds' can picture the boy Hardy observing a family party from one of the wide window-seats, for he makes the room bigger than it really was and notes details with the clear eyes of a child – seeing the bluish mist being raised by the dust from the floor, waistcoats having to be unbuttoned, ladies' back-hair 'looking forlorn and dissipated', skirts torn out of their gathers, and the fiddlers' chairs moving, as a result of their frantic playing, 'to a distance of about two feet from where they originally stood'.

In a series of vivid scenes the story continues and Dick's courtship of Fancy Day results at last in the young lady accepting him, in spite of open competition from Mr Shiner and overtures from the vicar about which Dick knows nothing. The choir, on the other hand, cannot persuade the vicar to let them remain as the providers of the church music and they attend the Harvest Thanksgiving service at last and sit around awkwardly in the congregation instead of in their usual place in the gallery, and watch their supplanter with her 'curls and a hat and feather', playing in the chancel. Hardy comments: 'The venerable body of musicians could not help thinking that the simpler notes they had been wont to bring forth were more in keeping with the simplicity of their old church than the crowded chords and interludes it was her pleasure to produce.' This is also Hardy's opinion, for he regretted the disappearance of the old choirs. In spite of this sad end to their activities, some of the choir members, however, join in Fancy's wedding celebrations and walk in the wedding procession afterwards, 'Now among dark perpendicular firs, like the shafted columns of a cathedral; now through a hazel copse, matted with primroses and wild hyacinths; now under broad beeches in bright young leaves'.

There is another dance on the wedding night, under the great tree by the house of Fancy's father in Yalbury Wood, a dance somehow more decorous than the first one, a marriage celebration with 'Haste to the Wedding' as one of the five tunes for the country dances, and everyone behaving with great propriety under the influence of the rather snobbish little heroine who quickly becomes accustomed to her matronly position. It is a charming picture of rural England, with the young people a 'whirling throng' in the centre and the older ones sitting under the trunk of the tree commenting on the happy married life that lies before the lucky couple.

Characters

There are evidences all through the book, however, that Hardy is not as sure as these old people are that Dick and Fancy have a very placid future before them.

His handling of the love theme is especially clever in this
novel and Fancy is a subtly drawn character, who gives
clear indications of Hardy's attitude to women at this stage
in his life. As a very young man he had an impressionable
nature and was romantically attracted to various young
women, some of whom he only knew from passing them in
the lane near his home or in the neighbouring towns. He was
very fond of his cousins in Puddletown, the Sparks family,
and even wanted to marry two of the girls, Martha and
Tryphena, and became engaged to the latter before he met
his first wife, Emma. One can see in Fancy the first sketch of
a very Hardyish heroine, who may well have been based on
this cousin and who later in the novels develops into more
complicated characters, such as Sue Bridehead in *Jude the
Obscure*. Fancy is elusive, tantalising, flirtatious, not altogether truthful and frank as Dick is and not, perhaps, quite
a suitable wife for him. Hardy speaks in a rather sardonic
way about 'those beautiful eyes of hers – too refined and
beautiful for a tranter's wife' and grandfather James asks, 'I
wonder which she thinks most about, Dick or her wedding
raiment?' The author seems to feel a little pity for Dick and
the tranter defines his son's love as a 'zickness. Distance
belongs to it, shyness belongs to it, queerest things on earth
belong to it! There, 'tmay as well come early as late s'far as I
know. The sooner begun, the sooner over; for come it will.'
Hardy's views on the courtship seem fairly optimistic and at
least he makes Fancy refuse the offer of marriage from the
vicar, though she is sorely tempted by the thought of what
being a vicar's wife would mean – among other things, 'a
pony-carriage, birds, pleasant society'. But this proposal she
is obviously going to keep secret from Dick all her life, even
though the trusting young husband believes they are happy
'because there is such full confidence between us'.

Dick develops during the course of the novel from the
carefree young man who first appears singing as he walks

round the lanes of Mellstock to the rather bewildered but still determined lover and finally to the newly married man beginning to realise what his responsibilities are going to be towards his wife. He is long-suffering but yet capable of an outburst of temper when Fancy tries him too hard, then is easily disheartened by Geoffrey Day's insistence that his daughter is too good for a tranter's son. Most of the characters in this novel, apart from Parson Maybold, are villagers, but Hardy takes great pains to point out the subtle class distinctions that existed even in this community, and Dick is made to see that he should not aspire to marry a 'Government teacher'. Fancy also has her moments of doubt when she is told of a rival who has danced with Dick: 'Her father farms five hundred acres and she could marry a doctor or a curate or anything of that kind if she contrived a little,' and although the vicar proposes to Fancy herself he makes it clear that they could not go on living in Mellstock if they were married. That Hardy did not agree with these snobbish notions is clear from the way in which he draws the other figures in the story, the sensible, kindly elder Dewys, and the lovable members of the choir. Here and in his poems on the choir's activities Hardy has made these singers and players into almost legendary characters. They are much more than a chorus commenting on the actions of the other people in the book, they are important actors in the drama and have a greatness of their own. Hardy repeats their names like a chant – Reuben Dewy, Robert Penny, Elias Spinks, Joseph Bowman, Thomas Leaf. Perhaps the most rugged of all of them is Grandfather William, likened to the greenwood tree itself as Hardy describes him standing nobly in the light of the setting sun 'which gave him a Titanic shadow at least thirty feet in length, stretching away to the east in outlines of imposing magnitude, his head finally terminating upon the trunk of a grand old oak tree'.

Geoffrey Day and his second wife are realistically drawn,

the man so silent, stubborn, and single-minded yet easily worked upon by his clever daughter who gets her own way with him just as she will probably do with her husband. The stepmother shows great snobbery and sensitivity which are qualities already shared in a minor degree by Fancy herself. Farmer Shiner and the vicar make up the list of characters, the first a coarse yet not totally unlikeable man, the latter described as 'a good-looking young man with courageous eyes, timid mouth and a neutral nose', who does in the end show great tact and understanding in his attitude to Fancy's real attachment to Dick.

The qualities and appeal of the novel

It seems obvious that this is a book Hardy enjoyed writing, and one that he regarded with affection. In 1896, at the end of his career as a novelist, with the great tragic characters of Eustacia, Giles, Tess, and Jude all created, he wrote in a letter from Max Gate to his friend, Mrs Henniker:

> I have been all right in health, and have had a
> Christmas of the dull kind which contents
> so-called 'pessimists' like me – in its freedom
> from positive sorrows. An old choir of waits,
> however, came from a village a few nights ago,
> and sang to us the same carols that used to be sung
> by the 'Mellstock' Choir – (the characters that I like
> best in my own novels).

This love of his for the characters of Mellstock he passes on to his readers. He is not a detached observer of the rustic scene, describing it from the outside, as a novelist with a different background might have done. He is part of the life of the hamlets described. Like most of the truly great writers, Hardy can be appreciated on various levels. For those who want a good light story with a satisfactory and entertaining plot this is certainly the book to read. For those who are interested in the social history of England there are these vivid sketches, both in the dialogue and in the descriptive passages, of the fields and woods, the dusty roads, the interior of the houses, the church services, the textures of the clothes of the men and women, their food and drink and social customs. It is not entirely a picture of a golden age, for Hardy was above all a realist. There are references even here to darker aspects of Victorian rural England, when we learn of the infant mortality rate in Thomas Leaf's family, for instance; 'Mother had twelve regular,' he tells us, 'One after another, and they all, except myself, died very young; either before they were born or just afterwards.' The choir have a 'toilsome week' and then walk many miles to sing and play on their instruments in the church and around the parish. Dick and Fancy seem likely to have a comfortable future for ' 'Tis always so when a couple is so exactly in tune with one another as Dick and she,'; but grandfather James adds darkly: 'When they be'n't too poor to have time to sing,' thinking of other, less fortunate couples. Girls still consult witches in matters of romance, even though Mrs Endorfield, the Mellstock 'Deep Body', solves Fancy's problems more by common sense than magic. People are still put in the stocks for punishment, to be jeered at by passers-by. Hardy does not speak of greater rural problems, of the labourers' revolts so cruelly suppressed or of the Tolpuddle Martyrs' trial, which took place shortly before he was born, in a village not five miles away from his home. This may have been because he was more interested in individuals than in causes and already in this book he shows that tenderness and compassion for the underdog, for the poorer, more gullible members of society, which is characteristic of all his later writing. Notice, for instance, how easily the vicar, with his persuasive and almost patronising ways, gets the better of the simple members of the choir in the matter of introducing the organ into the church and making them redundant.

There is a great deal of wit in this novel, especially in the conversation of the members of the choir and in Hardy's descriptions of them and, in spite of his later apology about his treatment of these rustics, he seems rather to be laughing with his characters than at them. Note the gentle satire of whole passages on the relative merits of the outgoing Parson Grinham and the new vicar as seen by the villagers. 'Ah, Mr Grinham was the man! . . . He never troubled us wi' a visit from year's end to year's end', whereas Parson Maybold keeps on about 'being good and upright to such a pitch' that he irritates most of his parishioners. Of Geoffrey Day it is said: 'He can hold his tongue well. That man's dumbness is wonderful to listen to.' When the tranter describes Fancy's stepmother as 'a very good woman at bottom', her husband replies, 'She's terrible deep then.' Thomas Leaf stands in the vicar's study 'with his elbows nailed back to a bookcase' and the bridesmaids arrive at Fancy's home so transformed in their muslin dresses that they look like 'some very rich sisters of theirs that nobody knew they had'.

On yet another level Hardy can be seen in this book as a great stylist. His similes here are particularly apt and occur frequently. On the first page he speaks of the stars twinkling 'so vehemently that their flickering seemed like the flapping of wings'. The tranter comes in from his 'great Sunday wash' smelling like 'a summer fog', butterflies hover round the hollyhocks in summer 'like female idlers round a bonnet shop', while in Mellstock church there could be heard 'through the floor overhead a little world of undertones and creaks from the halting clockwork, which . . . raised in the more meditative minds a fancy that here lay the direct pathway of time'. Hardy's descriptions stick in the mind like familiar sayings: 'A curl of wood-smoke came from the chimney and drooped over the roof like a blue feather in a lady's hat'; and, 'I see her eyes mooning through the pane of glass like a pot-sick winder-flower'. There are other passages that are more like poetry than prose, the opening lines of the chapter entitled 'A Confession', for example, where he describes 'a morning of the latter summer-time; a morning of lingering dews, when the grass is never dry in the shade' or the picture of the sun descending in a 'nebulous blaze of amber light, its outline being lost in cloudy masses hanging round it like wild locks of hair', or the first paragraph of the Conclusion when the prosaic phrase 'The last day of the story is dated just subsequent to that point in the development of the seasons' is succeeded by the magical 'when country people go to bed among nearly naked trees, are lulled to sleep by a fall of rain, and awake next morning among green ones . . .' These are not purple passages but an integral part of the structure of the novel and forerunners of greater things to come in the later novels.

This novel is interesting also because of the insight it gives into Hardy's own character. His hatred of false values, his compassion, his humour have already been noted and his attitude to women as enigmatic, unreliable creatures is obvious. The tone of the book is on the whole cheerful but there is already at least one hint of Hardy's later pessimism in the title to the Conclusion of the novel, 'The Knot there's no Untying'. This comes from a song by Thomas Campbell, a popular poet who lived from 1774 to 1844. The song is called 'How Delicious is the Winning' and although it begins happily it ends on a gloomy note:

> Can you keep the bee from ranging,
> Or the ringdove's neck from changing?
> No! Nor fettered love from dying
> In the knot there's no untying.

This comment, half hidden though it is, at the start of the satisfactory ending to the story is a strange forecast of his own sombre views on marriage when he had endured years of incompatibility with Emma. In Hardy's world anyone

who wants complete possession of another person is doomed
to disappointment and the man who gets a wife very often
finds that she is not what he imagined her to be. In the poem
entitled 'The Well-Beloved' he addresses such a person:

> O fatuous man, this truth infer
> Brides are not what they seem;
> Thou lovest what thou dreamest her . . .

In his later novels this theme is often repeated and although
the divorce laws that were passed in the latter part of the nineteenth century made it easier for couples to find a way out of
their difficulties, this was not a way that Hardy or his tragic
heroes and heroines could easily take.

The quotation from Campbell, then, is the sting in the tail
that Hardy was fond of administering in his prose works and
in his poems, many of which begin lightheartedly and end
with a melancholy line. We see this, for example, in the poem
entitled 'The Self-Unseeing', which describes Hardy's return
in later life to the Bockhampton home of his childhood.

> Here is the ancient floor,
> Footworn and hollowed and thin,
> Here was the former door
> Where the dead feet walked in.
>
> She sat here in her chair,
> Smiling into the fire;
> He who played stood there,
> Bowing it higher and higher.
>
> Childlike, I danced in a dream;
> Blessings emblazoned that day;
> Everything glowed with a gleam;
> Yet we were looking away!

There is much in this poem to remind us of *Under the
Greenwood Tree* yet after reading the novel it could scarcely
be said that Hardy was 'looking away' since he has re-created

here so vividly his boyhood home and immortalised the men and women of his parish.

Short Bibliography

Hardy, Florence Emily, *The Life of Thomas Hardy* (Macmillan 1962)

Howe, Irving, *Thomas Hardy* (Macmillan 1967)

Millgate, Michael, *Thomas Hardy: His Career as a Novelist* (Bodley Head 1971)

Preface

This story of the Mellstock Quire[1] and its old-established west-gallery[2] musicians, with some supplementary descriptions of similar officials in *Two on a Tower*,[3] *A Few Crusted Characters*,[4] and other places, is intended to be a fairly true picture, at first hand, of the personages, ways, and customs which were common among such orchestral bodies in the villages of fifty or sixty years ago.

One is inclined to regret the displacement of these ecclesiastical bandsmen by an isolated organist (often at first a barrel-organist[5]) or harmonium[6] player; and despite certain advantages in point of control and accomplishment which were, no doubt, secured by installing the single artist, the change has tended to stultify the professed aims of the clergy, its direct result being to curtail and extinguish the interest of parishioners in church doings. Under the old plan, from half a dozen to ten full-grown players, in addition to the numerous more or less grown-up singers, were officially occupied with the Sunday routine, and concerned in trying their best to make it an artistic outcome of the combined musical taste of the congregation. With a musical executive limited, as it mostly is limited now, to the parson's wife or daughter and the school-children, or to the school-teacher and the children, an important union of interests has disappeared.

The zest of these bygone instrumentalists must have been keen and staying, to take them, as it did, on foot every Sunday after a toilsome week through all weathers to the church, which often lay at a distance from their homes. They usually received so little in payment for their performances that their efforts were really a labour of love. In the parish I had in my mind when writing the present tale, the gratuities[7] received yearly by the musicians at Christmas were somewhat as follows: from the manor-house ten shillings[8] and a supper; from the vicar ten shillings; from the farmers five shillings[9] each; from each cottage-household one shilling;[10] amounting altogether to not more than ten shillings a head annually – just enough, as an old executant told me, to pay for their fiddle-strings, repairs, rosin,[11] and music-paper (which they mostly ruled themselves). Their music in those days was all in their own manuscript, copied in the evenings after work, and their music-books[12] were home-bound.

It was customary to inscribe a few jigs, reels, hornpipes, and ballads in the same book, by beginning it at the other end, the insertions being continued from front and back till sacred and secular met together in the middle, often with bizarre effect, the words of some of the songs exhibiting that ancient and broad humour which our grandfathers, and possibly grandmothers, took delight in, and is in these days unquotable.

The aforesaid fiddle-strings, rosin, and music-paper were supplied by a pedlar, who travelled exclusively in such wares from parish to parish, coming to each village about every six months. Tales are told of the consternation once caused among the church fiddlers when, on the occasion of their producing a new Christmas anthem, he did not come to time, owing to being snowed up on the downs, and the straits they were in through having to make shift with whip-cord[13] and twine[14] for strings. He was generally a musician himself, and sometimes a composer in a small way, bringing his own new tunes, and tempting each choir to adopt them for a consideration. Some of these compositions which now lie before me, with their repetitions of lines, half-lines, and half-words, their fugues[15] and their intermediate symphonies,[16] are good singing still, though they would hardly be admitted into such hymn-books as are popular in the churches of fashionable society at the present time.

August 1896

Under the Greenwood Tree was first brought out in the summer of 1872 in two volumes. The name of the story was originally intended to be, more appropriately, *The Mellstock Quire*, and this has been appended as a sub-title since the early editions, it having been thought unadvisable to displace for it the title by which the book first became known.

In re-reading the narrative after a long interval there occurs the inevitable reflection that the realities out of which it was spun were material for another kind of study of this little group of church musicians than is found in the chapters here penned so lightly, even so farcically and flippantly at times. But circumstances would have rendered any aim at a deeper, more essential, more transcendent[17] handling unadvisable at the date of writing; and the exhibition of the Mellstock Quire in the following pages must remain the only extant[18] one, except for the few glimpses of that perished band which I have given in verse elsewhere.[19]

April 1912   T.H.

Part the First

Winter

1 Mellstock Lane

To dwellers in a wood almost every species of tree has its voice as well as its feature.[1] At the passing of the breeze the fir-trees sob and moan no less distinctly than they rock; the holly whistles as it battles with itself; the ash hisses amid its quivering; the beech rustles while its flat boughs rise and fall. And winter, which modifies the note of such trees as shed their leaves, does not destroy its individuality.

On a cold and starry Christmas-eve within living memory[2] a man was passing up a lane towards Mellstock Cross in the darkness of a plantation that whispered thus distinctively to his intelligence. All the evidences of his nature were those afforded by the spirit of his footsteps, which succeeded each other lightly and quickly, and by the liveliness of his voice as he sang in a rural cadence:

> 'With the rose and the lily
> And the daffodowndilly,[3]
> The lads and the lasses a-sheep-shearing go.'

The lonely lane he was following connected one of the hamlets of Mellstock parish with Upper Mellstock and Lewgate, and to his eyes, casually glancing upward, the silver and black-stemmed birches with their characteristic tufts, the pale grey boughs of beech, the dark-creviced elm, all appeared now as black and flat outlines upon the sky, wherein the white stars twinkled so vehemently that their flickering seemed like the flapping of wings. Within the woody pass, at a level anything lower than the horizon, all was dark as the grave. The copsewood forming the sides of the bower interlaced its branches so densely, even at this season of the year, that the draught from the north-east flew along the channel with scarcely an interruption from lateral breezes.

After passing the plantation and reaching Mellstock Cross the white surface of the lane revealed itself between the dark hedgerows like a ribbon jagged at the edges; the irregularity being caused by temporary accumulations of leaves extending from the ditch on either side.

The song (many times interrupted by flitting thoughts which took the place of several bars, and resumed at a point it would have reached had its continuity been un-broken) now received a more palpable check, in the shape of 'Ho-i-i-i-i-i!' from the crossing lane to Lower Mellstock, on the right of the singer who had just emerged from the trees.

'Ho-i-i-i-i-i!' he answered, stopping and looking round, though with no idea of seeing anything more than imagination pictured.

'Is that thee, young Dick Dewy?' came from the dark-ness.

'Ay, sure, Michael Mail.'

'Then why not stop for fellow-craters[4] – going to thy own father's house too, as we be, and knowen us so well?'

Dick Dewy faced about and continued his tune in an under-whistle, implying that the business of his mouth could not be checked at a moment's notice by the placid emotion of friendship.

Having come more into the open he could now be seen rising against the sky, his profile appearing on the light background like the portrait of a gentleman in black card-board.[5] It assumed the form of a low-crowned hat, an ordinary-shaped nose, an ordinary chin, an ordinary neck, and ordinary shoulders. What he consisted of further down was invisible from lack of sky low enough to picture him on.

Shuffling, halting, irregular footsteps of various kinds were now heard coming up the hill, and presently there emerged from the shade severally[6] five men of different ages and gaits, all of them working villagers of the parish of Mellstock. They, too, had lost their rotundity with the daylight, and advanced against the sky in flat outlines, which suggested some processional design on Greek or Etruscan[7] pottery. They represented the chief portion of Mellstock parish choir.

The first was a bowed and bent man, who carried a fiddle under his arm, and walked as if engaged in studying some subject connected with the surface of the road. He was Michael Mail, the man who had hallooed to Dick.

The next was Mr Robert Penny, boot- and shoe-maker; a little man who, though rather round-shouldered, walked as if that fact had not come to his own knowledge, moving on with his back very hollow and his face fixed on the north-east quarter of the heavens before him, so that his lower waist-coat-buttons came first, and then the remainder of his figure. His features were invisible; yet when he occasionally looked round, two faint moons of light gleamed for an instant from the precincts of his eyes, denoting that he wore spectacles of a circular form.

The third was Elias Spinks, who walked perpendicularly and dramatically. The fourth outline was Joseph Bowman's, who had now no distinctive appearance beyond that of a human being. Finally came a weak lath-like[8] form, trotting and stumbling along with one shoulder forward and his head inclined to the left, his arms dangling nervelessly in the wind as if they were empty sleeves. This was Thomas Leaf.

'Where be the boys?' said Dick to this somewhat indifferently-matched assembly.

The eldest of the group, Michael Mail, cleared his throat from a great depth.

'We told them to keep back at home for a time, thinken they wouldn't be wanted yet awhile; and we could choose the tuens, and so on.'

'Father and grandfather William have expected ye a little sooner. I have just been for a run round by Ewelease Stile[9] and Hollow Hill to warm my feet.'

'To be sure father did! To be sure 'a did expect us – to taste the little barrel beyond compare that he's going to tap.'

' ''Odd rabbit it all![10] Never heard a word of it!' said Mr Penny, gleams of delight appearing upon his spectacle-glasses, Dick meanwhile singing parenthetically[11]—

'The lads and the lasses a-sheep-shearing go.'

'Neighbours, there's time enough to drink a sight of drink now afore bedtime?' said Mail.

'True, true – time enough to get as drunk as lords!' replied Bowman cheerfully.

This opinion being taken as convincing they all advanced between the varying hedges and the trees dotting them here and there, kicking their toes occasionally among the crumpled leaves. Soon appeared glimmering indications of the few cottages forming the small hamlet of Upper Mellstock for which they were bound, whilst the faint sound of church-bells ringing a Christmas peal could be heard floating over upon the breeze from the direction of Longpuddle and Weatherbury parishes on the other side of the hills. A little wicket[12] admitted them to the garden, and they proceeded up the path to Dick's house.

2 The Tranter's

It was a long low cottage with a hipped[1] roof of thatch, having dormer[2] windows breaking up into the eaves, a chimney standing in the middle of the ridge and another at each end. The window-shutters[3] were not yet closed, and the fire- and candle-light within radiated forth upon the thick bushes of box[4] and laurestinus[5] growing in clumps outside, and upon the bare boughs of several codlin-trees[6] hanging about in various distorted shapes, the result of early training as espaliers[7] combined with careless climbing, into their boughs in later years. The walls of the dwelling were for the most part covered with creepers, though these were rather beaten back from the doorway – a feature which was worn and scratched by much passing in and out, giving it by day the appearance of an old keyhole. Light streamed through the cracks and joints of outbuildings a little way from the cottage, a sight which nourished a fancy that the purpose of the erection must be rather to veil bright attractions than to shelter unsightly necessaries. The noise of a beetle[8] and wedges[9] and the splintering of wood was periodically heard from this direction; and at some little distance further a steady regular munching and the occasional scurr[10] of a rope betokened a stable, and horses feeding within it.

The choir stamped severally on the door-stone to shake from their boots any fragment of earth or leaf adhering thereto, then entered the house and looked around to survey the condition of things. Through the open doorway of a small inner room on the right hand, of a character between pantry and cellar, was Dick Dewy's father Reuben, by vocation a 'tranter', or irregular carrier. He was a stout florid man about forty years of age, who surveyed people up and down when first making their acquaintance, and generally smiled at the horizon or other distant object during conversations with friends, walking about with a steady sway, and turning out his toes very considerably. Being now occupied in bending over a hogshead[11] that stood in the pantry ready horsed[12] for the process of broaching,[13] he did not take the trouble to turn or raise his eyes at the entry of his visitors, well knowing by their footsteps that they were the expected old comrades.

The main room, on the left, was decked with bunches of holly and other evergreens, and from the middle of the beam bisecting the ceiling hung the mistletoe, of a size out of all proportion to the room, and extending so low that it became necessary for a full-grown person to walk round it in passing, or run the risk of entangling his hair. This apartment contained Mrs Dewy the tranter's wife, and the four remaining children, Susan, Jim, Bessy, and Charley, graduating uniformly though at wide stages from the age of sixteen to that of four years – the eldest of the series being separated from Dick the firstborn by a nearly equal interval.

Some circumstance had apparently caused much grief to Charley just previous to the entry of the choir, and he had absently taken down a small looking-glass, holding it before his face to learn how the human countenance appeared when engaged in crying, which surveyed him to pause at the various points in each wail that were more than ordinarily striking, for a thorough appreciation of the general effect. Bessy was leaning against a chair, and glancing under the plaits[14] about the waist of the plaid frock she wore, to notice the original unfaded pattern of the material as there preserved, her face bearing an expression of regret that the brightness had passed away from the visible portions. Mrs Dewy sat in a brown settle[15] by the side of the glowing wood fire – so glowing that with a heedful compression of the lips she would now and then rise and put her hand upon the hams and flitches[16] of bacon lining the chimney,[17] to reassure herself that they were not being broiled[18] instead of smoked – a misfortune that had been known to happen now and then at Christmas-time.

'Hullo, my sonnies, here you be, then!' said Reuben Dewy at length, standing up and blowing forth a vehement gust of breath. 'How the blood do puff up in anybody's head, to be sure, a-stooping like that! I was just going out to gate to hark for ye.' He then carefully began to wind a strip of brown paper round a brass tap he held in his hand. 'This in the cask here is a drop o' the right sort' (tapping the cask); ''tis a real drop o' cordial from the best picked apples – Sansoms,[19] Stubbards,[20] Five-corners,[21] and such-like – you d'mind[22] the sort, Michael?' (Michael nodded.) 'And there's a sprinkling of they that grow down by the orchard-rails – streaked ones – rail apples we d'call 'em, as 'tis by the rails they grow, and not knowing the right name. The water-cider from 'em is as good as most people's best cider is.'

'Ay, and of the same make too,' said Bowman. '"It rained when we wrung it out, and the water got into it," folk will say. But 'tis on'y an excuse. Watered cider is too common among us.'

'Yes, yes; too common it is!' said Spinks with an inward sigh, whilst his eyes seemed to be looking at the case in an abstract form rather than at the scene before him. 'Such poor liquor do make a man's throat feel very melancholy – and is a disgrace to the name of stimmilent.'[23]

'Come in, come in, and draw up to the fire; never mind your shoes,' said Mrs Dewy, seeing that all except Dick had paused to wipe them upon the doormat. 'I am glad that you've stepped up-along at last; and, Susan, you run down to Grammer Kaytes's[24] and see if you can borrow some larger candles than these fourteens.[25] Tommy Leaf, don't ye be afeard! Come and sit here in the settle.'

This was addressed to the young man before mentioned, consisting chiefly of a human skeleton and a smock-frock,[26] who was very awkward in his movements, apparently on account of having grown so very fast that before he had had time to get used to his height he was higher.

'Hee – hee – ay!' replied Leaf, letting his mouth continue to smile for some time after his mind had done smiling, so that his teeth remained in view as the most conspicuous members of his body.

'Here, Mr Penny,' resumed Mrs Dewy, 'you sit in this chair. And how's your daughter, Mrs Brownjohn?'

'Well, I suppose I must say pretty fair.' He adjusted his spectacles a quarter of an inch to the right. 'But she'll be worse before she's better, 'a b'lieve.'

'Indeed – poor soul! And how many will that make in all, four or five?'

'Five; they've buried three. Yes, five; and she not much more than a maid yet. She do know the multiplication table[27] onmistakable well. However, 'twas to be, and none can gainsay it.'

Mrs Dewy resigned Mr Penny. 'Wonder where your grandfather James is?' she inquired of one of the children. 'He said he'd drop in tonight.'

'Out in fuel-house with grandfather William,' said Jimmy.

'Now let's see what we can do,' was heard spoken about this time by the tranter in a private voice to the barrel, beside which he had again established himself, and was stooping to cut away the cork.

'Reuben, don't make such a mess o' tapping that barrel

as is mostly made in this house,' Mrs Dewy cried from the
fireplace. 'I'd tap a hundred without wasting more than you
do in one. Such a squizzling[28] and squirting job as 'tis in
your hands! There, he always was such a clumsy man indoors.'

'Ay, ay; I know you'd tap a hundred beautiful, Ann – I
know you would; two hundred, perhaps. But I can't promise. This is a' old cask, and the wood's rotted away about
the tap-hole. The husbird[29] of a feller Sam Lawson – that
ever I should call'n such, now he's dead and gone, poor
heart! – took me in completely upon the feat of buying this
cask. "Reub," says he – 'a always used to call me plain
Reub, poor old heart! – "Reub," he said says he, "that
there cask, Reub, is as good as new; yes, good as new. 'Tis
a wine-hogshead; the best port-wine in the commonwealth
have been in that there cask; and you shall have en for ten
shillens,[30] Reub," – 'a said says he – "he's worth twenty, ay,
five-and-twenty, if he's worth one; and an iron hoop or two
put round en among the wood ones will make en worth
thirty shillens of any man's money, if—" '

'I think I should have used the eyes that Providence gave
me to use afore I paid any ten shillens for a jimcrack[31]
wine-barrel; a saint is sinner enough not to be cheated. But
'tis like all your family was, so easy to be deceived.'

'That's as true as gospel of this member,' said Reuben.

Mrs Dewy began a smile at the answer, then altering her
lips and refolding them so that it was not a smile, com-
menced smoothing little Bessy's hair; the tranter having
meanwhile suddenly become oblivious to conversation, oc-
cupying himself in a deliberate cutting and arrangement of
some more brown paper for the broaching operation.

'Ah, who can believe sellers!' said old Michael Mail in a
carefully-cautious voice, by way of tiding-over this critical
point of affairs.

'No one at all,' said Joseph Bowman, in the tone of a man fully agreeing with everybody.

'Ay,' said Mail, in the tone of a man who did not agree with everybody as a rule, though he did now; 'I knowed a' auctioneering feller once – a very friendly feller 'a was too. And so one hot day as I was walking down the front street o' Casterbridge, jist below the King's Arms,[32] I passed a' open winder and see him inside, stuck upon his perch, a-selling off. I jist nodded to en in a friendly way as I passed, and went my way, and thought no more about it. Well, next day, as I was oilen[33] my boots by fuel-house door, if a letter didn't come wi' a bill charging me with a feather-bed, bolster, and pillers, that I had bid for at Mr Taylor's sale. The slim-faced martel[34] had knocked 'em down to me because I nodded to en in my friendly way; and I had to pay for 'em too. Now, I hold that that was coming it very close, Reuben?'

' 'Twas close, there's no denying,' said the general voice.

'Too close, 'twas,' said Reuben, in the rear of the rest. 'And as to Sam Lawson – poor heart! now he's dead and gone too! – I'll warrant, that if so be I've spent one hour in making hoops for that barrel, I've spent fifty, first and last. That's one of my hoops' – touching it with his elbow – 'that's one of mine, and that, and that, and all these.'

'Ah, Sam was a man,' said Mr Penny, contemplatively.

'Sam was!' said Bowman.

'Expecially for a drap o' drink,' said the tranter.

'Good, but not religious-good,' suggested Mr Penny.

The tranter nodded. Having at last made the tap and hole quite ready, 'Now then, Suze, bring a mug,' he said. 'Here's luck to us, my sonnies!'

The tap went in, and the cider immediately squirted out in a horizontal shower over Reuben's hands, knees, and leggings, and into the eyes and neck of Charley, who, having temporarily put off his grief under pressure of more interesting proceedings, was squatting down and blinking near his father.

'There 'tis again!' said Mrs Dewy.

'Devil take the hole, the cask, and Sam Lawson too, that good cider should be wasted like this!' exclaimed the tranter. 'Your thumb! Lend me your thumb, Michael! Ram it in here, Michael! I must get a bigger tap, my sonnies.'

'Idd it cold inthide te hole?'[35] inquired Charley of Michael, as he continued in the stooping posture with his thumbs in the cork-hole.

'What wonderful odds and ends that chiel[36] has in his head to be sure!' Mrs Dewy admiringly exclaimed from the distance. 'I lay a wager that he thinks more about how 'tis inside that barrel than in all the other parts of the world put together.'

All persons present put on a speaking countenance of admiration for the cleverness alluded to, in the midst of which Reuben returned. The operation was then satisfactorily performed; when Michael arose and stretched his head to the extremest fraction of height that his body would allow of, to restraighten his back and shoulders – thrusting out his arms and twisting his features to a mass of wrinkles to emphasize the relief acquired. A quart or two of the beverage was then brought to table, at which all the new arrivals reseated themselves with wide-spread knees, their eyes meditatively seeking out any speck or knot in the board upon which the gaze might precipitate itself.

'Whatever is father a-biding out in fuel-house so long for?' said the tranter. 'Never such a man as father for two things – cleaving up old dead apple-tree wood and playing the bass-viol.[37] 'A'd pass his life between the two, that 'a would.' He stepped to the door and opened it.

'Father!'

'Ay!' rang thinly from round the corner.

'Here's the barrel tapped, and we all a-waiting!'

A series of dull thuds, that had been heard without for some time past, now ceased; and after the light of a lantern had passed the window and made wheeling rays upon the ceiling inside the eldest of the Dewy family appeared.

3 The Assembled Quire

William Dewy – otherwise grandfather William – was now about seventy; yet an ardent vitality still preserved a warm and roughened bloom upon his face, which reminded gardeners of the sunny side of a ripe ribstone-pippin;[1] though a narrow strip of forehead, that was protected from the weather by lying above the line of his hat-brim, seemed to belong to some town man, so gentlemanly was its whiteness. His was a humorous and kindly nature, not unmixed with a frequent melancholy; and he had a firm religious faith. But to his neighbours he had no character in particular. If they saw him pass by their windows when they had been bottling off old mead,[2] or when they had just been called long-headed[3] men who might do anything in the world if they chose, they thought concerning him, 'Ah, there's that good-hearted man – open as a child!' If they saw him just after losing a shilling or half-a-crown,[4] or accidentally letting fall a piece of crockery, they thought, 'There's that poor weak-minded man Dewy again! Ah, he's never done much in the world either!' If he passed when fortune neither smiled nor frowned on them, they merely thought him old William Dewy.

'Ah, so's – here you be! – Ah, Michael and Joseph and John – and you too, Leaf! a merry Christmas all! We shall have a rare log-wood fire directly, Reub, to reckon by the toughness of the job I had in cleaving[5] 'em.' As he spoke he threw down an armful of logs which fell in the chimney-corner with a rumble, and looked at them with something

of the admiring enmity he would have bestowed on living
people who had been very obstinate in holding their own.
'Come in, grandfather James.'

Old James (grandfather on the maternal side) had simply
called as a visitor. He lived in a cottage by himself, and
many people considered him a miser; some, rather slovenly
in his habits. He now came forward from behind grandfather William, and his stooping figure formed a well-
illuminated picture as he passed towards the fire-place.
Being by trade a mason, he wore a long linen apron reaching
almost to his toes, corduroy breeches and gaiters, which, together with his boots, graduated in tints of whitish-brown
by constant friction against lime and stone. He also wore a
very stiff fustian[6] coat, having folds at the elbows and shoulders as unvarying in their arrangement as those in a pair of
bellows: the ridges and the projecting parts of the coat col-
lectively exhibiting a shade different from that of the
hollows, which were lined with small ditch-like accumulations of stone and mortar-dust. The extremely large side-
pockets, sheltered beneath wide flaps, bulged out convexly
whether empty or full; and as he was often engaged to work
at buildings far away – his breakfasts and dinners being
eaten in a strange chimney-corner, by a garden wall, on a
heap of stones, or walking along the road – he carried in
these pockets a small tin canister of butter, a small canister
of sugar, a small canister of tea, a paper of salt, and a paper
of pepper; the bread, cheese and meat, forming the substance of his meals, hanging up behind him in his basket
among the hammers and chisels. If a passer-by looked hard
at him when he was drawing forth any of these, 'My
buttery,'[7] he said, with a pinched smile.

'Better try over number seventy-eight before we start, I
suppose?' said William, pointing to a heap of old Christ-
mas-carol books on a side table.

'Wi' all my heart,' said the choir generally.

'Number seventy-eight was always a teaser – always. I can mind him ever since I was growing up a hard boy-chap.'[8]

'But he's a good tune, and worth a mint o' practice,'[9] said Michael.

'He is; though I've been mad enough wi' that tune at times to seize en and tear en all to linnit.[10] Ay, he's a splendid carrel[11] – there's no denying that.'

'The first line is well enough,' said Mr Spinks; 'but when you come to "O, thou man", you make a mess o't.'

'We'll have another go into en, and see what we can make of the mantel. Half-an-hour's hammering at en will conquer the toughness of en; I'll warn it.'

''Od rabbit it all!' said Mr Penny, interrupting with a flash of his spectacles, and at the same time clawing at something in the depths of a large side-pocket, 'If so be I hadn't been as scatter-brained and thirtingill[12] as a chiel I should have called at the schoolhouse wi' a boot as I cam up along. Whatever is coming to me I really can't estimate at all!'

'The brain has its weaknesses,' murmured Mr Spinks, waving his head ominously. Mr Spinks was considered to be a scholar, having once kept a night-school, and always spoke up to that level.

'Well, I must call with en the first thing tomorrow. And I'll empt my pocket o' this last[13] too, if you don't mind, Mrs Dewy.' He drew forth a last, and placed it on a table at his elbow. The eyes of three or four followed it.

'Well,' said the shoemaker, seeming to perceive that the interest the object had excited was greater than he had anticipated, and warranted the last's being taken up again and exhibited; 'now, whose foot do ye suppose this last was made for? It was made for Geoffrey Day's father, over at Yalbury Wood. Ah, many's the pair o' boots he've had off the last! Well, when 'a died, I used the last for Geoffrey, and have ever since, though a little doctoring was wanted to make it do. Yes, a very queer natured last it is now, 'a b'lieve,' he continued, turning it over caressingly. 'Now, you notice that there' (pointing to a lump of leather bradded[14] to the toe), 'that's a very bad bunion that he've had ever since 'a was a boy. Now, this remarkable large piece' (pointing to a patch nailed to the side), 'shows a' accident he received by the tread of a horse, that squashed his foot a'most to a pomace.[15] The horse-shoe came full-butt[16] on this point, you see. And so I've just been over to Geoffrey's, to know if he wanted his bunion altered or made bigger in the new pair I'm making.'

During the latter part of this speech Mr Penny's left hand wandered towards the cider-cup as if the hand had no connection with the person speaking; and bringing his sentence to an abrupt close all but the extreme margin of the bootmaker's face was eclipsed by the circular brim of the vessel.

'However, I was going to say,' continued Penny, putting down the cup, 'I ought to have called at the school' – here he went groping again in the depths of his pocket – 'to leave this without fail, though I suppose the first thing tomorrow will do.'

He now drew forth and placed upon the table a boot – small, light, and prettily shaped – upon the heel of which he had been operating.

'The new schoolmistress's!'

'Ay, no less, Miss Fancy Day; as neat a little figure of fun as ever I see, and just husband-high.'[17]

'Never Geoffrey's daughter Fancy?' said Bowman, as all glances present converged like wheel-spokes upon the boot in the centre of them.

'Yes, sure,' resumed Mr Penny, regarding the boot as if that alone were his auditor; ''tis she that's come here schoolmistress. You knowed his daughter was in training?'

'Strange, isn't it, for her to be here Christmas night, Master Penny?'

'Yes; but here she is, 'a b'lieve.'

'I know how she comes here – so I do!' chirruped one of the children.

'Why?' Dick inquired with subtle interest.

'Pa'son Maybold was afraid he couldn't manage us all tomorrow at the dinner, and he talked o' getting her jist to come over and help him hand about the plates, and see we didn't make pigs of ourselves; and that's what she's come for!'

'And that's the boot, then,' continued its mender imaginatively, 'that she'll walk to church in tomorrow morning. I don't care to mend boots I don't make; but there's no knowing what it may lead to, and her father always comes to me.'

There, between the cider-mug and the candle, stood this interesting receptacle of the little unknown's foot; and a very pretty boot it was. A character, in fact – the flexible bend at the instep, the rounded localities of the small nestling toes, scratches from careless scampers now forgotten – all, as repeated in the tell-tale leather, evidencing a nature and a bias. Dick surveyed it with a delicate feeling that he had no right to do so without having first asked the owner of the foot's permission.

'Now, neighbours, though no common eye can see it,' the shoemaker went on, 'a man in the trade can see the likeness between this boot and that last, although that is so deformed as hardly to recall one of God's creatures, and this is one of as pretty a pair as you'd get for ten-and-sixpence in Casterbridge. To you, nothing; but 'tis father's voot[18] and daughter's voot to me, as plain as houses.'

'I don't doubt there's a likeness, Master Penny – a mild likeness – a fantastical[19] likeness,' said Spinks. 'But *I* hadn't got imagination enough to see it, perhaps.'

Mr Penny adjusted his spectacles.

'Now, I'll tell ye what happened to me once on this very point. You used to know Johnson the dairyman, William?'

'Ay, sure; I did.'

'Well, 'twasn't opposite his house, but a little lower down – by his paddock, in front o' Parkmaze Pool. I was a-bearing across towards Bloom's End, and lo and behold, there was a man just brought out o' the Pool, dead; he had un'rayed[20] for a dip, but not being able to pitch it[21] just there had gone in flop over his head. Men looked at en; women looked at en; children looked at en; nobody knowed en. He was covered wi' a sheet; but I catched sight of his voot, just showing out as they carried en along. "I don't care what name that man went by," I said, in my way, "but he's John Woodward's brother; I can swear to the family voot." At that very moment up comes John Woodward, weeping and teaving,[22] "I've lost my brother! I've lost my brother!"'

'Only to think of that!' said Mrs Dewy.

''Tis well enough to know this foot and that foot,' said Mr Spinks. ''Tis long-headed, in fact, as far as feet do go. I know little, 'tis true – I say no more; but show *me* a man's foot, and I'll tell you that man's heart.'

'You must be a cleverer feller, then, than mankind in jineral,'[23] said the tranter.

'Well, that's nothing for me to speak of,' returned Mr Spinks. 'A man lives and learns. Maybe I've read a leaf[24] or two in my time. I don't wish to say anything large, mind you; but nevertheless, maybe I have.'

'Yes, I know,' said Michael soothingly, 'and all the parish knows, that ye've read sommat[25] of everything a'most, and have been a great filler of young folks' brains. Learning's a worthy thing, and ye've got it, Master Spinks.'

'I make no boast, though I may have read and thought a little; and I know – it may be from much perusing, but I make no boast – that by the time a man's head is finished 'tis almost time for him to creep underground. I am over forty-five.'

Mr Spinks emitted a look to signify that if his head was not finished, nobody's head ever could be.

'Talk of knowing people by their feet!' said Reuben. 'Rot me,[26] my sonnies, then, if I can tell what a man is from all his members put together, oftentimes.'

'But still, look is a good deal,' observed grandfather William absently, moving and balancing his head till the tip of grandfather James's nose was exactly in a right line with William's eye and the mouth of a miniature cavern he was discerning in the fire. 'By the way,' he continued in a fresher voice, and looking up, 'that young creature, the school-mis'ess, must be sung to tonight wi' the rest? If her ear is as fine as her face, we shall have enough to do to be upsides with[27] her.'

'What about her face?' said young Dewy.

'Well, as to that,' Mr Spinks replied ' 'tis a face you can hardly gainsay.[28] A very good pink face, as far as that do go. Still, only a face, when all is said and done.'

'Come, come, Elias Spinks, say she's a pretty maid and have done wi' her,' said the tranter, again preparing to visit the cider-barrel.

4 Going the Rounds

Shortly after ten o'clock the singing-boys arrived at the tranter's house, which was invariably the place of meeting, and preparations were made for the start. The older men and musicians wore thick coats, with stiff perpendicular collars, and coloured handkerchiefs wound round and round the neck till the end came to hand, over all which they just showed their ears and noses, like people looking over a wall. The remainder, stalwart ruddy men and boys, were dressed mainly in snow-white smock-frocks, embroidered upon the shoulders and breasts in ornamental forms of hearts, diamonds, and zigzags. The cider-mug was emptied for the ninth time, the music-books were arranged and the pieces finally decided upon. The boys in the meantime put the old horn-lanterns[1] in order, cut candles into short lengths to fit the lanterns; and, a thin fleece of snow having fallen since the early part of the evening, those who had no leggings went to the stable and wound wisps of hay round their ankles to keep the insidious flakes from the interior of their boots.

Mellstock was a parish of considerable acreage, the hamlets composing it lying at a much greater distance from each other than is ordinarily the case. Hence several hours were consumed in playing and singing within hearing of every family, even if but a single air were bestowed on each. There was Lower Mellstock, the main village; half a mile from this were the church and vicarage, and a few other houses, the spot being rather lonely now, though in past centuries it had been the most thickly-populated quarter of

the parish. A mile north-east lay the hamlet of Upper Mellstock, where the tranter lived; and at other points knots of
cottages, besides solitary farmsteads and dairies.

Old William Dewy, with the violoncello, played the bass;
his grandson Dick the treble violin; and Reuben and
Michael Mail the tenor and second violins respectively. The
singers consisted of four men and seven boys, upon whom
devolved the task of carrying and attending to the lanterns,
and holding the books open for the players. Directly music
was the theme old William ever and instinctively came to
the front.

'Now mind, neighbours,' he said, as they all went out one
by one at the door, he himself holding it ajar and regarding
them with a critical face as they passed, like a shepherd
counting out his sheep. 'You two counter-boys,[2] keep your
ears open to Michael's fingering, and don't ye go straying
into the treble part along o' Dick and his set, as ye did last
year; and mind this especially when we be in "Arise, and
hail". Billy Chimlen, don't you sing quite so raving mad as
you fain would; and, all o' ye, whatever ye do, keep from
making a great scuffle on the ground when we go in at
people's gates; but go quietly, as to strike up all of a sudden,
like spirits.'

'Farmer Ledlow's[3] first?'

'Farmer Ledlow's first; the rest as usual.'

'And, Voss,' said the tranter terminatively, 'you keep
house here till about half-past two; then heat the metheglin[4] and cider in the warmer[5] you'll find turned up upon
the copper; and bring it wi' the victuals to church-hatch,[6]
as th'st know.'

Just before the clock struck twelve they lighted the lanterns
and started. The moon, in her third quarter, had risen since
the snowstorm; but the dense accumulation of snow-cloud
weakened her power to a faint twilight which was rather

pervasive of the landscape than traceable to the sky. The breeze had gone down, and the rustle of their feet and tones of their speech echoed with an alert rebound from every post, boundary-stone, and ancient wall they passed, even where the distance of the echo's origin was less than a few yards. Beyond their own slight noises nothing was to be heard save the occasional bark of foxes in the direction of Yalbury Wood, or the brush of a rabbit among the grass now and then as it scampered out of their way.

Most of the outlying homesteads and hamlets had been visited by about two o'clock; they then passed across the outskirts of a wooded park toward the main village, nobody being at home at the Manor.[7] Pursuing no recognized track, great care was necessary in walking lest their faces should come in contact with the low-hanging boughs of the old lime-trees, which in many spots formed dense overgrowths of interlaced branches.

'Times have changed from the times they used to be,' said Mail, regarding nobody can tell what interesting old panoramas[8] with an inward eye, and letting his outward glance rest on the ground because it was as convenient a position as any. 'People don't care much about us now! I've been thinking we must be almost the last left in the country of the old string players? Barrel-organs, and the things next door to 'em that you blow wi' your foot,[9] have come in terribly of late years.'

'Ay!' said Bowman shaking his head; and old William on seeing him did the same thing.

'More's the pity,' replied another. 'Time was – long and merry ago now! – when not one of the varmits[10] was to be heard of; but it served some of the quires right. They should have stuck to strings as we did, and kept out clarinets, and done away with serpents.[11] If you'd thrive in musical-religion, stick to strings, says I.'

'Strings be safe soul-lifters, as far as that do go,' said Mr Spinks.

'Yet there's worse things than serpents,' said Mr Penny. 'Old things pass away, 'tis true; but a serpent was a good old note: a deep rich note was the serpent.'

'Clar'nets,[12] however, be bad at all times,' said Michael Mail. 'One Christmas – years agone now, years – I went the rounds wi' the Weatherbury quire. 'Twas a hard frosty night, and the keys of all the clar'nets froze – ah, they did freeze! – so that 'twas like drawing a cork every time a key was opened; and the players o' 'em had to go into a hedger-and-ditcher's[13] chimley-corner,[14] and thaw their clar'nets every now and then. An icicle o' spet[15] hung down from the end of every man's clar'net a span[16] long; and as to fingers – well, there, if ye'll believe me, we had no fingers at all, to our knowing.'

'I can well bring back to my mind,' said Mr Penny, 'what I said to poor Joseph Ryme (who took the treble part in Chalk-Newton Church for two-and-forty year) when they thought of having clar'nets there. "Joseph," I said says I, "depend upon't, if so be you have them tooting clar'nets you'll spoil the whole set-out. Clar'nets were not made for the service of the Lard;[17] you can see it by looking at 'em," I said. And what came o't? Why, souls, the parson set up a barrel-organ on his own account within two years o' the time I spoke, and the old quire went to nothing.'

'As far as look is concerned,' said the tranter, 'I don't for my part see that a fiddle is much nearer heaven than a clar'net. 'Tis further off. There's always a rakish, scampish twist about a fiddle's looks that seems to say the Wicked One[18] had a hand in making o'en; while angels be supposed to play clar'nets in heaven, or som'at like 'em if ye may believe picters.'

'Robert Penny, you was in the right,' broke in the eldest Dewy. 'They should ha' stuck to strings. Your brass-man is a

rafting[19] dog – well and good; your reed-man[20] is a dab
at[21] stirring ye – well and good; your drum-man is a rare
bowel-shaker – good again. But I don't care who hears me
say it, nothing will spak to your heart wi' the sweetness o'
the man of strings!'

'Strings for ever!' said little Jimmy.

'Strings alone would have held their ground against all
the new-comers in creation.' ('True, true!' said Bowman.)
'But clarinets was death.' ('Death they was!' said Mr
Penny.) 'And harmonions,' William continued in a louder
voice, and getting excited by these signs of approval, 'harmonions and barrel-organs' ('Ah!' and groans from Spinks)
'be miserable – what shall I call 'em? – miserable—'

'Sinners,' suggested Jimmy, who made large strides like
the men and did not lag behind with the other little boys.

'Miserable dumbledores!'[22]

'Right, William, and so they be – miserable dumbledores!' said the choir with unanimity.

By this time they were crossing to a gate in the direction
of the school which, standing on a slight eminence at the
junction of three ways, now rose in unvarying and dark
flatness against the sky. The intruments were re-tuned, and
all the band entered the school enclosure, enjoined by old
William to keep upon the grass.[23]

'Number seventy-eight,' he softly gave out as they formed
round in a semicircle, the boys opening the lanterns to get a
clearer light, and directing their rays on the books.

Then passed forth into the quiet night an ancient and
time-worn hymn, embodying a quaint Christianity in words
orally transmitted from father to son through several gen-
erations down to the present characters, who sang them out
right earnestly:

'Remember Adam's fall,
O thou Man:

Remember Adam's fall
　　From Heaven to Hell.
Remember Adam's fall;
How he hath condemn'd all
In Hell perpetual
　　There for to dwell.

Remember God's goodnesse,
　　O thou Man:
Remember God's goodnesse,
　　His promise made.
Remember God's goodnesse;
He sent His Son sinlesse
Our ails for to redress;
　　Be not afraid!

In Bethlehem He was born,
　　O thou Man:
In Bethlehem He was born,
　　For mankind's sake.
In Bethlehem He was born,
Christmas-day i' the morn:
Our Saviour thought no scorn
　　Our faults to take.

Give thanks to God alway,
　　O thou Man:
Give thank to God alway
　　With heart-most joy.
Give thanks to God alway
On this our joyful day:
Let all men sing and say,
　　Holy, Holy!'

Having concluded the last note they listened for a minute
or two, but found that no sound issued from the school-
house.

'Four breaths, and then, "O, what unbounded good-ness!", number fifty-nine,' said William.

This was duly gone through, and no notice whatever seemed to be taken of the performance.

'Good guide us, surely 'tisn't a' empty house, as befell us in the year thirty-nine and forty-three!'[24] said old Dewy.

'Perhaps she's jist come from some musical city, and sneers at our doings?' the tranter whispered.

' 'Od rabbit her!' said Mr Penny, with an annihilating look at a corner of the school chimney, 'I don't quite stom-ach her, if this is it. Your plain music well done is as worthy as your other sort done bad, a' b'lieve, souls; so say I.'

'Four breaths, and then the last,' said the leader authori-tatively. ' "Rejoice, ye Tenants of the Earth", number sixty-four.'

At the close, waiting yet another minute, he said in a clear loud voice, as he had said in the village at that hour and season for the previous forty years –

'A merry Christmas to ye!'

5   The Listeners

When the expectant stillness consequent upon the exclamation had nearly died out of them all, an increasing light made itself visible in one of the windows of the upper floor. It came so close to the blind that the exact position of the flame could be perceived from the outside. Remaining steady for an instant, the blind went upward from before it, revealing to thirty concentrated eyes a young girl framed as a picture by the window architrave,[1] and unconsciously illuminating her countenance to a vivid brightness by a candle she held in her left hand, close to her face, her right hand being extended to the side of the window. She was wrapped in a white robe of some kind, whilst down her shoulders fell a twining profusion of marvellously rich hair, in a wild disorder which proclaimed it to be only during the invisible hours of the night that such a condition was discoverable. Her bright eyes were looking into the grey world outside with an uncertain expression, oscillating between courage and shyness, which, as she recognized the semicircular group of dark forms gathered before her, transformed itself into pleasant resolution.

Opening the window, she said lightly and warmly —

'Thank you, singers, thank you!'

Together went the window quickly and quietly, and the blind started downward on its return to its place. Her fair forehead and eyes vanished; her little mouth; her neck and shoulders; all of her. Then the spot of candlelight shone nebulously as before; then it moved away.

'How pretty!' exclaimed Dick Dewy.

'If she'd been rale[2] wexwork she couldn't ha' been come-lier,' said Michael Mail.

'As near a thing to a spiritual vision as ever *I* wish to see!' said tranter Dewy.

'O, sich[3] I never, never see!' said Leaf fervently.

All the rest, after clearing their throats and adjusting their hats, agreed that such a sight was worth singing for.

'Now to Farmer Shiner's, and then replenish our insides, father?' said the tranter.

'Wi' all my heart,' said old William, shouldering his bass-viol.

Farmer Shiner's was a queer lump of a house, standing at the corner of a lane that ran into the principal thorough-fare. The upper windows were much wider than they were high, and this feature, together with a broad bay-window where the door might have been expected, gave it by day the aspect of a human countenance turned askance, and wearing a sly and wicked leer. Tonight nothing was visible but the outline of the roof upon the sky.

The front of this building was reached, and the prelimin-aries arranged as usual.

'Four breaths, and number thirty-two, "Behold the Morn-ing Star",' said old William.

They had reached the end of the second verse, and the fiddlers were doing the up bow-stroke previously to pouring forth the opening chord of the third verse, when, without a light appearing or any signal being given a roaring voice exclaimed –

'Shut up, woll 'ee![4] Don't make your blaring row here! A feller wi' a headache enough to split his skull likes a quiet night!'

Slam went the window.

'Hullo, that's a' ugly blow for we!' said the tranter, in a keenly appreciative voice, and turning to his companions.

'Finish the carrel, all who be friends of harmony!' commanded old William; and they continued to the end.

'Four breaths, and number nineteen!' said William firmly. 'Give it him well; the quire can't be insulted in this manner!'

A light now flashed into existence, the window opened, and the farmer stood revealed as one in a terrific passion.

'Drown en! – drown en!' the tranter cried, fiddling frantically. 'Play fortissimy,[5] and drown his spaking!'[6]

'Fortissimy!' said Michael Mail, and the music and singing waxed so loud that it was impossible to know what Mr Shiner had said, was saying, or was about to say; but wildly flinging his arms and body about in the forms of capital Xs and Ys, he appeared to utter enough invectives to consign the whole parish to perdition.

'Very onseemly – very!' said old William, as they retired. 'Never such a dreadful scene in the whole round o' my carrel practice – never! And he a churchwarden!'

'Only a drap o' drink got into his head,' said the tranter. 'Man's well enough when he's in his religious frame. He's in his worldly frame now. Must ask en to our bit of a party tomorrow night, I suppose, and so put en in humour again. We bear no mortal man ill-will.'

They now crossed Mellstock Bridge, and went along an embowered path beside the Froom towards the church and vicarage, meeting Voss with the hot mead and bread-and-cheese as they were approaching the churchyard. This determined them to eat and drink before proceeding further, and they entered the church and ascended to the gallery. The lanterns were opened, and the whole body sat round against the walls on benches and whatever else was available, and made a hearty meal. In the pauses of conversation there could be heard through the floor overhead a little world of undertones and creaks from the halting clockwork, which never spread further than the tower they were born in, and raised in the more meditative minds a fancy that here lay the direct pathway of Time.

Having done eating and drinking they again tuned the instruments, and once more the party emerged into the night air.

'Where's Dick?' said old Dewy.

Every man looked round upon every other man, as if Dick might have been transmuted into one or the other; and then they said they didn't know.

'Well, now, that's what I call very nasty of Master Dicky, that I do,' said Michael Mail.

'He've clinked off home-along,[7] depend upon't,' another suggested, though not quite believing that he had.

'Dick!' exclaimed the tranter, and his voice rolled sonorously forth among the yews.

He suspended his muscles rigid as stone whilst listening for an answer, and finding he listened in vain, turned to the assemblage.

'The treble man[8] too! Now if he'd been a tenor or counter chap,[9] we might ha' contrived the rest o't without en, you see. But for a quire to lose the treble, why, my sonnies, you may so well lose your. . . .' The tranter paused, unable to mention an image vast enough for the occasion.

'Your head at once,' suggested Mr Penny.

The tranter moved a pace as if it were puerile of people to complete sentences when there were more pressing things to be done.

'Was ever heard such a thing as a young man leaving his work half done and turning tail like this!'

'Never,' replied Bowman, in a tone signifying that he was the last man in the world to wish to withhold the formal finish required of him.

'I hope no fatal tragedy has overtook the lad!' said his grandfather.

'Oh no,' replied tranter Dewy placidly. 'Wonder where

he's put that there fiddle of his. Why, that fiddle cost thirty shillings, and good words besides. Somewhere in the damp, without doubt; that instrument will be unglued and spoilt in ten minutes – ten! ay, two.'

'What in the name o' righteousness can have happened?' said old William, more uneasily. 'Perhaps he's drowned!'[10]

Leaving their lanterns and instruments in the belfry they retraced their steps along the waterside track. 'A strapping lad like Dick d'know better than let anything happen on-awares,' Reuben remarked. 'There's sure to be some poor little scram[11] reason for't staring us in the face all the while.' He lowered his voice to a mysterious tone: 'Neighbours, have ye noticed any sign of a scornful woman in his head, or suchlike?'

'Not a glimmer of such a body. He's as clear as water yet.'

'And Dicky said he should never marry,' cried Jimmy, 'but live at home always along wi' mother and we!'

'Ay, ay, my sonny; every lad has said that in his time.'

They had now again reached the precincts of Mr Shiner's, but hearing nobody in that direction, one or two went across to the schoolhouse. A light was still burning in the bedroom, and though the blind was down the window had been slightly opened, as if to admit the distant notes of the carollers to the ears of the occupant of the room.

Opposite the window, leaning motionless against a beech tree, was the lost man, his arms folded, his head thrown back, his eyes fixed upon the illuminated lattice.

'Why, Dick, is that thee? What b'st[12] doing here?'

Dick's body instantly flew into a more rational attitude, and his head was seen to turn east and west in the gloom as if endeavouring to discern some proper answer to that question; and at last he said in rather feeble accents –

'Nothing, father.'

'Th'st take long enough time about it then, upon my body,' said the tranter as they all turned anew towards the vicarage.

'I thought you hadn't done having snap[13] in the gallery,' said Dick.

'Why, we've been traypsing[14] and rambling about, looking everywhere, and thinking you'd done fifty deathly things, and here have you been at nothing at all!'

'The stupidness lies in that point of it being nothing at all,' murmured Mr Spinks.

The vicarage front was their next field of operation, and Mr Maybold, the lately-arrived incumbent,[15] duly received his share of the night's harmonies. It was hoped that by reason of his profession he would have been led to open the window, and an extra carol in quick time was added to draw him forth. But Mr Maybold made no stir.

'A bad sign!' said old William, shaking his head.

However, at that same time a musical voice was heard exclaiming from inner depths of bedclothes –

'Thanks, villagers!'

'What did he say?' asked Bowman, who was rather dull of hearing. Bowman's voice, being therefore loud, had been heard by the vicar within.

'I said, "Thanks, villagers!"' cried the vicar again.

'Oh, we didn't hear 'ee the first time!' cried Bowman.

'Now don't for heaven's sake spoil the young man's temper by answering like that!' said the tranter.

'You won't do that, my friends!' the vicar shouted.

'Well to be sure, what ears!' said Mr Penny in a whisper. 'Beats any horse or dog in the parish, and depend upon't that's a sign he's a proper clever chap.'

'We shall see that in time,' said the tranter.

Old William, in his gratitude for such thanks from a comparatively new inhabitant, was anxious to play all the tunes over again; but renounced his desire on being reminded by Reuben that it would be best to leave well alone.

minded by Reuben that it would be best to leave well alone.

'Now putting two and two together,' the tranter continued, as they went their way over the hill, and across to the last remaining houses; 'that is, in the form of that young female vision we zeed[16] just now, and this young tenor-voiced parson, my belief is she'll wind en round her finger, and twist the pore young feller about like the figure of 8 – that she will, my sonnies.'

6 Christmas Morning

The choir at last reached their beds, and slept like the rest of the parish. Dick's slumbers, through the three or four hours remaining for rest, were disturbed and slight; an exhaustive variation upon the incidents that had passed that night in connection with the school-window going on in his brain every moment of the time.

In the morning, do what he would – go upstairs, downstairs, out of doors, speak of the wind and weather, or what not – he could not refrain from an unceasing renewal, in imagination, of that interesting enactment. Tilted on the edge of one foot he stood beside the fireplace, watching his mother grilling rashers; but there was nothing in grilling, he thought, unless the Vision grilled. The limp rasher hung down between the bars of the gridiron[1] like a cat in a child's arms; but there was nothing in similes unless She uttered them. He looked at the daylight shadows of a yellow hue, dancing with the firelight shadows in blue on the whitewashed chimney corner, but there was nothing in shadows. 'Perhaps the new young wom – sch – Miss Fancy Day will sing in church with us this morning,' he said.

The tranter looked a long time before he replied, 'I fancy she will; and yet I fancy she won't.'

Dick implied that such a remark was rather to be tolerated than admired; though deliberateness in speech was known to have, as a rule, more to do with the machinery of the tranter's throat than with the matter enunciated.

They made preparations for going to church as usual;

Dick with extreme alacrity, though he would not definitely consider why he was so religious. His wonderful nicety in brushing and cleaning his best light boots had features which elevated it to the rank of an art. Every particle and speck of last week's mud was scraped and brushed from toe and heel; new blacking[2] from the packet was carefully mixed and made use of, regardless of expense. A coat was laid on and polished; then another coat for increased blackness; and lastly a third, to give the perfect and mirror-like jet which the hoped-for rencounter[3] demanded.

It being Christmas-day, the tranter prepared himself with Sunday particularity. Loud sousing and snorting noises were heard to proceed from a tub in the back quarters of the dwelling, proclaiming that he was there performing his great Sunday wash, lasting half-an-hour, to which his washings on working-day mornings were mere flashes in the pan.[4] Vanishing into the outhouse with a large brown towel, and the above-named bubblings and snortings being carried on for about twenty minutes, the tranter would appear round the edge of the door, smelling like a summer fog, and looking as if he had just narrowly escaped a watery grave with the loss of much of his clothes, having since been weeping bitterly till his eyes were red; a crystal drop of water hanging ornamentally at the bottom of each ear, one at the tip of his nose, and others in the form of spangles about his hair.

After a great deal of crunching upon the sanded stone floor by the feet of father, son, and grandson as they moved to and fro in these preparations, the bass-viol and fiddles were taken from their nook, and the strings examined and screwed a little above concert-pitch, that they might keep their tone when the service began, to obviate the awkward contingency of having to re-tune them at the back of the gallery during a cough, sneeze, or amen – an inconvenience which had been known to arise in damp wintry weather.

The three left the door and paced down Mellstock Lane
and across the ewelease, bearing under their arms the instruments in faded green-baize bags, and old brown music-
books in their hands; Dick continually finding himself in
advance of the other two, and the tranter moving on with
toes turned outwards to an enormous angle.

At the foot of an incline the church became visible
through the north gate, or 'church hatch', as it was called
here. Seven agile figures in a clump were observable beyond, which proved to be the choristers waiting; sitting on
an altar-tomb[5] to pass the time, and letting their heels
dangle against it. The musicians being now in sight the
youthful party scampered off and rattled up the old wooden
stairs of the gallery like a regiment of cavalry; the other
boys of the parish waiting outside and observing birds,
cats, and other creatures till the vicar entered, when they
suddenly subsided into sober churchgoers, and passed
down the aisle with echoing heels.

The gallery of Mellstock Church had a status and
sentiment of its own. A stranger there was regarded with a
feeling altogether differing from that of the congregation below towards him. Banished from the nave[6] as an intruder
whom no originality could make interesting, he was received above as a curiosity that no unfitness could render
dull. The gallery, too, looked down upon and knew the
habits of the nave to its remotest peculiarity, and had an
extensive stock of exclusive information about it; whilst the
nave knew nothing of the gallery folk, as gallery folk,[7] beyond their loud-sounding minims[8] and chest notes. Such
topics as that the clerk[9] was always chewing tobacco except at the moment of crying amen; that he had a dust-
hole[10] in his pew; that during the sermon certain young
daughters of the village had left off caring to read anything
so mild as the marriage service for some years, and now
regularly studied the one which chronologically follows

it;[11] that a pair of lovers touched fingers through a knot-hole[12] between their pews in the manner ordained by their great exemplars,[13] Pyramus and Thisbe;[14] that Mrs Led-low, the farmer's wife, counted her money and reckoned her week's marketing expenses during the first lesson – all news to those below – were stale subjects here.

Old William sat in the centre of the front row, his violoncello between his knees and two singers on each hand. Behind him, on the left, came the treble singers and Dick; and on the right the tranter and the tenors. Further back was old Mail with the altos[15] and supernumeraries.[16]

But before they had taken their places, and whilst they were standing in a circle at the back of the gallery practising a psalm or two, Dick cast his eyes over his grandfather's shoulder, and saw the vision of the past night enter the porch-door as methodically as if she had never been a vision at all. A new atmosphere seemed suddenly to be puffed into the ancient edifice by her movement, which made Dick's body and soul tingle with novel sensations. Directed by Shiner, the churchwarden, she proceeded to the small aisle on the north side of the chancel,[17] a spot now allotted to a throng of Sunday-school girls, and distinctly visible from the gallery-front by looking under the curve of the furthermost arch on that side.

Before this moment the church had seemed comparatively empty – now it was thronged; and as Miss Fancy rose from her knees and looked around her for a permanent place in which to deposit herself – finally choosing the remotest corner – Dick began to breathe more freely the warm new air she had brought with her; to feel rushings of blood, and to have impressions that there was a tie between her and himself visible to all the congregation.

Ever afterwards the young man could recollect individually each part of the service of that bright Christmas morning, and the trifling occurrences which took place as its minutes slowly drew along; the duties of that day dividing themselves by a complete line from the services of other times. The tunes they that morning essayed remained with him for years, apart from all others; also the text; also the appearance of the layer of dust upon the capitals of the piers;[18] that the holly-bough in the chancel archway was hung a little out of the centre – all the ideas, in short, that creep into the mind when reason is only exercising its lowest activity through the eye.

By chance or by fate, another young man who attended Mellstock Church on that Christmas morning had towards the end of the service the same instinctive perception of an interesting presence, in the shape of the same bright maiden, though his emotion reached a far less developed stage. And there was this difference, too, that the person in question was surprised at his condition, and sedulously endeavoured to reduce himself to his normal state of mind. He was the young vicar, Mr Maybold.

The music on Christmas mornings was frequently below the standard of church-performances at other times. The boys were sleepy from the heavy exertions of the night; the men were slightly wearied; and now, in addition to these constant reasons, there was a dampness in the atmosphere that still further aggravated the evil. Their strings, from the recent long exposure to the night air, rose whole semitones, and snapped with a loud twang at the most silent moment; which necessitated more retiring than ever to the back of the gallery, and made the gallery throats quite husky with the quantity of coughing and hemming[19] required for tuning in. The vicar looked cross.

When the singing was in progress there was suddenly discovered to be a strong and shrill reinforcement from some point, ultimately found to be the school-girls' aisle. At every attempt it grew bolder and more distinct. At the third time of singing, these intrusive feminine voices were as

mighty as those of the regular singers; in fact, the flood of
sound from this quarter assumed such an individuality, that
it had a time, a key, almost a tune of its own, surging upwards when the gallery plunged downwards, and the reverse.

Now this had never happened before within the memory
of man. The girls, like the rest of the congregation, had
always been humble and respectful followers of the gallery;
singing at sixes and sevens if without gallery leaders; never
interfering with the ordinances of these practised artists –
having no will, union, power, or proclivity[20] except it was
given them from the established choir enthroned above
them.

A good deal of desperation became noticeable in the gallery throats and strings, which continued throughout the
musical portion of the service. Directly the fiddles were
laid down, Mr Penny's spectacles put in their sheath,
and the text had been given out, an indignant whispering
began.

'Did ye hear that, souls?' Mr Penny said, in a groaning
breath.

'Brazen-faced hussies!' said Bowman.

'True; why, they were every note as loud as we, fiddles
and all, if not louder!'

'Fiddles and all!' echoed Bowman bitterly.

'Shall anything saucier be found than united 'ooman?'[21]
Mr Spinks murmured.

'What I want to know is,' said the tranter (as if he knew
already, but that civilization required the form of words),
'what business people have to tell maidens to sing like that
when they don't sit in a gallery, and never have entered one
in their lives? That's the question, my sonnies.'

' 'Tis the gallery have got to sing, all the world knows,'
said Mr Penny. 'Why, souls, what's the use o' the ancients
spending scores of pounds to build galleries if people down

in the lowest depths of the church sing like that at a moment's notice?'

'Really, I think we useless ones had better march out of church, fiddles and all!' said Mr Spinks, with a laugh which, to a stranger, would have sounded mild and real. Only the initiated body of men he addressed could understand the horrible bitterness of irony that lurked under the quiet words 'useless ones', and the ghastliness of the laughter apparently so natural.

'Never mind! Let 'em sing too – 'twill make it all the louder – hee, hee!' said Leaf.

'Thomas Leaf, Thomas Leaf! Where have you lived all your life?' said grandfather William sternly.

The quailing Leaf tried to look as if he had lived nowhere at all.

'When all's said and done, my sonnies,' Reuben said, 'there'd have been no real harm in their singing if they had let nobody hear 'em, and only jined[22] in now and then.'

'None at all,' said Mr Penny. 'But though I don't wish to accuse people wrongfully, I'd say before my lord judge that I could hear every note o' that last psalm come from 'em as much as from us – every note as if 'twas their own.'

'Know it! ah, I should think I did know it!' Mr Spinks was heard to observe at this moment without reference to his fellow-players – shaking his head at some idea he seemed to see floating before him, and smiling as if he were attending a funeral at the time. 'Ah, do I or don't I know it!'

No one said 'Know what?' because all were aware from experience that what he knew would declare itself in process of time.

'I could fancy last night that we should have some trouble wi' that young man,' said the tranter, pending the continuance of Spinks's speech, and looking towards the unconscious Mr Maybold in the pulpit.

'*I* fancy,' said old William, rather severely, 'I fancy there's too much whispering going on to be of any spiritual use to gentle or simple.'[23] Then folding his lips and concentrating his glance on the vicar, he implied that none but the ignorant would speak again; and accordingly there was silence in the gallery, Mr Spinks's telling speech remaining for ever unspoken.

Dick had said nothing, and the tranter little, on this episode of the morning; for Mrs Dewy at breakfast expressed it as her intention to invite the youthful leader of the culprits to the small party it was customary with them to have on Christmas-night – a piece of knowledge which had given a particular brightness to Dick's reflections since he had received it. And in the tranter's slightly cynical nature, party feeling was weaker than in the other members of the choir, though friendliness and faithful partnership still sustained in him a hearty earnestness on their account.

7 The Tranter's Party

During the afternoon unusual activity was seen to prevail about the precincts of tranter Dewy's house. The flagstone floor was swept of dust, and a sprinkling of the finest yellow sand from the innermost stratum[1] of the adjoining sand-pit lightly scattered thereupon. Then were produced large knives and forks, which had been shrouded in darkness and grease since the last occasion of the kind, and bearing upon their sides, 'Shear-steel,[2] warranted', in such emphatic letters of assurance, that the warranter's name was not required as further proof, and not given. The key was left in the tap of the cider-barrel instead of being carried in a pocket. And finally the tranter had to stand up in the room and let his wife wheel him round like a turnstile, to see if anything discreditable was visible in his appearance.

'Stand still till I've been for the scissors,' said Mrs Dewy.

The tranter stood as still as a sentinel at the challenge.

The only repairs necessary were a trimming of one or two whiskers that had extended beyond the general contour of the mass; a like trimming of a slightly-frayed edge visible on his shirt-collar; and a final tug at a grey hair – to all of which operations he submitted in resigned silence, except the last, which produced a mild 'Come, come, Ann,' by way of expostulation.

'Really, Reuben, 'tis quite a disgrace to see such a man,' said Mrs Dewy, with the severity justifiable in a long-tried companion, giving him another turn round, and picking several of Smiler's hairs from the shoulder of his coat. Reuben's thoughts seemed engaged elsewhere, and he yawned. 'And the collar of your coat is a shame to behold – so plastered with dirt, or dust, or grease, or something. Why, wherever could you have got it?'

' 'Tis my warm nater[3] in summer-time, I suppose. I always did get in such a heat when I bustle about.'

'Ay, the Dewys always were such a coarse-skinned family. There's your brother Bob just as bad – as fat as a porpose – wi' his low, mean, "How'st do, Ann?" whenever he meets me. I'd "How'st do" him indeed! If the sun only shines out a minute, there be you all streaming in the face – I never see!'

'If I be hot week-days, I must be hot Sundays.'

'If any of the girls should turn after their father 'twill be a bad look-out for 'em, poor things! None of my family was sich vulgar sweaters, not one of 'em. But, Lord-a-mercy, the Dewys! I don't know how ever I cam' into such a family!'

'Your woman's weakness when I asked ye to jine us. That's how it was, I suppose.' But the tranter appeared to have heard some such words from his wife before, and hence his answer had not the energy it might have shown if the inquiry had possessed the charm of novelty.

'You never did look so well in a pair o' trousers as in them,' she continued in the same unimpassioned voice, so that the unfriendly criticism of the Dewy family seemed to have been more normal than spontaneous. 'Such a cheap pair as 'twas too. As big as any man could wish to have, and lined inside, and double-lined in the lower parts, and an extra piece of stiffening at the bottom. And 'tis a nice high cut that comes up right under your armpits, and there's enough turned down inside the seams to make half a pair more, besides a piece of cloth left that will make an honest waistcoat – all by my contriving in buying the stuff at a bargain, and having it made up under my eye. It only shows what may be done by taking a little trouble, and not going straight to the rascally tailors.'

The discourse was cut short by the sudden appearance of Charley on the scene, with a face and hands of hideous blackness, and a nose like a guttering candle. Why, on that particularly cleanly afternoon, he should have discovered that the chimney-crook[4] and chain from which the hams were suspended should have possessed more merits and general interest as playthings than any other articles in the house, is a question for nursing mothers to decide. However, the humour seemed to lie in the result being, as has been seen, that any given player with these articles was in the long-run daubed with soot. The last that was seen of Charley by daylight after this piece of ingenuity was when in the act of vanishing from his father's presence round the corner of the house – looking back over his shoulder with an expression of great sin on his face, like Cain[5] as the Outcast in Bible pictures.

The guests had all assembled, and the tranter's party had reached that degree of development which accords with ten o'clock p.m. in rural assemblies. At that hour the sound of a fiddle in process of tuning was heard from the inner pantry.

'That's Dick,' said the tranter. 'That lad's crazy for a jig.'

'Dick! Now I cannot – really, I cannot have any dancing at all till Christmas-day is out,' said old William emphatically. 'When the clock ha' done striking twelve, dance as much as ye like.'

'Well, I must say there's reason in that, William,' said Mrs Penny. 'If you do have a party on Christmas-night, 'tis only fair and honourable to the sky-folk[6] to have it a sit-still party. Jigging parties be all very well on the Devil's holidays; but a jigging party looks suspicious now. O yes;

stop till the clock strikes, young folk – so say I.'

It happened that some warm mead accidentally got into Mr Spinks's head about this time.

'Dancing,' he said, 'is a most strengthening, livening, and courting movement, 'specially with a little beverage added! And dancing is good. But why disturb what is ordained, Richard and Reuben, and the company zhinerally?[7] Why, I ask, as far as that do go?'

'Then nothing till after twelve,' said William.

Though Reuben and his wife ruled on social points, religious questions were mostly disposed of by the old man, whose firmness on this head quite counterbalanced a certain weakness in his handling of domestic matters. The hopes of the younger members of the household were therefore relegated to a distance of one hour and three-quarters – a result that took visible shape in them by a remote and listless look about the eyes – the singing of songs being permitted in the interim.

At five minutes to twelve the soft tuning was again heard in the back quarters; and when at length the clock had whizzed forth the last stroke, Dick appeared ready primed, and the instruments were boldly handled; old William very readily taking the bass-viol from its accustomed nail, and touching the strings as irreligiously as could be desired.

The country-dance called the 'Triumph, or Follow my Lover', was the figure with which they opened. The tranter took for his partner Mrs Penny, and Mrs Dewy was chosen by Mr Penny, who made so much of his limited height by a judicious carriage of the head, straightening of the back, and important flashes of his spectacle-glasses, that he seemed almost as tall as the tranter. Mr Shiner, age about thirty-five, farmer and churchwarden, a character principally composed of a crimson stare, vigorous breath, and a watch-chain, with a mouth hanging on a dark smile but never smiling, had come quite willingly to the party, and showed a wondrous obliviousness of all his antics on the previous night. But the comely, slender, prettily-dressed prize Fancy Day fell to Dick's lot, in spite of some private machinations of the farmer, for the reason that Mr Shiner, as a richer man, had shown too much assurance in asking the favour, whilst Dick had been duly courteous.

We gain a good view of our heroine as she advances to her place in the ladies' line. She belonged to the taller division of middle height. Flexibility was her first characteristic, by which she appeared to enjoy the most easeful rest when she was in gliding motion. Her dark eyes – arched by brows of so keen, slender, and soft a curve that they resembled nothing so much as two slurs in music[8] – showed primarily a bright sparkle each. This was softened by a frequent thoughtfulness, yet not so frequent as to do away, for more than a few minutes at a time, with a certain coquettishness; which in its turn was never so decided as to banish honesty. Her lips imitated her brows in their clearly-cut outline and softness of bend; and her nose was well shaped – which is saying a great deal, when it is remembered that there are a hundred pretty mouths and eyes for one pretty nose. Add to this, plentiful knots of dark-brown hair, a gauzy dress of white with blue facings; and the slightest idea may be gained of the young maiden who showed, amidst the rest of the dancing-ladies, like a flower among vegetables. And so the dance proceeded. Mr Shiner, according to the interesting rule laid down, deserted his own partner and made off down the middle with this fair one of Dick's – the pair appearing from the top of the room like two persons tripping down a lane to be married. Dick trotted behind with what was intended to be a look of composure, but which was, in fact, a rather silly expression of feature – implying, with too much earnestness, that such an elopement could not be tolerated. Then they turned and came back, when Dick grew more rigid around his mouth,

and blushed with ingenuous ardour as he joined hands with
the rival and formed the arch over his lady's head, which
presumably gave the figure its name; relinquishing her
again at setting to partners, when Mr Shiner's new chain
quivered in every link, and all the loose flesh upon the
tranter – who here came into action again – shook like
jelly. Mrs Penny, being always rather concerned for her
personal safety when she danced with the tranter, fixed her
face to a chronic smile of timidity the whole time it lasted –
a peculiarity which filled her features with wrinkles, and
reduced her eyes to little straight lines like hyphens, as she
jigged up and down opposite him; repeating in her own
person not only his proper movements, but also the minor
flourishes which the richness of the tranter's imagination
led him to introduce from time to time – an imitation which
had about it something of slavish obedience, not unmixed
with fear.

The ear-rings of the ladies now flung themselves wildly
about, turning violent summersaults, banging this way and
that, and then swinging quietly against the ears sustaining
them. Mrs Crumpler – a heavy woman, who, for some
reason which nobody ever thought worth inquiry, danced in
a clean apron – moved so smoothly through the figure that
her feet were never seen; conveying to imaginative minds
the idea that she rolled on castors.

Minute after minute glided by, and the party reached the
period when ladies' back-hair begins to look forgotten and
dissipated; when a perceptible dampness makes itself apparent upon the faces even of delicate girls – a ghastly dew
having for some time rained from the features of their masculine partners; when skirts begin to be torn out of their
gathers; when elderly people, who have stood up to please
their juniors, begin to feel sundry small tremblings in the
region of the knees, and to wish the interminable dance was
at Jericho;[9] when (at country parties of the thorough sort)

waistcoats begin to be unbuttoned, and when the fiddlers' chairs have been wriggled, by the frantic bowing[10] of their occupiers, to a distance of about two feet from where they originally stood.

Fancy was dancing with Mr Shiner. Dick knew that Fancy, by the law of good manners, was bound to dance as pleasantly with one partner as with another; yet he could not help suggesting to himself that she need not have put *quite* so much spirit into her steps, nor smiled *quite* so frequently whilst in the farmer's hands.

'I'm afraid you didn't cast off,'[11] said Dick mildly to Mr Shiner, before the latter man's watch-chain had done vibrating from a recent whirl.

Fancy made a motion of accepting the correction; but her partner took no notice, and proceeded with the next movement with an affectionate bend towards her.

'That Shiner's too fond of her,' the young man said to himself as he watched them. They came to the top again, Fancy smiling warmly towards her partner, and went to their places.

'Mr Shiner, you didn't cast off,' said Dick, for want of something else to demolish him with; casting off himself, and being put out at the farmer's irregularity.

'Perhaps I shan't cast off for any man,' said Mr Shiner.

'I think you ought to, sir.'

Dick's partner, a young lady of the name of Lizzy – called Lizz for short – tried to mollify.

'I can't say that I myself have much feeling for casting off,' she said.

'Nor I,' said Mrs Penny, following up the argument; 'especially if a friend and neighbour is set against it. Not but that 'tis a terrible tasty thing in good hands and well done; yes, indeed, so say I.'

'All I meant was,' said Dick, rather sorry that he had spoken correctingly to a guest, 'that 'tis in the dance; and a man has hardly any right to hack and mangle what was ordained by the regular dancemaker, who, I daresay, got his living by making 'em, and thought of nothing else all his life.'

'I don't like casting off: then very well; I cast off for no dancemaker that ever lived.'

Dick now appeared to be doing mental arithmetic, the act being really an effort to present to himself, in an abstract form, how far an argument with a formidable rival ought to be carried when that rival was his mother's guest. The deadlock was put an end to by the stamping arrival up the middle of the tranter, who, despising minutiae[12] on principle, started a theme of his own.

'I assure you, neighbours,' he said, 'the heat of my frame no tongue can tell!' He looked around and endeavoured to give, by a forcible gaze of self-sympathy, some faint idea of the truth.

Mrs Dewy formed one of the next couple.

'Yes,' she said in an auxiliary tone, 'Reuben always was such a hot man.'

Mrs Penny implied the species of sympathy that such a class of affliction required by trying to smile and to look grieved at the same time.

'If he only walk round the garden of a Sunday morning his shirt-collar is as limp as no starch at all,' continued Mrs Dewy, her countenance lapsing parenthetically into a housewifely expression of concern at the reminiscence.

'Come, come, you women-folk; 'tis hands-across[13] – come, come!' said the tranter; and the conversation ceased for the present.

8 They Dance more Wildly

Dick had at length secured Fancy for that most delightful of country-dances, opening with six-hands-round.[1]

'Before we begin,' said the tranter, 'my proposal is, that 'twould be a right and proper plan for every mortal man in the dance to pull off his jacket, considering the heat.'

'Such low notions as you have, Reuben! Nothing but strip will go down with you when you are a-dancing. Such a hot man as he is!'

'Well, now, look here, my sonnies,' he argued to his wife, whom he often addressed in the plural masculine for economy of epithet merely; 'I don't see that. You dance and get hot as fire; therefore you lighten your clothes. Isn't that nature and reason for gentle and simple? If I strip by myself and not necessary, 'tis rather pot-housey[2] I own; but if we stout chaps strip one and all, why, 'tis the native manners of the country, which no man can gainsay? Hey – what did you say, my sonnies?'

'Strip we will!' said the three other heavy men who were in the dance; and their coats were accordingly taken off and hung in the passage, whence the four sufferers from heat soon reappeared marching in close column, with flapping shirt-sleeves, and having as common to them all a general glance of being now a match for any man or dancer in England or Ireland. Dick, fearing to lose ground in Fancy's good opinion, retained his coat like the rest of the thinner men; and Mr Shiner did the same from superior knowledge.

And now a further phase of revelry had disclosed itself.

It was the time of night when a guest may write his name in the dust upon the tables and chairs, and a bluish mist pervades the atmosphere, becoming the distinct halo round the candles; when people's nostrils, wrinkles, and crevices in general seem to be getting gradually plastered up; when the very fiddlers as well as the dancers get red in the face, the dancers having advanced further still towards incandescence,[3] and entered the cadaverous[4] phase; the fiddlers no longer sit down, but kick back their chairs and saw madly at the strings with legs firmly spread and eyes closed, regardless of the visible world. Again and again did Dick share his Love's hand with another man, and wheel round; then, more delightfully, promenade in a circle with her all to himself, his arm holding her waist more firmly each time, as his elbow getting further and further behind her back, till the distance reached was rather noticeable; and, most blissful, swinging to places shoulder to shoulder, her breath curling round his neck like a summer zephyr[5] that had strayed from its proper date. Threading the couples one by one they reached the bottom, when there arose in Dick's mind a minor misery lest the tune should end before they could work their way to the top again, and have anew the same exciting run down through. Dick's feelings on actually reaching the top in spite of his doubts were supplemented by a mortal fear that the fiddling might even stop at this supreme moment; which prompted him to convey a stealthy whisper to the far-gone musicians to the effect that they were not to leave off till he and his partner had reached the bottom of the dance once more, which remark was replied to by the nearest of those convulsed and quivering men by a private nod to the anxious young man between two semiquavers of the tune, and a simultaneous 'All right, ay, ay,' without opening the eyes. Fancy was now held so closely that Dick and she were practically one person. The room became to Dick like a picture in a dream; all that he could remember of it afterwards being the look of the fiddlers going to sleep as humming-tops sleep,[6] by increasing their motion and hum, together with the figures of grandfather James and old Simon Crumpler sitting by the chimney-corner talking and nodding in dumb-show, and beating the air to their emphatic sentences like people near a threshing machine.

The dance ended. 'Piph-h-h-h!' said tranter Dewy, blowing out his breath in the very finest stream of vapour that a man's lips could form. 'A regular tightener, that one, sonnies!' He wiped his forehead, and went to the cider and ale mugs on the table.

'Well!' said Mrs Penny, flopping into a chair, 'my heart haven't been in such a thumping state of uproar since I used to sit up on old Midsummer-eves[7] to see who my husband was going to be.'

'And that's getting on for a good few years ago now, from what I've heard you tell,' said the tranter without lifting his eyes from the cup he was filling. Being now engaged in the business of handing round refreshments he was warranted in keeping his coat off still, though the other heavy men had resumed theirs.

'And a thing I never expected would come to pass, if you'll believe me, came to pass then,' continued Mrs Penny. 'Ah, the first spirit ever I see on a Midsummer-eve was a puzzle to me when he appeared, a hard puzzle, so say I!'

'So I should have fancied,' said Elias Spinks.

'Yes,' said Mrs Penny, throwing her glance into past times and talking on in a running tone of complacent abstraction, as if a listener were not a necessity. 'Yes; never was I in such a taking as on that Midsummer-eve! I sat up, quite determined to see if John Wildway was going to marry me or no. I put the bread-and-cheese and beer quite ready, as the witch's book ordered, and I opened the door, and I waited till the clock struck twelve, my nerves all alive and so strained that I could feel every one of 'em twitching like bell-wires. Yes, sure! and when the clock had struck, lo and behold I could see through the door a *little small* man in the lane wi' a shoemaker's apron on.'

Here Mr Penny stealthily enlarged himself half an inch.

'Now, John Wildway,' Mrs Penny continued, 'who courted me at that time, was a shoemaker, you see, but he was a very fair-sized man, and I couldn't believe that any such a little small man had anything to do wi' me, as anybody might. But on he came, and crossed the threshold – not John, but actually the same little small man in the shoemaker's apron—'

'You needn't be so mighty particular about little and small!' said her husband.

'In he walks, and down he sits, and O my goodness me, didn't I flee upstairs, body and soul hardly hanging together! Well, to cut a long story short, by-long and by-late[8] John Wildway and I had a miff[9] and parted; and lo and behold, the coming man came! Penny asked me if I'd go snacks with him,[10] and afore I knew what I was about a'most, the thing was done.'

'I've fancied you never knew better in your life; but I mid[11] be mistaken,' said Mr Penny in a murmur.

After Mrs Penny had spoken, there being no new occupation for her eyes she still let them stay idling on the past scenes just related, which were apparently visible to her in the centre of the room. Mr Penny's remark received no reply.

During this discourse the tranter and his wife might have been observed standing in an unobtrusive corner in mysterious closeness to each other, a just perceptible current of intelligence passing from each to each, which had apparently no relation whatever to the conversation of their guests, but much to their sustenance. A conclusion of some kind having at length been drawn, the palpable confederacy of man and wife was once more obliterated, the tranter marching off into the pantry humming a tune that he couldn't quite recollect, and then breaking into the words of a song of which he could remember about one line and a quarter. Mrs Dewy spoke a few words about the preparations for a bit of supper.

That elder portion of the company which loved eating and drinking put on a look to signify that till this moment they had quite forgotten that it was customary to expect suppers on these occasions; going even further than this politeness of feature, and starting irrelevant subjects, the exceeding flatness and forced tone of which rather betrayed their object. The younger members said they were quite hungry, and that supper would be delightful though it was so late.

Good luck attended Dick's love-passes during the meal. He sat next Fancy, and had the thrilling pleasure of using permanently a glass which had been taken by Fancy in mistake; of letting the outer edge of the sole of his boot touch the lower verge of her skirt; and to add to these delights the cat, which had lain unobserved in her lap for several minutes, crept across into his own, touching him with fur that had touched her hand a moment before. There were, besides, some little pleasures in the shape of helping her to vegetable she didn't want, and when it had nearly alighted on her plate taking it across for his own use, on the plea of waste not, want not. He also, from time to time, slipped sweet sly glances at her profile; noticing the set of her head, the curve of her throat, and other artistic properties of the lively goddess, who the while kept up a rather free, not to say too free, conversation with Mr Shiner sitting opposite; which, after some uneasy criticism, and much shifting of argument backwards and forwards in Dick's mind, he decided not to consider of alarming significance.

'A new music greets our ears now,' said Miss Fancy,

alluding, with the sharpness that her position as village sharpener[12] demanded, to the contrast between the rattle of knives and forks and the late notes of the fiddlers.

'Ay; and I don't know but what 'tis sweeter in tone when you get above forty,' said the tranter; 'except, in faith, as regards father there. Never such a mortal man as he for tunes. They do move his soul; don't 'em, father?'

The eldest Dewy smiled across from his distant chair an assent to Reuben's remark.

'Spaking of being moved in soul,' said Mr Penny, 'I shall never forget the first time I heard the "Dead March".[13] 'Twas at poor Corp'l Nineman's funeral at Casterbridge. It fairly made my hair creep and fidget about like a vlock[14] of sheep – ah, it did, souls! And when they had done, and the last trump[15] had sounded, and the guns was fired over the dead hero's grave, a' icy-cold drop o' moist sweat hung upon my forehead, and another upon my jawbone. Ah, 'tis a very solemn thing!'

'Well, as to father in the corner there,' the tranter said, pointing to old William, who was in the act of filling his mouth; 'he'd starve to death for music's sake now, as much as when he was a boy-chap of fifteen.'

'Truly, now,' said Michael Mail, clearing the corner of his throat in the manner of a man who meant to be convincing; 'there's a friendly tie of some sort between music and eating.' He lifted the cup to his mouth, and drank himself gradually backwards from a perpendicular position to a slanting one, during which time his looks performed a circuit from the wall opposite him to the ceiling overhead. Then clearing the other corner of his throat: 'Once I was a-setting in the little kitchen of the Dree Mariners[16] at Casterbridge, having a bit of dinner, and a brass band struck up in the street. Such a beautiful band as that were! I was setting eating fried liver and lights,[17] I well can mind – ah, I was! and to save my life, I couldn't help chawing[18]

to the tune. Band played six-eight time;[19] six-eight chaws
I, willynilly. Band plays common; common time[20] went
my teeth among the liver and lights as true as a hair. Beautiful 'twere! Ah, I shall never forget that there band!'

'That's as tuneful a thing as ever I heard of,' said grandfather James, with the absent gaze which accompanies pro-
found criticism.

'I don't like Michael's tuneful stories then,' said Mrs
Dewy. 'They are quite coarse to a person o' decent taste.'

Old Michael's mouth twitched here and there, as if he
wanted to smile but didn't know where to begin, which
gradually settled to an expression that it was not displeas-
ing for a nice woman like the tranter's wife to correct him.

'Well, now,' said Reuben, with decisive earnestness, 'that
sort o' coarse touch that's so upsetting to Ann's feelings is
to my mind a recommendation; for it do always prove a
story to be true. And for the same reason, I like a story
with a bad moral. My sonnies, all true stories have a coarse
touch or a bad moral, depend upon't. If the story-tellers
could ha' got decency and good morals from true stories,
who'd have troubled to invent parables?' Saying this the
tranter arose to fetch a new stock of cider, ale, mead, and
home-made wines.

Mrs Dewy sighed and appended a remark (ostensibly
behind her husband's back, though that the words should
reach his ears distinctly was understood by both): 'Such a
man as Dewy is! Nobody do know the trouble I have to
keep that man barely respectable. And did you ever hear
too – just now at supper-time – talking about "taties" with
Michael in such a work-folk way. Well, 'tis what I was
never brought up to! With our family 'twas never less than
"taters", and very often "pertatoes" outright; mother was
so particular and nice with us girls: there was no family in
the parish that kept themselves up more than we.'

The hour of parting came. Fancy could not remain for

the night because she had engaged a woman to wait up for her. She disappeared temporarily from the flagging party of dancers, and then came downstairs wrapped up and looking altogether a different person from whom she had been hitherto, in fact (to Dick's sadness and disappointment), a woman somewhat reserved and of a phlegmatic temperament – nothing left in her of the romping girl that she had seemed but a short quarter-hour before, who had not minded the weight of Dick's hand upon her waist, nor shirked the purlieus of the mistletoe.[21]

'What a difference!' thought the young man – hoary synic *pro tem*.[22] 'What a miserable deceiving difference between the manners of a maid's life at dancing times and at others! Look at this lovely Fancy! Through the whole past evening touchable, squeezable – even kissable! For whole half-hours I held her so close to me that not a sheet of paper could have been slipped between us; and I could feel her heart only just outside my own, her life beating on so close to mine, that I was aware of every breath in it. A flit is made upstairs – a hat and a cloak put on – and I no more dare to touch her than—' Thought failed him, and he returned to realities.

But this was an endurable misery in comparison with what followed. Mr Shiner and his watch-chain, taking the intrusive advantage that ardent bachelors who are going homeward along the same road as a pretty young woman always do take of that circumstance, came forward to assure Fancy – with a total disregard of Dick's emotions, and in tones which were certainly not frigid – that he (Shiner) was not the man to go to bed before seeing his Lady Fair safe within her own door – not he, nobody should say he was that; – and that he would not leave her side an inch till the thing was done – drown him if he would. The proposal was assented to by Miss Day, in Dick's foreboding judgement, with one degree – or at any rate, an appreciable fraction of a degree – of warmth beyond that required by a disinterested desire for protection from the dangers of the night.

All was over; and Dick surveyed the chair she had last occupied, looking now like a setting from which the gem has been torn. There stood her glass, and the romantic teaspoonful of elder wine[23] at the bottom that she couldn't drink by trying ever so hard, in obedience to the mighty arguments of the tranter (his hand coming down upon her shoulder the while like a Nasmyth hammer[24]); but the drinker was there no longer. There were the nine or ten pretty little crumbs she had left on her plate; but the eater was no more seen.

There seemed a disagreeable closeness of relationship between himself and the members of his family now that they were left alone again face to face. His father seemed quite offensive for appearing to be in just as high spirits as when the guests were there; and as for grandfather James (who had not yet left), he was quite fiendish in being rather glad they were gone.

'Really,' said the tranter, in a tone of placid satisfaction, 'I've had so little time to attend to myself all the evenen that I mean to enjoy a quiet meal now! A slice of this here ham – neither too fat nor too lean – so; and then a drop of this vinegar and pickles – there, that's it – and I shall be as fresh as a lark again! And to tell the truth, my sonny, my inside has been as dry as a lime-basket[25] all night.'

'I like a party very well once in a while,' said Mrs Dewy, leaving off the adorned tones she had been bound to use throughout the evening and returning to the natural marriage voice; 'but, Lord, 'tis such a sight of heavy work next day! What with the dirty plates, and knives and forks, and dust and smother, and bits kicked off your furniture, and I don't know what all, why, a body could a'most wish there were no such things as Christmases.... Ah-h dear!' she yawned, till the clock in the corner had ticked several beats. She cast her eyes round upon the displaced, dust-laden furniture, and sat down overpowered at the sight.

'Well, I be getting all right by degrees, thank the Lord for't!' said the tranter cheerfully through a mangled mass of ham and bread, without lifting his eyes from his plate, and chopping away with his knife and fork as if he were felling trees. 'Ann, you may as well go on to bed at once, and not bide there making such sleepy faces; you look as long-favoured as a fiddle, upon my life, Ann. There, you must be wearied out, 'tis true. I'll do the doors and draw up the clock;[26] and you go on, or you'll be as white as a sheet tomorrow.'

'Ay; I don't know whether I shan't or no.' The matron passed her hand across her eyes to brush away the film of sleep till she got upstairs.

Dick wondered how it was that when people were married they could be so blind to romance; and was quite certain that if he ever took to wife that dear impossible Fancy, he and she would never be so dreadfully practical and undemonstrative of the Passion as his father and mother were. The most extraordinary thing was that all the fathers and mothers he knew were just as undemonstrative as his own.

9 Dick calls at the School

The early days of the year drew on, and Fancy, having spent the holiday weeks at home, returned again to Mellstock.

Every spare minute of the week following her return was used by Dick in accidentally passing the schoolhouse in his journeys about the neighbourhood; but not once did she make herself visible. A handkerchief belonging to her had been providentially found by his mother in clearing the rooms the day after that of the dance; and by much contrivance Dick got it handed over to him, to leave with her at any time he should be near the school after her return. But he delayed taking the extreme measure of calling with it lest, had she really no sentiment of interest in him, it might be regarded as a slightly absurd errand, the reason guessed, and the sense of the ludicrous, which was rather keen in her, do his dignity considerable injury in her eyes; and what she thought of him, even apart from the question of her loving, was all the world to him now.

But the hour came when the patience of love at twenty-one could endure no longer. One Saturday he approached the school with a mild air of indifference, and had the satisfaction of seeing the object of his quest at the further end of her garden, trying, by the aid of a spade and gloves, to root a bramble that had intruded itself there.

He disguised his feelings from some suspicious-looking cottage-windows opposite by endeavouring to appear like a man in a great hurry of business, who wished to leave the handkerchief and have done with such trifling errands.

This endeavour signally failed; for on approaching the gate he found it locked to keep the children, who were playing 'cross-dadder'[1] in the front, from running into her private grounds.

She did not see him; and he could only think of one thing to be done, which was to shout her name.

'Miss Day!'

The words were uttered with a jerk and a look meant to imply to the cottages opposite that he was now simply one who liked shouting as a pleasant way of passing his time, without any reference to persons in gardens. The name died away, and the unconscious Miss Day continued digging and pulling as before.

He screwed himself up to enduring the cottage-windows yet more stoically, and shouted again. Fancy took no notice whatever.

He shouted the third time, with desperate vehemence, turning suddenly about and retiring a little distance as if it were by no means for his own pleasure that he had come.

This time she heard him, came down the garden, and entered the school at the back. Footsteps echoed across the interior, the door opened, and three-quarters of the blooming young schoolmistress's face and figure stood revealed before him; a slice on her left-hand side being cut off by the edge of the door. Having surveyed and recognized him she came to the gate.

At sight of him had the pink of her cheeks increased, lessened, or did it continue to cover its normal area of ground? It was a question meditated several hundreds of times by her visitor in after-hours – the meditation, after wearying involutions, always ending in one way, that it was impossible to say.

'Your handkerchief: Miss Day: I called with.' He held it out spasmodically and awkwardly. 'Mother found it: under a chair.'

'Oh, thank you very much for bringing it, Mr Dewy. I couldn't think where I had dropped it.'

Now Dick, not being an experienced lover – indeed, never before having been engaged in the practice of love-making at all, except in a small schoolboy way – could not take advantage of the situation; and out came the blunder which afterwards cost him so many bitter moments and a sleepless night:

'Good morning, Miss Day.'

'Good morning, Mr Dewy.'

The gate was closed; she was gone; and Dick was standing outside, unchanged in his condition from what he had been before he called. Of course the Angel was not to blame – a young woman living alone in a house could not ask him indoors unless she had known him better – he should have kept her outside before floundering into that fatal farewell. He wished that before he called he had realized more fully than he did the pleasure of being about to call; and turned away.

Part the Second

Spring

1   Passing by the School

It followed that as the spring advanced Dick walked
abroad much more frequently than had hitherto been usual
with him, and was continually finding that his nearest way
to or from home lay by the road which skirted the garden of
the school. The first-fruits of his perseverance were that, on
turning the angle on the nineteenth journey by that track,
he saw Miss Fancy's figure, clothed in a dark-grey dress,
looking from a high open window upon the crown of his
hat. The friendly greeting resulting from this rencounter
was considered so valuable an elixir[1] that Dick passed still
oftener; and by the time he had almost trodden a little path
under the fence where never a path was before, he was
rewarded with an actual meeting face to face on the open
road before her gate. This brought another meeting, and
another, Fancy faintly showing by her bearing that it was a
pleasure to her of some kind to see him there; but the sort
of pleasure she derived, whether exultation at the hope her
exceeding fairness inspired, or the true feeling which was
alone Dick's concern, he could not anyhow decide, although he meditated on her every little movement for hours
after it was made.

2 A Meeting of the Quire

It was the evening of a fine spring day. The descending sun appeared as a nebulous[1] blaze of amber light, its outline being lost in cloudy masses hanging round it like wild locks of hair.

The chief members of the Mellstock parish choir were standing in a group in front of Mr Penny's workshop in the lower village. They were all brightly illuminated, and each was backed up by a shadow as long as a steeple; the lowness of the source of light rendering the brims of their hats of no use at all as a protection to the eyes.

Mr Penny's was the last house in that part of the parish, and stood in a hollow by the roadside; so that cart-wheels and horses' legs were about level with the sill of his shop-window. This was low and wide, and was open from morning till evening, Mr Penny himself being invariably seen working inside like a framed portrait of a shoemaker by some modern Moroni.[2] He sat facing the road, with a boot on his knees and the awl[3] in his hand, only looking up for a moment as he stretched out his arms and bent forward at the pull, when his spectacles flashed in the passer's face with a shine of flat whiteness, and then returned again to the boot as usual. Rows of lasts, small and large, stout and slender, covered the wall which formed the background, in the extreme shadow of which a kind of dummy was seen sitting, in the shape of an apprentice with a string tied round his hair (probably to keep it out of his eyes). He smiled at remarks that floated in from without, but was never known to answer them in Mr Penny's presence. Outside the window the upper-leather of a Wellington-boot[4] was usually hung, pegged to a board as if to dry. No sign was over his door; in fact – as with old banks and mercan-tile[5] houses – advertising in any shape was scorned, and it would have been felt as beneath his dignity to paint up, for the benefit of strangers, the name of an establishment whose trade came solely by connection based on personal respect.

His visitors now came and stood on the outside of his window, sometimes leaning against the sill, sometimes mov-ing a pace or two backwards and forwards in front of it. They talked with deliberate gesticulations to Mr Penny, en-throned in the shadow of the interior.

'I do like a man to stick to men who be in the same line o' life – o' Sundays, anyway – that I do so.'

' 'Tis like all the doings of folk who don't know what a day's work is, that's what I say.'

'My belief is the man's not to blame; 'tis *she* – she's the bitter weed!'

'No, not altogether. He's a poor gawk-hammer.[6] Look at his sermon yesterday.'

'His sermon was well enough, a very good guessable sermon, only he couldn't put it into words and speak it. That's all was the matter wi' the sermon. He hadn't been able to get it past his pen.'

'Well – ay, the sermon might have been good; for, 'tis true, the sermon of Old Eccl'iastes[7] himself lay in Eccl'i-astes's ink-bottle afore he got it out.'

Mr Penny, being in the act of drawing the last stitch tight, could afford time to look up and throw in a word at this point.

'He's no spouter[8] – that must be said, 'a b'lieve.'

' 'Tis a terrible muddle sometimes with the man, as far as spout do go,' said Spinks.

'Well, we'll say nothing about that,' the tranter answered; 'for I don't believe 'twill make a penneth[9] o' difference to we poor martels here or hereafter whether his sermons be good or bad, my sonnies.'

Mr Penny made another hole with his awl, pushed in the thread, and looked up and spoke again at the extension of arms.[10]

' 'Tis his goings-on, souls, that's what it is.' He clenched his features for an Herculean[11] addition to the ordinary pull, and continued, 'The first thing he done when he came here was to be hot and strong about church business.'

'True,' said Spinks; 'that was the very first thing he done.'

Mr Penny, having now been offered the ear of the assembly, accepted it, ceased stitching, swallowed an unimportant quantity of air as if it were a pill, and continued:

'The next thing he do do is to think about altering the church, until he found 'twould be a matter o' cost and what not, and then not to think no more about it.'

'True: that was the next thing he done.'

'And the next thing was to tell the young chaps that they were not on no account to put their hats in the christening font during service.'

'True.'

'And then 'twas this, and then 'twas that, and now 'tis—'

Words were not forcible enough to conclude the sentence, and Mr Penny gave a huge pull to signify the concluding word.

'Now 'tis to turn us out of the quire neck and crop,'[12] said the tranter after an interval of half a minute, not by way of explaining the pause and pull, which had been quite understood, but as a means of keeping the subject well before the meeting.

Mrs Penny came to the door at this point in the discussion. Like all good wives, however much she was inclined to play the Tory[13] to her husband's Whiggism,[14] and *vice versa*, in times of peace, she coalesced with[15] him heartily enough in time of war.

'It must be owned he's not all there,' she replied in a general way to the fragments of talk she had heard from indoors. 'Far below poor Mr Grinham' (the late vicar).

'Ay, there was this to be said for he, that you were quite sure he'd never come mumbudgeting[16] to see ye, just as you were in the middle of your work, and put you out with his fuss and trouble about ye.'

'Never. But as for this new Mr Maybold, though he mid be a very well-intending party in that respect, he's unbearable; for as to sifting your cinders, scrubbing your floors, or emptying your slops, why, you can't do it. I assure you I've not been able to empt them for several days, unless I throw 'em up the chimley or out of winder; for as sure as the sun you meet him at the door, coming to ask how you are, and 'tis such a confusing thing to meet a gentleman at the door when ye are in the mess o' washing.'

''Tis only for want of knowing better, poor gentleman,' said the tranter. 'His meaning's good enough. Ay, your pa'son comes by fate: 'tis heads or tails, like pitch-half-penny,[17] and no choosing; so we must take en as he is, my sonnies, and thank God he's no worse, I suppose.'

'I fancy I've seen him look across at Miss Day in a warmer way than Christianity asked for,' said Mrs Penny musingly; 'but I don't quite like to say it.'

'O no; there's nothing in that,' said grandfather William.

'If there's nothing, we shall see nothing,' Mrs Penny replied in the tone of a woman who might possibly have private opinions still.

'Ah, Mr Grinham was the man!' said Bowman. 'Why, he never troubled us wi' a visit from year's end to year's end. You might go anywhere, do anything: you'd be sure never to see him.'

'Yes; he was a right sensible pa'son,' said Michael. 'He

never entered our door but once in his life, and that was to tell my poor wife – ay, poor soul, dead and gone now, as we all shall! – that as she was such a' old aged person, and lived so far from the church, he didn't at all expect her to come any more to the service.'

'And 'a was a very jinerous[18] gentleman about choosing the psalms and hymns o' Sundays. "Confound ye," says he, "blare and scrape what ye will, but don't bother me!"'

'And he was a very honourable man in not wanting any of us to come and hear him if we were all on-end for[19] a jaunt or spree, or to bring the babies to be christened if they were inclined to squalling. There's good in a man's not putting a parish to unnecessary trouble.'

'And there's this here man never letting us have a bit o' peace; but keeping on about being good and upright till 'tis carried to such a pitch as I never see the like afore nor since!'

'No sooner had he got here than he found the font wouldn't hold water, as it hadn't for years off and on; and when I told him that Mr Grinham never minded it, but used to spet upon his vinger[20] and christen 'em just as well, 'a said, "Good Heavens! Send for a workman immediate. What place have I come to!" Which was no compliment to us, come to that.'

'Still, for my part,' said old William, 'though he's arrayed against us, I like the hearty borus-snorus[21] ways of the new pa'son.'

'You, ready to die for the quire,' said Bowman reproachfully, 'to stick up for the quire's enemy, William!'

'Nobody will feel the loss of our church-work so much as I,' said the old man firmly: 'that you d'all know. I've a-been in the quire man and boy ever since I was a chiel of eleven. But for all that 'tisn't in me to call the man a bad man, because I truly and sincerely believe en to be a good young feller.'

Some of the youthful sparkle that used to reside there animated William's eye as he uttered the words, and a certain nobility of aspect was also imparted to him by the setting sun, which gave him a Titanic[22] shadow at least thirty feet in length, stretching away to the east in outlines of imposing magnitude, his head finally terminating upon the trunk of a grand old oak-tree.

'Mayble's a hearty feller enough,' the tranter replied, 'and will spak to you be you dirty or be you clane.[23] The first time I met en was in a drong,[24] and though 'a didn't know me no more than the dead 'a passed the time of day. "D'ye do!" he said says he, nodding his head. "A fine day." Then the second time I met en was full-bluff[25] in town street, when my breeches were tore into a long strent[26] by getting through a copse of thorns and brimbles[27] for a short cut home-along; and not wanting to disgrace the man by spaking in that state, I fixed my eye on the weathercock to let en pass me as a stranger. But no: "How d'ye do, Reuben?" says he, right hearty, and shook my hand. If I'd been dressed in silver spangles from top to toe the man couldn't have been civiller.'

At this moment Dick was seen coming up the village street, and they turned and watched him.

3   A Turn in the Discussion

'I'm afraid Dick's a lost man,' said the tranter.

'What? – no!' said Mail, implying by his manner that it was a far commoner thing for his ears to report what was not said than that his judgment should be at fault.

'Ay,' said the tranter, still gazing at Dick's unconscious advance. 'I don't at all like what I see! There's too many o' them looks out of the winder without noticing anything; too much shining of boots; too much peeping round corners; too much looking at the clock; telling about clever things *she* did till you be sick of it, and then upon a hint to that effect a horrible silence about her. I've walked the path once in my life and know the country, neighbours; and Dick's a lost man!' The tranter turned a quarter round and smiled a smile of miserable satire at the setting new moon, which happened to catch his eye.

The others became far too serious at his announcement to allow them to speak; and they still regarded Dick in the distance.

' 'Twas his mother's fault,' the tranter continued, 'in asking the young woman to our party last Christmas. When I eyed the blue frock and light heels o' the maid, I had my thoughts directly. "God bless thee, Dicky my sonny," I said to myself, "there's a delusion for thee!"'

'They seemed to be rather distant in manner last Sunday, I thought?' Mail tentatively observed, as became one who was not a member of the family.

'Ay, that's a part of the zickness. Distance belongs to it,

slyness belongs to it, queerest things on earth belongs to it! There, 'tmay[1] as well come early as late s'far as I know. The sooner begun, the sooner over; for come it will.'

'The question I ask is,' said Mr Spinks, connecting into one thread the two subjects of discourse, as became a man learned in rhetoric, and beating with his hand in a way which signified that the manner rather than the matter of his speech was to be observed, 'how did Mr Maybold know she could play the organ? You know we had it from her own lips, as far as lips go, that she has never, first or last, breathed such a thing to him; much less that she ever would play.'

In the midst of this puzzle Dick joined the party, and the news which had caused such a convulsion among the ancient musicians was unfolded to him. 'Well,' he said, blushing at the allusion to Miss Day, 'I know by some words of hers that she has a particular wish not to play, because she is a friend of ours; and how the alteration comes I don't know.'

'Now, this is my plan,' said the tranter, reviving the spirit of the discussion by the infusing of new ideas, as was his custom – 'this is my plan; if you don't like it, no harm's done. We all know one another very well, don't we, neighbours?'

That they knew one another very well was received as a statement which, though familiar, should not be omitted in introductory speeches.

'Then I say this' – and the tranter in his emphasis slapped down his hand on Mr Spinks's shoulder with a momentum of several pounds, upon which Mr Spinks tried to look not in the least startled – 'I say that we all move down-along[2] straight as a line to Pa'son Mayble's when the clock has gone six tomorrow night. There we one and all stand in the passage; then one or two of us go in and spak to en, man and man, and say, "Pa'son Mayble, every tradesman

d'like to have his own way in his workshop, and Mellstock
Church is yours. Instead of turning us out neck and crop, let
us stay on till Christmas, and we'll gie way to the young
woman, Mr Mayble, and make no more ado about it. Add
we shall always be quite willing to touch our hats when we
meet ye, Mr Mayble, just as before." That sounds very
well? Hey?'

'Proper well, in faith, Reuben Dewy.'

'And we won't sit down in his house; 'twould be looking
too familiar when only just reconciled?'

'No need at all to sit down. Just do our duty man and
man, turn round, and march out – he'll think all the more
of us for it.'

'I hardly think Leaf had better go wi' us?' said Michael,
turning to Leaf and taking his measure from top to bottom
by the eye. 'He's so terrible silly that he might ruin the
concern.'

'He don't want to go much; do ye, Thomas Leaf?' said
William.

'Hee-hee! no; I don't want to. Only a teeny bit!'

'I be mortal afeard, Leaf, that you'll never be able to tell
how many cuts d'take to sharpen a spar,'[3] said Mail.

'I never had no head, never! that's how it happened to
happen, hee-hee!'

They all assented to this, not with any sense of humiliating Leaf by disparaging him after an open confession, but
because it was an accepted thing that Leaf didn't in the
least mind having no head, that deficiency of his being an
unimpassioned matter of parish history.

'But I can sing my treble!' continued Thomas Leaf, quite
delighted at being called a fool in such a friendly way; 'I
can sing my treble as well as any maid, or married woman
either, and better! And if Jim had lived, I should have had
a clever brother! Tomorrow is poor Jim's birthday. He'd
ha' been twenty-six if he'd lived till tomorrow.'

'You always seem very sorry for Jim,' said old William musingly.

'Ah! I do. Such a stay to mother as he'd always have been! She'd never have had to work in her old age if he had continued strong, poor Jim!'

'What was his age when a' died?'

'Four hours and twenty minutes, poor Jim. 'A was born as might be at night; and 'a didn't last as might be till the morning. No, 'a didn't last. Mother called en Jim on the day that would ha' been his christening-day if he had lived; and she's always thinking about en. You see, he died so very young.'

'Well, 'twas rather youthful,' said Michael.

'Now to my mind that woman is very romantical on the matter o' children?' said the tranter, his eye sweeping his audience.

'Ah, well she mid be,' said Leaf. 'She had twelve regular one after another, and they all, except myself, died very young;[4] either before they was born or just afterwards.'

'Pore feller, too. I suppose th'st want to come wi' us?' the tranter murmured.

'Well, Leaf, you shall come wi' us as yours is such a melancholy family,' said old William rather sadly.

'I never see such a melancholy family as that afore in my life,' said Reuben. 'There's Leaf's mother, poor woman! Every morning I see her eyes mooning out through the panes of glass like a pot-sick winder-flower;[5] and as Leaf sings a very high treble, and we don't know what we should do without en for upper G, we'll let en come as a trate,[6] poor feller.'

'Ay, we'll let en come, 'a b'lieve,' said Mr Penny, looking up, as the pull happened to be at that moment.

'Now,' continued the tranter, dispersing by a new tone of voice these digressions about Leaf; 'as to going to see the pa'son, one of us might call and ask en his meaning, and 'twould be just as well done; but it will add a bit of a flourish to the cause if the quire waits on him as a body. Then the great thing to mind is, not for any of our fellers to be nervous; so before starting we'll one and all come to my house and have a rasher of bacon; then every man-jack[7] het[8] a pint of cider into his inside; then we'll warm up an extra drop wi' some mead and a bit of ginger; every one take a thimbleful – just a glimmer of a drop, mind ye, no more, to finish off his inner man – and march off to Pa'son Mayble. Why, sonnies, a man's not himself till he is fortified wi' a bit and a drop! We shall be able to look any gentle-man in the face then without shrink or shame.'

Mail recovered from a deep meditation and downward glance into the earth in time to give a cordial approval to this line of action, and the meeting adjourned.

1   Thomas Hardy in 1872

~~The Mellstock Quire~~
or
Under the Greenwood Tree

A rural painting of the Dutch School.

Part I. Winter.

Chapter I

Mellstock Lane.

To dwellers in a wood, almost every species of tree has its voice as well as its feature. At the passing of the breeze the fir-trees sob & moan no less distinctly than they rock: the holly whistles as it battles with itself: the ash hisses amid its quivering: the beech rustles as its flat boughs rise & fall. And winter, which modifies the notes of such trees as shed their leaves, does not destroy their individuality.

On a cold & starry Christmas-eve, not less than a generation ago a man was passing along a lane in the darkness of a plantation that whispered thus distinctly to his intelligence. All the evidences of his nature were those afforded by the spirit of his footsteps, which succeeded each other lightly & quickly, & by the liveliness of his voice as he sang in a rural cadence.

"... With the rose & the lily
And the daffadowndilly,
The lads & the lasses a-sheep-shearing go."

they were bound, whilst the faint sound of college bells *(crimson above "college")*
ringing a Christmas peal could be heard floating over upon
the breeze from the direction of Mintfield parish on the other
side of the hills. A little wicket admitted them to a
garden, & they proceeded up the path to Dick's house.

Chapter II.

~~[crossed out line]~~

The tranter's.

It was a small low cottage with a thatched pyramidal
roof, & having dormer windows breaking up into the eaves,
a single chimney standing in the very midst. The window-shutters
were not yet closed, & the fire & candle-light within radiated
forth upon the bushes of variegated box & thick laurestinus
growing in a throng outside, & upon the bare boughs of
several codlin trees hanging above, in various distorted
shapes — the result of early training as espaliers, & of
careless climbing into their boughs in later years. The walls
of the dwelling were for the most part covered with creepers,
though these were rather beaten back from the doorway —
~~a feature which was worn and scratched by much~~ *(crossed out)*
(giving it by day the appearance of) passing in & out, an old keyhole. Light streamed
through the cracks & joints of a wooden shed at the end of the
cottage — ~~[crossed out]~~ which nourished a fancy that
the purpose of the erection must be rather to veil bright
attractions than to shelter unsightly necessaries. The
noise of a beetle & wedges & the splintering of wood was
sometimes heard from this direction, & at the other end
of the house, a steady regular munching & the *occasional* scurr of a
rope betokened a stable, & horses feeding *within it* ~~[crossed out]~~.

The choir stamped severally on the door-stone to shake
from their boots any fragment of dirt or leaf adhering thereto

4 & 5 Thomas Hardy's cottage at Higher Bockhampton: (*above*) exterior view and (*below*) looking out from Hardy's bedroom

4   The Interview with the Vicar

At six o'clock next day the whole body of men in the choir
emerged from the tranter's door, and advanced with a firm
step down the lane. This dignity of march gradually became obliterated as they went on, and by the time they
reached the hill behind the vicarage a faint resemblance to
a flock of sheep might have been discerned in the venerable
party. A word from the tranter, however, set them right
again; and as they descended the hill, the regular tramp,
tramp, tramp of the united feet was clearly audible from
the vicarage garden. At the opening of the gate there was
another short interval of irregular shuffling, caused by a
rather peculiar habit the gate had, when swung open
quickly, of striking against the bank and slamming back
into the opener's face.

'Now keep step again, will ye?' said the tranter. 'It looks
better, and more becomes the high class of arrant[1] which
has brought us here.' Thus they advanced to the door.

At Reuben's ring the more modest of the group turned
aside, adjusted their hats, and looked critically at any shrub
that happened to lie in the line of vision; endeavouring thus
to give a person who chanced to look out of the windows
the impression that their request, whatever it was going to
be, was rather a casual thought occurring whilst they were
inspecting the vicar's shrubbery and grass-plot than a pre-
determined thing. The tranter who, coming frequently to the
vicarage with luggage, coals, firewood, etc., had none of the
awe for its precincts that filled the breasts of most of the

others, fixed his eyes firmly on the knocker during this interval of waiting. The knocker having no characteristic
worthy of notice he relinquished it for a knot in one of the
door-panels, and studied the winding lines of the grain.

'O, sir, please, here's Tranter Dewy, and old William
Dewy, and young Richard Dewy, O, and all the quire too,
sir, except the boys, a-come to see you!' said Mr Maybold's
maid-servant to Mr Maybold, the pupils of her eyes dilating
like circles in a pond.[2]

'All the choir?' said the astonished vicar (who may be
shortly described as a good-looking young man with courageous eyes, timid mouth, and neutral nose), abandoning
his writing and looking at his parlour-maid after speaking,
like a man who fancied he had seen her face before but
couldn't recollect where.

'And they looks very firm, and Tranter Dewy do turn
neither to the right hand nor to the left,[3] but stares quite
straight and solemn with his mind made up!'

'O, all the choir,' repeated the vicar to himself, trying by
that simple device to trot out his thoughts on what the choir
could come for.

'Yes; every man-jack of 'em, as I be alive!' (The parlour-
maid was rather local in manner, having in fact been raised
in the same village.) 'Really, sir, 'tis thoughted by many in
town and country that—'

'Town and country—! Heavens, I had no idea that I was
public property in this way!' said the vicar, his face acquir-
ing a hue somewhere between that of the rose and the
peony. 'Well, "It is thought in town, and country that—"'

'It is thought that you be going to get it hot and strong! –
excusen my incivility, sir.'

The vicar suddenly recalled to his recollection that he had
long ago settled it to be decidedly a mistake to encourage
his servant Jane in giving personal opinions. The servant
Jane saw by the vicar's face that he recalled this fact to his
mind; and removing her forehead from the edge of the

door, and rubbing away the indent that edge had made, vanished into the passage as Mr Maybold remarked, 'Show them in, Jane.'

A few minutes later a shuffling and jostling (reduced to as refined a form as was compatible with the nature of shuffles and jostles) was heard in the passage; then an earnest and prolonged wiping of shoes, conveying the notion that volumes of mud had to be removed; but the roads being so clean that not a particle of dirt appeared on the choir's boots (those of all the elder members being newly oiled, and Dick's brightly polished), this wiping might have been set down simply as a desire to show that respectable men had no wish to take a mean advantage of clean roads for curtailing proper ceremonies. Next there came a powerful whisper from the same quarter:

'Now stand stock-still there, my sonnies, one and all! And don't make no noise; and keep your backs close to the wall, that company may pass in and out easy if they want to without squeezing through ye; and we two are enough to go in.' ... The voice was the tranter's.

'I wish I could go in too and see the sight!' said a reedy[4] voice – that of Leaf.

''Tis a pity Leaf is so terribly silly, or else he might,' another said.

'I never in my life seed a quire go into a study to have it out about the playing and singing,' pleaded Leaf; 'and I should like to see it just once!'

'Very well; we'll let en come in,' said the tranter. 'You'll be like chips[5] in porridge, Leaf – neither good nor hurt. All right, my sonny, come along'; and immediately himself, old William, and Leaf appeared in the room.

'We took the liberty to come and see 'ee, sir,' said Reuben, letting his hat hang in his left hand, and touching with his right the brim of an imaginary one on his head. 'We've come to see 'ee, sir, man and man and no offence, I hope?'

'None at all,' said Mr Maybold.

'This old aged man standing by my side is father; William Dewy by name, sir.'

'Yes; I see it is,' said the vicar, nodding aside to old William, who smiled.

'I thought ye mightn't know en without his bass-viol,' the tranter apologized. 'You see, he always wears his best clothes and his bass-viol a-Sundays, and it do make such a difference in a' old man's look.'

'And who's that young man?' the vicar said.

'Tell the pa'son yer name,' said the tranter, turning to Leaf, who stood with his elbows nailed back to a book-case.

'Please, Thomas Leaf, your holiness!'[6] said Leaf, trembling.

'I hope you'll excuse his looks being so very thin,' continued the tranter deprecatingly, turning to the vicar again. 'But 'tisn't his fault, poor feller. He's rather silly by nature, and could never get fat; though he's a' excellent treble, and so we keep him on.'

'I never had no head, sir,' said Leaf, eagerly grasping at this opportunity for being forgiven his existence.

'Ah, poor young man!' said Mr Maybold.

'Bless you, he don't mind it a bit, if you don't, sir,' said the tranter assuringly. 'Do ye, Leaf?'

'Not I – not a morsel – hee, hee! I was afeard it mightn't please your holiness, sir, that's all.'

The tranter, finding Leaf get on so very well through his negative qualities, was tempted in a fit of generosity to advance him still higher, by giving him credit for positive ones. 'He's very clever for a silly chap, good-now,[7] sir. You never knowed a young feller keep his smock-frocks so clane; very honest too. His ghastly[8] looks is all there is against en, poor feller; but we can't help our looks, you know, sir.'

'True: we cannot. You live with your mother, I think, Leaf?'

The tranter looked at Leaf to express that the most friendly assistant to his tongue could do no more for him now, and that he must be left to his own resources.

'Yes, sir: a widder, sir. Ah, if brother Jim had lived she'd have had a clever son to keep her without work!'

'Indeed! poor woman. Give her this half-crown. I'll call and see your mother.'

'Say, "Thank you, sir,"' the tranter whispered imperatively towards Leaf.

'Thank you, sir!' said Leaf.

'That's it, then; sit down, Leaf,' said Mr Maybold.

'Y-yes, sir!'

The tranter cleared his throat after this accidental parenthesis about Leaf, rectified his bodily position, and began his speech.

'Mr Mayble,' he said, 'I hope you'll excuse my common way, but I always like to look things in the face.'

Reuben made a point of fixing this sentence in the vicar's mind by gazing hard at him at the conclusion of it, and then out of the window.

Mr Maybold and old William looked in the same direction, apparently under the impression that the things' faces alluded to were there visible.

'What I have been thinking' – the tranter implied by this use of the past tense that he was hardly so discourteous as to be positively thinking it then – 'is that the quire ought to be gie'd a little time, and not done away wi' till Christmas, as a fair thing between man and man. And, Mr Mayble, I hope you'll excuse my common way?'

'I will, I will. Till Christmas,' the vicar murmured, stretching the two words to a great length, as if the distance to Christmas might be measured in that way. 'Well, I want you all to understand that I have no personal fault to find, and that I don't wish to change the church music by forcible means, or in a way which should hurt the feelings of any parishioners. Why I have at last spoken definitely on the subject is that a player has been brought under – I may say pressed upon – my notice several times by one of the churchwardens. And as the organ I brought with me is here waiting' (pointing to a cabinet-organ⁹ standing in the study), 'there is no reason for longer delay.'

'We made a mistake I suppose then, sir? But we understood the young woman didn't want to play particularly?' The tranter arranged his countenance to signify that he did not want to be inquisitive in the least.

'No, nor did she. Nor did I definitely wish her to just yet; for your playing is very good. But, as I said, one of the churchwardens has been so anxious for a change that, as matters stand, I couldn't consistently refuse my consent.'

Now for some reason or other the vicar at this point seemed to have an idea that he had prevaricated; and as an honest vicar it was a thing he determined not to do. He corrected himself, blushing as he did so, though why he should blush was not known to Reuben.

'Understand me rightly,' he said: 'the churchwarden proposed it to me, but I had thought myself of getting – Miss Day to play.'

'Which churchwarden might that be who proposed her, sir? – excusing my common way.' The tranter intimated by his tone that so far from being inquisitive he did not even wish to ask a single question.

'Mr Shiner, I believe.'

'Clk, my sonny! – beg your pardon, sir, that's only a form of words of mine, and slipped out accidental – he nourishes enmity against us for some reason or another; perhaps because we played rather hard upon en Christmas night. Anyhow 'tis certain sure that Mr Shiner's real love for music of a particular kind isn't his reason. He've no more ear than that chair. But let that be.'

'I don't think you should conclude that, because Mr Shiner wants a different music, he has any ill-feeling for you. I myself, I must own, prefer organ-music to any other. I consider it most proper, and feel justified in endeavouring to introduce it; but then, although other music is better, I don't say yours is not good.'

'Well then, Mr Mayble, since death's to be, we'll die like men any day you name (excusing my common way).'

Mr Maybold bowed his head.

'All we thought was, that for us old ancient singers to be choked off quiet at no time in particular, as now, in the Sundays after Easter, would seem rather mean in the eyes of other parishes, sir. But if we fell glorious with a bit of a flourish at Christmas, we should have a respectable end, and not dwindle away at some nameless paltry second-Sunday-after or Sunday-next-before something, that's got no name of his own.'

'Yes, yes, that's reasonable; I own it's reasonable.'

'You see, Mr Mayble, we've got – do I keep you inconvenient long, sir?'

'No, no.'

'We've got our feelings – father there especially.'

The tranter, in his earnestness, had advanced his person to within six inches of the vicar's.

'Certainly, certainly!' said Mr Maybold, retreating a little for convenience of seeing. 'You are all enthusiastic on the subject, and I am all the more gratified to find you so. A Laodicean[10] lukewarmness is worse than wrongheadedness itself.'

'Exactly, sir. In fact now, Mr Mayble,' Reuben continued more impressively, and advancing a little closer still to the vicar, 'father there is a perfect figure o' wonder, in the way of being fond of music!'

The vicar drew back a little further, the tranter suddenly also standing back a foot or two to throw open the view of his father, and pointing to him at the same time.

Old William moved uneasily in the large chair, and with a minute smile on the mere edge of his lips for good manners, said he was indeed very fond of tunes.

'Now, you see exactly how it is,' Reuben continued, appealing to Mr Maybold's sense of justice by looking sideways into his eyes. The vicar seemed to see how it was so well that the gratified tranter walked up to him again with even vehement eagerness, so that his waistcoat buttons almost rubbed against the vicar's as he continued: 'As to father, if you or I, or any man or woman of the present generation, at the time music is a-playing, was to shake your fist in father's face, as may be this way, and say, "Don't you be delighted with that music!"' – the tranter went back to where Leaf was sitting, and held his fist so close to Leaf's face that the latter pressed his head back against the wall: 'All right, Leaf, my sonny, I won't hurt you; 'tis just to show my meaning to Mr Mayble. – As I was saying, if you or I, or any man, was to shake your fist in father's face this way, and say, "William, your life or your music!" he'd say, "My life!" Now that's father's nature all over; and you see, sir, it must hurt the feelings of a man of that kind for him and his bass-viol to be done away wi' neck and crop.'

The tranter went back to the vicar's front and again looked earnestly at his face.

'True, true, Dewy,' Mr Maybold answered, trying to withdraw his head and shoulders without moving his feet; but finding this impracticable, edging back another inch. These frequent retreats had at last jammed Mr Maybold between his easy chair and the edge of the table.

And at the moment of the announcement of the choir Mr Maybold had just re-dipped the pen he was using; at their

entry, instead of wiping it, he had laid it on the table with
the nib overhanging. At the last retreat his coat-tails came
in contact with the pen, and down it rolled, first against the
back of the chair, thence turning a somersault into the seat,
thence falling to the floor with a rattle.

The vicar stooped for his pen, and the tranter, wishing to
show that, however great their ecclesiastical difference, his
mind was not so small as to let this affect his social feelings,
stooped also.

'And have you anything else you want to explain to me,
Dewy?' said Mr Maybold from under the table.

'Nothing, sir. And, Mr Mayble, you be not offended? I
hope you see our desire is reason?' said the tranter from
under the chair.

'Quite, quite; and I shouldn't think of refusing to listen to
such a reasonable request,' the vicar replied. Seeing that
Reuben had secured the pen he resumed his vertical position, and added, 'You know, Dewy, it is often said how difficult a matter it is to act up to our convictions and please all
parties. It may be said with equal truth, that it is difficult for
a man of any appreciativeness to have convictions at all.
Now in my case, I see right in you, and right in Shiner. I see
that violins are good, and that an organ is good; and when
we introduce the organ it will not be that fiddles were bad,
but that an organ was better. That you'll clearly understand, Dewy?'

'I will; and thank you very much for such feelings, Sir.
Piph-h-h-h! How the blood do get into my head, to be
sure, whenever I quat[11] down like that!' said Reuben, who
having also risen to his feet stuck the pen vertically in the
inkstand and almost through the bottom, that it might not
roll down again under any circumstances whatever.

Now the ancient body of minstrels in the passage felt
their curiosity surging higher and higher as the minutes
passed. Dick, not having much affection for this errand,

soon grew tired, and went away in the direction of the
school. Yet their sense of propriety would probably have
restrained them from any attempt to discover what was
going on in the study had not the vicar's pen fallen to the
floor. The conviction that the movement of chairs, etc.,
necessitated by the search, could only have been caused by
the catastrophe of a bloody fight beginning, overpowered
all other considerations; and they advanced to the door,
which had only just fallen to. Thus, when Mr Maybold
raised his eyes after the stooping he beheld glaring through
the door Mr Penny in full-length portraiture, Mail's face
and shoulders above Mr Penny's head, Spinks's forehead
and eyes over Mail's crown, and a fractional part of Bowman's countenance under Spinks's arm – crescent-shaped
portions of other heads and faces being visible behind these
– the whole dozen and odd eyes bristling with eager inquiry.

Mr Penny, as is the case with excitable bootmakers and
men, seeing the vicar look at him and hearing no word
spoken, thought it incumbent upon himself to say something of any kind. Nothing suggested itself till he had
looked for about half a minute at the vicar.

'You'll excuse my naming of it, sir,' he said, regarding
with much commiseration the mere surface of the vicar's
face; 'but perhaps you don't know that your chin have bust
out a-bleeding where you cut yourself a-shaving this morning, sir.'

'Now, that was the stooping, depend upon't,' the tranter
suggested, also looking with much interest at the vicar's
chin. 'Blood always will bust out again if you hang down
the member[12] that's been bleeding.'

Old William raised his eyes and watched the vicar's
bleeding chin likewise; and Leaf advanced two or three
paces from the bookcase, absorbed in the contemplation of
the same phenomenon with parted lips and delighted eyes.

'Dear me, dear me!' said Mr Maybold hastily, looking very red and brushing his chin with his hand, then taking out his handkerchief and wiping the place.

'That's it, sir; all right again now, 'a b'lieve – a mere nothing,' said Mr Penny. 'A little bit of fur off your hat will stop it in a minute if it should bust out again.'

'I'll let 'ee have a bit off mine,' said Reuben, to show his good feelings; 'my hat isn't so new as yours, sir, and 'twon't hurt mine a bit.'

'No, no; thank you, thank you,' Mr Maybold again nervously replied.

' 'Twas rather a deep cut seemingly?' said Reuben, feeling these to be the kindest and best remarks he could make.

'O, no; not particularly.'

'Well, sir, your hand will shake sometimes a-shaving, and just when it comes into your head that you may cut yourself, there's the blood.'

'I have been revolving in my mind that question of the time at which we make the change,' said Mr Maybold, 'and I know you'll meet me half-way. I think Christmas Day as much too late for me as the present time is too early for you. I suggest Michaelmas[13] or thereabout as a convenient time for both parties; for I think your objection to a Sunday which has no name is not one of any real weight.'

'Very good, sir. I suppose mortal men mustn't expect their own way entirely; and I express in all our names that we'll make shift and be satisfied with what you say.' The tranter touched the brim of his imaginary hat again, and all the choir did the same. 'About Michaelmas, then, as far as you are concerned, sir, and then we make room for the next generation.'

'About Michaelmas,' said the vicar.

5 Returning Homeward

' 'A took it very well, then?' said Mail, as they all walked up the hill.

'He behaved like a man; 'a did so,' said the tranter. 'And I'm glad we've let en know our minds. And though, beyond that, we ha'n't got much by going, 'twas worthwhile. He won't forget it. Yes, he took it very well. Supposing this tree here was Pa'son Mayble, and I standing here, and thik gr't[1] stone is father sitting in the easy chair. "Dewy," says he, "I don't wish to change the church music in a forcible way." '

'That was very nice o' the man, even though words be wind.'

'Proper nice – out and out nice. The fact is,' said Reuben confidentially, ' 'tis how you take a man. Everybody must be managed. Queens must be managed: kings must be managed; for men want managing almost as much as women, and that's saying a good deal.'

' 'Tis truly!' murmured the husbands.

'Pa'son Mayble and I were as good friends all through it as if we'd been sworn brothers. Ay, the man's well enough; 'tis what's put in his head that spoils him, and that's why we've got to go.'

'There's really no believing half you hear about people nowadays.'

'Bless ye, my sonnies, 'tisn't the pa'son's move at all. That gentleman over there' (the tranter nodded in the direction of Shiner's farm) 'is at the root of the mischty.'[2]

'What! Shiner?'

'Ay; and I see what the pa'son don't see. Why, Shiner is for putting forward that young woman that only last night I was saying was our Dick's sweetheart, but I suppose can't be, and making much of her in the sight of the congregation, and thinking he'll win her by showing her off. Well, perhaps 'a woll.'[3]

'Then the music is second to the woman, the other churchwarden is second to Shiner, the pa'son is second to the churchwardens, and God A'mighty is nowhere at all.'

'That's true; and you see,' continued Reuben, 'at the very beginning it put me in a stud[4] as to how to quarrel wi' en. In short, to save my soul, I couldn't quarrel wi' such a civil man without belying my conscience. Says he to father there, in a voice as quiet as a lamb's, "William, you are a' old aged man, as all shall be, so sit down in my easy chair, and rest yourself." And down father zot.[5] I could fain ha' laughed at thee, father; for thou'st take it so unconcerned at first, and then looked so frightened when the chair-bottom sunk in.'

'You see,' said old William, hastening to explain, 'I was scared to find the bottom gie way – what should I know o' spring bottoms?[6] – and thought I had broke it down; and of course as to breaking down a man's chair, I didn't wish any such thing.'

'And, neighbours, when a feller, ever so much up for a miff, d'see his own father sitting in his enemy's easy chair, and a poor chap like Leaf made the best of, as if he almost had brains – why, it knocks all the wind out of his sail at once: it did out of mine.'

'If that young figure of fun – Fance Day, I mean,' said Bowman, 'hadn't been so mighty forward wi' showing herself off to Shiner and Dick and the rest, 'tis my belief we should never ha' left the gallery.'

' 'Tis my belief that though Shiner fired the bullets, the

parson made 'em,' said Mr Penny. 'My wife sticks to it that he's in love wi' her.'

'That's a thing we shall never know. I can't onriddle her,[7] nohow.'

'Thou'st ought to be able to onriddle such a little chiel as she,' the tranter observed.

'The littler the maid, the bigger the riddle, to my mind. And coming of such a stock, too, she may well be a twister.'[8]

'Yes; Geoffrey Day is a clever man if ever there was one. Never says anything: not he.'

'Never.'

'You might live wi' that man, my sonnies, a hundred years, and never know there was anything in him.'

'Ay; one o' these up-country London ink-bottle chaps[9] would call Geoffrey a fool.'

'Ye never find out what's in that man: never,' said Spinks. 'Close? ah, he is close! He can hold his tongue well. That man's dumbness is wonderful to listen to.'

'There's so much sense in it. Every moment of it is brimmen over wi' sound understanding.'

''A can hold his tongue very clever – very clever truly,' echoed Leaf. ''A do look at me as if 'a could see my thoughts running round like the works of a clock.'

'Well, all will agree that the man can halt well in his talk, be it a long time or be it a short time. And though we can't expect his daughter to inherit his closeness, she may have a few driblets[10] from his sense.'

'And his pocket, perhaps.'

'Yes; the nine hundred pound that everybody says he's worth; but I call it four hundred and fifty; for I never believe more than half I hear.'

'Well, he've made a pound or two, and I suppose the maid will have it, since there's nobody else. But 'tis rather sharp upon her, if she's born to fortune, to bring her up as if not born for it, and letting her work so hard.'

''Tis all upon his principle. A long-headed feller!'

'Ah,' murmured Spinks, ''twould be sharper upon her if she were born for fortune, and not to it! I suffer from that affliction.'

6 Yalbury Wood and the Keeper's House

A mood of blitheness rarely experienced even by young men was Dick's on the following Monday morning. It was the week after the Easter holidays, and he was journeying along with Smart the mare and the light spring-cart,[1] watching the damp slopes of the hill-sides as they streamed in the warmth of the sun, which at this unsettled season shone on the grass with the freshness of an occasional inspector rather than as an accustomed proprietor. His errand was to fetch Fancy, and some additional household goods, from her father's house in the neighbouring parish to her dwelling at Mellstock. The distant view was darkly shaded with clouds; but the nearer parts of the landscape were whitely illumined by the visible rays of the sun streaming down across the heavy grey shade behind.

The tranter had not yet told his son of the state of Shiner's heart that had been suggested to him by Shiner's movements. He preferred to let such delicate affairs right themselves; experience having taught him that the uncertain phenomenon of love, as it existed in other people, was not a groundwork upon which a single action of his own life could be founded.

Geoffrey Day lived in the depths of Yalbury Wood, which formed portion of one of the outlying estates of the Earl of Wessex,[2] to whom Day was head game-keeper, timber-steward, and general overlooker for this district. The wood was intersected by the highway from Caster-

bridge to London at a place not far from the house, and
some trees had of late years been felled between its windows and the ascent of Yalbury Hill, to give the solitary
cottager a glimpse of the passers-by.

It was a satisfaction to walk into the keeper's house, even
as a stranger, on a fine spring morning like the present. A
curl of wood-smoke came from the chimney and drooped
over the roof like a blue feather in a lady's hat; and the sun
shone obliquely upon the patch of grass in front, which
reflected its brightness through the open doorway and up
the staircase opposite, lighting up each riser[3] with a shiny
green radiance and leaving the top of each step in shade.

The window-sill of the front room was between four and
five feet from the floor, dropping inwardly to a broad low
bench, over which, as well as over the whole surface of the
wall beneath, there always hung a deep shade, which was
considered objectionable on every ground save one, namely,
that the perpetual sprinkling of seeds and water by the
caged canary above was not noticed as an eyesore by visitors. The window was set with thickly-leaded diamond glaz-
ing, formed, especially in the lower panes, of knotty glass[4]
of various shades of green. Nothing was better known to
Fancy than the extravagant manner in which these circular
knots or eyes distorted everything seen through them from
the outside – lifting hats from heads shoulders from
bodies; scattering the spokes of cart-wheels, and bending the
straight fir-trunks into semicircles. The ceiling was carried
by a beam traversing its midst, from the side of which projected a large nail, used solely and constantly as a peg for
Geoffrey's hat; the nail was arched by a rainbow-shaped
stain, imprinted by the brim of the said hat when it was
hung there dripping wet.

The most striking point about the room was the furniture. This was a repetition upon inanimate objects of the
old principle introduced by Noah,[5] consisting for the most

part of two articles of every sort. The duplicate system of
furnishing owned its existence to the forethought of Fancy's
mother, exercised from the date of Fancy's birthday onwards. The arrangement spoke for itself: nobody who
knew the tone of the household could look at the goods
without being aware that the second set was a provision for
Fancy when she should marry and have a house of her
own. The most noticeable instance was a pair of green-
faced eight-day clocks ticking alternately, which were severally two-and-a-half minutes and three minutes striking
the hour of twelve, one proclaiming, in Italian flourishes,[6]
Thomas Wood as the name of its maker, and the other –
arched at the top, and altogether of more cynical appearance – that of Ezekiel Saunders. They were two departed
clockmakers of Casterbridge, whose desperate rivalry
throughout their lives was nowhere more emphatically per-
petuated than here at Geoffrey's. These chief specimens of
the marriage provision were supported on the right by a
couple of kitchen dressers, each fitted complete with their
cups, dishes, and plates, in their turn followed by two dumb-
waiters,[7] two family Bibles, two warming-pans,[8] and two
intermixed sets of chairs.

But the position last reached – the chimney-corner – was,
after all, the most attractive side of the parallelogram. It
was large enough to admit, in addition to Geoffrey himself,
Geoffrey's wife, her chair, and her work-table, entirely within the line of the mantel,[9] without danger or even inconvenience from the heat of the fire; and was spacious enough
overhead to allow of the insertion of wood poles for the
hanging of bacon, which were cloaked with long shreds of
soot floating on the draught like the tattered banners on the
walls of ancient aisles.

These points were common to most chimney-corners of
the neighbourhood; but one feature there was which made
Geoffrey's fireside not only an object of interest to casual

aristocratic visitors – to whom every cottage fireside was more or less a curiosity – but the admiration of friends who were accustomed to fireplaces of the ordinary hamlet model. This peculiarity was a little window in the chimney-back almost over the fire, around which the smoke crept caressingly when it left the perpendicular course. The window-board was curiously stamped with black circles, burnt thereon by the heated bottoms of drinking-cups which had rested there after previously standing on the hot ashes of the hearth for the purpose of warming their contents, the result giving to the ledge the look of an envelope which has passed through innumerable post-offices.

Fancy was gliding about the room preparing dinner, her head inclining now to the right, now to the left, and singing the tips and ends of tunes that sprang up in her mind like mushrooms. The footsteps of Mrs Day could be heard in the room overhead. Fancy went finally to the door.

'Father! Dinner.'

A tall spare figure was seen advancing by the window with periodical steps, and the keeper entered from the garden. He appeared to be a man who was always looking down as if trying to recollect something he said yesterday. The surface of his face was fissured rather than wrinkled, and over and under his eyes were folds which seemed as a kind of exterior eyelids. His nose had been thrown backwards by a blow in a poaching fray,[10] so that when the sun was low and shining in his face people could see far into his head. There was in him a quiet grimness which would in his moments of displeasure have become surliness, had it not been tempered by honesty of soul, and which was often wrongheadedness because not allied with subtlety.

Although not an extraordinarily taciturn man among friends slightly richer than himself, he never wasted words upon outsiders, and to his trapper Enoch his ideas were seldom conveyed by any other means than nods and shakes of the head. Their long acquaintance with each other's ways, and the nature of their labours, rendered words between them almost superfluous as vehicles of thought, whilst the coincidence of their horizons, and the astonishing equality of their social views, by startling the keeper from time to time as very damaging to the theory of master and man, strictly forbade any indulgence in words as courtesies.

Behind the keeper came Enoch (who had been assisting in the garden) at the well-considered chronological distance of three minutes – an interval of non-appearance on the trapper's part not arrived at without some reflection. Four minutes had been found to express indifference to indoor arrangements, and simultaneousness had implied too great an anxiety about meals.

'A little earlier than usual, Fancy,' the keeper said, as he sat down and looked at the clocks. 'That Ezekiel Saunders o' thine is tearing on afore Thomas Wood again.'

'I kept in the middle between them,' said Fancy, also looking at the two clocks.

'Better stick to Thomas,' said her father. 'There's a healthy beat in Thomas that would lead a man to swear by en offhand. He is as true as the town time. How is it your stap-mother[11] isn't here?'

As Fancy was about to reply the rattle of wheels was heard, and 'Weh-hey, Smart!' in Mr Richard Dewy's voice rolled into the cottage from round the corner of the house.

'Hullo! there's Dewy's cart come for thee, Fancy – Dick driving – afore time, too. Well, ask the lad to have pot-luck[12] with us.'

Dick on entering made a point of implying by his general bearing that he took an interest in Fancy simply as in one of the same race and country as himself; and they all sat down. Dick could have wished her manner had not been so entirely free from all apparent consciousness of those accidental meetings of theirs; but he let the thought pass.

Enoch sat diagonally at a table afar off under the corner cupboard, and drank his cider from a long perpendicular pint cup having tall fir-trees done in brown on its sides. He threw occasional remarks into the general tide of conversation, and with this advantage to himself, that he participated in the pleasures of a talk (slight as it was) at meal-times, without saddling himself with the responsibility of sustaining it.

'Why don't your stap-mother come down, Fancy?' said Geoffrey. 'You'll excuse her, Mister Dick, she's a little queer sometimes.'

'O yes, – quite,' said Richard, as if he were in the habit of excusing people every day.

'She d'belong to that class of womankind that become second wives: a rum[13] class rather.'

'Indeed,' said Dick, with sympathy for an indefinite something.

'Yes; and 'tis trying to a female, especially if you'd been a first wife, as she have.'

'Very trying it must be.'

'Yes: you see, her first husband was a young man who let her go too far; in fact, she used to kick up Bob's-a-dying[14] at the least thing in the world. And when I'd married her and found it out, I thought, thinks I, " 'Tis too late now to begin to cure 'ee"; and so I let her bide. But she's queer, – very queer, at times!'

'I'm sorry to hear that.'

'Yes: there; wives be such a provoking class of society because, though they be never right, they be never more than half wrong.'

Fancy seemed uneasy under the infliction of this household moralizing, which might tend to damage the airy-fairy nature that Dick, as maiden shrewdness told her, had accredited her with. Her dead silence impressed Geoffrey with the notion that something in his words did not agree with her educated ideas, and he changed the conversation.

'Did Fred Shiner send the cask o' drink, Fancy?'

'I think he did: O yes, he did.'

'Nice solid feller, Fred Shiner!' said Geoffry to Dick as he helped himself to gravy, bringing the spoon round to his plate by way of the potato dish, to obviate a stain on the cloth in the event of a spll.

Now Geoffrey's eyes had been fixed upon his plate for the previous four or five minutes, and in removing them he had only carried them to the spoon, which, from its fulness and the distance of its transit, necessitated a steady watching through the whole of the route. Just as intently as the keeper's eyes had been fixed on the spoon Fancy's had been fixed on her father's, without premeditation or the slightest phase of furtiveness; but there they were fastened. This was the reason why:

Dick was sitting next to her on the right side, and on the side of the table opposite to her father. Fancy had laid her right hand lightly down upon the tablecloth for an instant, and to her alarm Dick, after dropping his fork and brushing his forehead as a reason, flung down his own left hand, overlapping a third of Fancy's with it, and keeping it there. So the innocent Fancy, instead of pulling her hand from the trap, settled her eyes on her father's, to guard against his discovery of this perilous game of Dick's. Dick finished his mouthful; Fancy finished her crumb, and nothing was done beyond watching Geoffrey's eyes. Then the hands slid apart; Fancy's going over six inches of cloth, Dick's over one. Geoffrey's eye had risen.

'I said Fred Shiner is a nice solid feller,' he repeated more emphatically.

'He is; yes, he is,' stammered Dick; 'but to me he is little more than a stranger.'

'O, sure. Now I know en as well as any man can be known. And you know en very well too, don't ye, Fancy?'

Geoffrey put on a tone expressing that these words signified at present about one hundred times the amount of meaning they conveyed literally.

Dick looked anxious.

'Will you pass me some bread?' said Fancy in a flurry, the red of her face becoming slightly disordered, and looking as solicitous as a human being could look about a piece of bread.

'Ay, that I will,' replied the unconscious Geoffrey. 'Ay,' he continued, returning to the displaced idea, 'we are likely to remain friendly wi' Mr Shiner if the wheels d'run smooth.'

'An excellent thing – a very capital thing, as I should say,' the youth answered with exceeding relevance, considering that his thoughts, instead of following Geoffrey's remark, were nestling at a distance of about two feet on his left the whole time.

'A young woman's face will turn the north wind,[15] Master Richard: my heart if 'twon't.' Dick looked more anxious and was attentive in earnest at these words. 'Yes; turn the north wind,' added Geoffrey after an impressive pause. 'And though she's one of my own flesh and blood....'

'Will you fetch down a bit of raw-mil' cheese[16] from pantry-shelf?' Fancy interrupted, as if she were famishing.

'Ay, that I will, chiel; chiel, says I, and Mr Shiner only asking last Saturday night ... cheese you said, Fancy?'

Dick controlled his emotion at these mysterious allusions to Mr Shiner, – the better enabled to do so by perceiving that Fancy's heart went not with her father's – and spoke like a stranger to the affairs of the neighbourhood. 'Yes, there's a great deal to be said upon the power of maiden faces in settling your courses,' he ventured, as the keeper retreated for the cheese.

'The conversation is taking a very strange turn: nothing

that *I* have ever done warrants such things being said!'
murmured Fancy with emphasis just loud enough to reach
Dick's ears.

'You think to yourself, 'twas to be,' cried Enoch from his
distant corner, by way of filling up the vacancy caused by
Geoffrey's momentary absence. 'And so you marry her,
Master Dewy, and there's an end o't.'

'Pray don't say such things, Enoch,' came Fancy severely, upon which Enoch relapsed into servitude.

'If we be doomed to marry, we marry; if we be doomed
to remain single, we do,' replied Dick.

Geoffrey had by this time sat down again, and now he
made his lips thin by severely straining them across his
gums, and looked out of the window along the vista to the
distant highway up Yalbury Hill. 'That's not the case with
some folk,' he said at length, as if he read the words on a
board at the further end of the vista.

Fancy looked interested, and Dick said, 'No?'

'There's that wife o' mine. It was her doom to be nobody's wife at all in the wide universe. But she made up her
mind that she would, and did it twice over. Doom? Doom
is nothing beside a elderly woman – quite a chiel in her
hands!'

A movement was now heard along the upstairs passage,
and footsteps descending. The door at the foot of the stairs
opened and the second Mrs Day appeared in view, looking
fixedly at the table as she advanced towards it, with apparent obliviousness of the presence of any other human
being than herself. In short, if the table had been the personages, and the persons the table, her glance would have
been the most natural imaginable.

She showed herself to possess an ordinary woman's face,
iron-grey hair, hardly any hips, and a great deal of clean-
liness in a broad white apron-string as it appeared upon the
waist of her dark stuff dress.

'People will run away with a story now, I suppose,' she began saying, 'that Jan Day's tablecloths are as poor and ragged as any union beggar's!'[17]

Dick now perceived that the tablecloth was a little the worse for wear, and reflecting for a moment concluded that 'people' in stepmother language probably meant himself. On lifting his eyes he found that Mrs Day had vanished again upstairs, and presently returned with an armful of new damask-linen[18] tablecloths folded square and hard as boards by long compression. These she flounced down into a chair; then took one, shook it out from its folds, and spread it on the table by instalments, transferring the plates and dishes one by one from the old to the new cloth.

'And I suppose they'll say, too, that she ha'n't a decent knife and fork in her house!'

'I shouldn't say any such ill-natured thing, I am sure—' began Dick. But Mrs Day had vanished into the next room. Fancy appeared distressed.

'Very strange woman, isn't she?' said Geoffrey, quietly going on with his dinner. 'But 'tis too late to attempt curing. My heart! 'tis so growed into her that 'twould kill her to take it out. Ay, she's very queer: you'd be amazed to see what valuable goods we've got stowed away upstairs.'

Back again came Mrs Day with a box of bright steel horn-handled knives,[19] silver-plated forks, carver, and all complete. These were wiped of the preservative oil which coated them, and then a knife and fork were laid down to each individual with a bang, the carving knife and fork thrust into the meat dish, and the old ones they had hither-to used tossed away.

Geoffrey placidly cut a slice with the new knife and fork, and asked Dick if he wanted any more.

The table had been spread for the mixed mid-day meal of dinner and tea which was common among frugal country-folk. 'The parishioners about here,' continued Mrs Day, not looking at any living being, but snatching up the brown delf[20] tea-things, 'are the laziest, gossipest, poachest, jail-est[21] set of any ever I came among. And they'll talk about my teapot and tea-things next, I suppose!' She vanished with the teapot, cups, and saucers, and reappeared with a tea-service in white china, and a packet wrapped in brown paper. This was removed, together with folds of tissue-paper underneath; and a brilliant silver teapot appeared.

'I'll help to put the things right,' said Fancy soothingly, and rising from her seat. 'I ought to have laid out better things, I suppose. But' (here she enlarged her looks so as to include Dick) 'I have been away from home a good deal, and I make shocking blunders in my housekeeping.' Smiles and suavity were then dispensed all around by this bright little bird.

After a little more preparation and modification Mrs Day took her seat at the head of the table, and during the latter or tea division of the meal presided with much composure. It may cause some surprise to learn that, now her vagary was over, she showed herself to be an excellent person with much common sense, and even a religious serious-ness of tone on matters pertaining to her afflictions.

7 Dick makes himself Useful

The effect of Geoffrey's incidental allusions to Mr Shiner was to restrain a considerable flow of spontaneous chat that would otherwse have burst from young Dewy along the drive homeward. And a certain remark he had hazarded to her, in rather too blunt and eager a manner, kept the young lady herself even more silent than Dick. On both sides there was an unwillingness to talk on any but the most trivial subjects, and their sentences rarely took a larger form than could be expressed in two or three words.

Owing to Fancy being later in the day than she had promised the charwoman[1] had given up expecting her; whereupon Dick could do no less than stay and see her comfortably tided over the disagreeable time of entering and establishing herself in an empty house after an absence of a week. The additional furniture and utensils that had been brought (a canary and cage among the rest) were taken out of the vehicle, and the horse was unharnessed and put in the plot opposite, where there was some tender grass. Dick lighted the fire already laid; and activity began to loosen their tongues a little.

'There!' said Fancy, 'we forgot to bring the fire-irons!'[2]

She had originally found in her sitting-room, to bear out the expression 'nearly furnished' which the school-manager had used in his letter to her, a table, three chairs, a fender, and a piece of carpet. This 'nearly' had been supplemented hitherto by a kind friend, who had lent her fire-irons and crockery until she should fetch some from home.

Dick attended to the young lady's fire, using his whip-handle for a poker till it was spoilt, and then flourishing a hurdle stick for the remainder of the time.

'The kettle boils; now you shall have a cup of tea,' said Fancy, diving into the hamper she had brought.

'Thank you,' said Dick, whose drive had made him ready for some, especially in her company.

'Well, here's only one cup-and-saucer, as I breathe! Whatever could mother be thinking about? Do you mind making shift,[3] Mr Dewy?'

'Not at all, Miss Day,' said that civil person.

'– And only having a cup by itself? or a saucer by itself?'

'Don't mind in the least.'

'Which do you mean by that?'

'I mean the cup if you like the saucer.'

'And the saucer if I like the cup?'

'Exactly, Miss Day.'

'Thank you, Mr Dewy, for I like the cup decidedly. Stop a minute; there are no spoons now!' She dived into the hamper again, and at the end of two or three minutes looked up and said, 'I suppose you don't mind if I can't find a spoon?'

'Not at all,' said the agreeable Richard.

'The fact is the spoons have slipped down somewhere; right under the other things. O yes, here's one, and only one. You would rather have one than not I suppose, Mr Dewy?'

'Rather not. I never did care much about spoons.'

'Then I'll have it. I do care about them. You must stir up your tea with a knife. Would you mind lifting the kettle off, that it may not boil dry?'

Dick leapt to the fireplace, and earnestly removed the kettle.

'There! you did it so wildly that you have made your hand black. We always use kettle-holders; didn't you learn housewifery as far as that, Mr Dewy? Well, never mind the soot on your hand. Come here. I am going to rinse mine, too.'

They went to a basin she had placed in the back room. 'This is the only basin I have,' she said. 'Turn up your sleeves, and by that time my hands will be washed, and you can come.'

Her hands were in the water now. 'O, how vexing!' she exclaimed. 'There's not a drop of water left for you unless you draw it, and the well is I don't know how many furlongs deep; all that was in the pitcher I used for the kettle and this basin. Do you mind dipping the tips of your fingers in the same?'

'Not at all. And to save time I won't wait till you have done, if you have no objection?'

Thereupon he plunged in his hands, and they paddled together. It being the first time in his life that he had touched female fingers under water, Dick duly registered the sensation as rather a nice one.

'Really, I hardly know which are my own hands and which are yours, they have got so mixed up together,' she said, withdrawing her own very suddenly.

'It doesn't matter at all,' said Dick, 'at least as far as I am concerned.'

'There! no towel! Whoever thinks of a towel till the hands are wet?'

'Nobody.'

' "Nobody." How very dull it is when people are so friendly! Come here, Mr Dewy. Now do you think you could lift the lid of that box with your elbow, and then, with something or other, take out a towel you will find under the clean clothes? Be *sure* don't touch any of them with your wet hands, for the things at the top are all Starched and Ironed.'

Dick managed by the aid of a knife and fork to extract a towel from under a muslin dress without wetting the latter;

and for a moment he ventured to assume a tone of criticism.

'I fear for that dress,' he said, as they wiped their hands together.

'What?' said Miss Day, looking into the box at the dress alluded to. 'O, I know what you mean – that the vicar will never let me wear muslin?'[5]

'Yes.'

'Well, I know it is condemned by all orders in the church as flaunting, and unfit for common wear for girls who've their living to get; but we'll see.'

'In the interest of the church I hope you don't speak seriously.'

'Yes, I do; but we'll see.' There was a comely determination on her lip, very pleasant to a beholder who was neither bishop, priest, nor deacon. 'I think I can manage any vicar's views about me if he's under forty.'

Dick rather wished she had never thought of managing vicars.

'I certainly shall be glad to get some of your delicious tea,' he said in rather a free way, yet modestly, as became one in a position between that of visitor and inmate, and looking wistfully at his lonely saucer.

'So shall I. Now is there anything else we want, Mr Dewy?'

'I really think there's nothing else, Miss Day.'

She prepared to sit down, looking musingly out of the window at Smart's enjoyment of the rich grass. 'Nobody seems to care about me,' she murmured, with large lost eyes fixed upon the sky beyond Smart.

'Perhaps Mr Shiner does,' said Dick, in the tone of a slightly injured man.

'Yes, I forgot – he does, I know.' Dick precipitately regretted that he had suggested Shiner since it had produced such a miserable result as this.

'I'll warrant you'll care for somebody very much indeed another day, won't you, Mr Dewy?' she continued, looking very feelingly into the mathematical centre of his eyes.

'Ah, I'll warrant I shall,' said Dick, feelingly too, and looking back into her dark pupils, whereupon they were turned aside.

'I meant,' she went on, preventing him from speaking just as he was going to narrate a forcible story about his feelings; 'I meant that nobody comes to see if I have returned – not even the vicar.'

'If you want to see him, I'll call at the vicarage directly we have had some tea.'

'No, no! Don't let him come down here, whatever you do, whilst I am in such a state of disarrangement. Parsons look so miserable and awkward when one's house is in a muddle; walking about and making impossible suggestions in quaint academic phrases till your flesh creeps and you wish them dead. Do you take sugar?'

Mr Maybold was at this instant seen coming up the path.

'There! That's he coming! How I wish you were not here! – that is, how awkward – dear, dear!' she exclaimed, with a quick ascent of blood to her face, and irritated with Dick rather than the vicar, as it seemed.

'Pray don't be alarmed on my account, Miss Day – good afternoon!' said Dick in a huff, putting on his hat and leaving the room hastily by the back door.

The horse was caught and put in, and on mounting the shafts to start he saw through the window the vicar, standing upon some books piled in a chair, and driving a nail into the wall; Fancy, with a demure glance, holding the canary-cage up to him as if she had never in her life thought of anything but vicars and canaries.

8 Dick meets his Father

For several minutes Dick drove along homeward, with the inner eye of reflection so anxiously set on his passages at arms with Fancy that the road and scenery were as a thin mist over the real pictures of his mind. Was she a coquette? The balance between the evidence that she did love him and that she did not was so nicely struck that his opinion had no stability. She had let him put his hand upon hers; she had allowed her gaze to drop plumb into the depths of his – his into hers – three or four times; her manner had been very free with regard to the basin and towel; she had appeared vexed at the mention of Shiner. On the other hand, she had driven him about the house like a quiet dog or cat, said Shiner cared for her, and seemed anxious that Mr Maybold should do the same.

Thinking thus as he neared the handpost[1] at Mellstock Cross, sitting on the front board of the spring-cart – his legs on the outside, and his whole frame jigging up and down like a candle-flame to the time of Smart's trotting – who should he see coming down the hill but his father in the light wagon, quivering up and down on a smaller scale of shakes, those merely caused by the stones in the road. They were soon crossing each other's front.

'Weh-hey!' said the tranter to Smiler.

'Weh-hey!' said Dick to Smart, in an echo of the same voice.

'Th'st[2] hauled her back, I suppose?' Reuben inquired peaceably.

'Yes,' said Dick, with such a clinching period at the end that it seemed he was never going to add another word. Smiler, thinking this the close of the conversation, prepared to move on.

'Weh-hey! said the tranter. 'I tell thee what it is, Dick. That there maid is taking up thy thoughts more than's good for thee, my sonny. Thou'rt never happy now unless th'rt making thyself miserable about her in one way or another.'

'I don't know about that, father,' said Dick rather stupidly.

'But I do – Wey, Smiler! – 'Od rot the women, 'tis nothing else wi' 'em nowadays but getting young men and leading 'em astray.'

'Pooh, father! you just repeat what all the common world says; that's all you do.'

'The world's a very sensible feller on things in jineral, Dick; very sensible indeed.'

Dick looked into the distance at a vast expanse of mortgaged estate. 'I wish I was as rich as a squire when he's as poor as a crow,' he murmured; 'I'd soon ask Fancy something.'

'I wish so too, wi' all my heart, sonny; that I do. Well, mind what beest about, that's all.'

Smart moved on a step or two. 'Supposing now, father, – We-hey, Smart! – I did think a little about her, and I had a chance, which I ha'n't; don't you think she's a very good sort of – of – one?'

'Ay, good; she's good enough. When you've made up your mind to marry, take the first respectable body that comes to hand – she's as good as any other; they be all alike in the groundwork; 'tis only in the flourishes[3] there's a difference. She's good enough; but I can't see what the nation[4] a young feller like you – wi' a comfortable house and home, and father and mother to take care o' thee, and who sent 'ee to a school so good that 'twas hardly fair to

the other children – should want to go hollering[5] after a
young woman for, when she's quietly making a husband in
her pocket,[6] and not troubled by chick nor chiel,[7] to make
a poverty-stric'[8] wife and family of her, and neither hat,
cap, wig, nor waistcoat to set 'em up with: be drowned if I
can see it, and that's the long and short o't, my sonny!'

Dick looked at Smart's ears, then up the hill; but no
reason was suggested by any object that met his gaze.

'For about the same reason that you did, father, I suppose.'

'Dang it,[9] my sonny, thou'st got me there!' And the
tranter gave vent to a grim admiration, with the mien[10] of
a man who was too magnanimous not to appreciate artistic-
ally a slight rap on the knuckles, even if they were his own.

'Whether or no,' said Dick, 'I asked her a thing going
along the road.'

'Come to that, is it? Turk![11] won't thy mother be in a
taking![12] Well, she's ready, I don't doubt?'

'I didn't ask her anything about having me; and if you'll
let me speak, I'll tell 'ee what I want to know. I just said,
Did she care about me?'

'Piph-ph-ph!'

'And then she said nothing for a quarter of a mile, and
then she said she didn't know. Now, what I want to know
is, what was the meaning of that speech?' The latter words
were spoken resolutely, as if he didn't care for the ridicule
of all the fathers in creation.

'The meaning of that speech is,' the tranter replied deliberately, 'that the meaning is meant to be rather hid at
present. Well, Dick, as an honest father to thee, I don't pretend to deny what you d'know well enough; that is, that her
father being rather better in the pocket than we, I should
welcome her ready enough if it must be somebody.'

'But what d'ye think she really did mean?' said the un-
satisfied Dick.

'I'm afeard I am not o' much account in guessing, especially as I was not there when she said it, and seeing that your mother was the only 'ooman I ever cam' into such close quarters as that with.'

'And what did mother say to you when you asked her?' said Dick musingly.

'I don't see that that will help 'ee.'

'The principle is the same.'

'Well – ay: what did she say? Let's see. I was oiling my working-day boots without taking 'em off, and wi' my head hanging down when she just brushed on by the garden hatch[13] like a flittering[14] leaf. "Anne," I said says I, and then, – but, Dick, I'm afeard 'twill be no help to thee; for we were such a rum couple, your mother and I, leastways one half was, that is myself – and your mother's charms was more in the manner than the material.'

'Never mind! "Ann," said you.'

'"Ann," said I, as I was saying … "Ann," I said to her when I was oiling my working-day boots wi' my head hanging down, "Woot hae me?"[15] … What came next I can't quite call up at this distance o' time. Perhaps your mother would know, – she's got a better memory for her little triumphs than I. However, the long and the short o' the story is that we were married somehow, as I found afterwards. 'Twas on White Tuesday,[16] – Mellstock Club[17] walked the same day, every man two and two, and a fine day 'twas, – hot as fire; how the sun did strike down upon my back going to church! I well can mind what a bath o' sweating I was in, body and soul! But Fance will ha' thee, Dick – she won't walk with another chap – no such good luck.'

'I don't know about that,' said Dick, whipping at Smart's flank in a fanciful way which, as Smart knew, meant nothing in connection with going on. 'There's Pa'son Maybold, too – that's all against me.'

'What about he? She's never been stuffing into thy

innocent heart that he's in love with her? Lord, the vanity o' maidens!'

'No, no. But he called, and she looked at him in such a way, and at me in such a way – quite different the ways were, – and as I was coming off there was he hanging up her birdcage.'

'Well, why shouldn't the man hang up her birdcage? Turk seize it all, what's that got to do wi' it? Dick, that thou beest a white-lyvered[18] chap I don't say, but if thou beestn't as made as a cappel-faced[19] bull let me smile no more.'

'O, ay.'

'And what's think now, Dick?'

'I don't know.'

'Here's another pretty kettle o' fish,[20] for thee. Who d'ye think's the bitter weed[21] in our being turned out? Did our party tell 'ee?'

'No. Why, Pa'son Maybold, I suppose.'

'Shiner, – because he's in love with thy young woman, and d'want to see her young figure sitting up at that queer instrument, and her young fingers rum-strumming[22] upon the keys.'

A sharp ado of sweet and bitter was going on in Dick during this communication from his father. 'Shiner's a fool! – no, that's not it; I don't believe any such thing, father. Why, Shiner would never take a bold step like that unless she'd been a little made up to, and had taken it kindly. Pooh!'

'Who's to say she didn't?'

'I do.'

'The more fool you.'

'Why, father of me?'

'Has she ever done more to thee?'

'No.'

'Then she has done as much to he – rot 'em! Now, Dick,

this is how a maid is. She'll swear she's dying for thee, and she is dying for thee, and she will die for thee; but she'll fling a look over t'other shoulder at another young feller, though never leaving off dying for thee just the same.'

'She's not dying for me, and so she didn't fling a look at him.'

'But she may be dying for him, for she looked at thee.'

'I don't know what to make of it at all,' said Dick gloomily.

'All I can make of it is,' the tranter said, raising his whip, arranging his different joints and muscles, and motioning to the horse to move on, 'that if you can't read a maid's mind by her motions, nature d'seem to say thou'st ought to be a bachelor. Clk, clk! Smiler!' And the tranter moved on.

Dick held Smart's rein firmly, and the whole concern of horse, cart, and man remained rooted in the lane. How long this condition would have lasted is unknown, had not Dick's thoughts, after adding up numerous items of misery, gradually wandered round to the fact that as something must be done it could not be done by staying there all night.

Reaching home he went up to his bedroom, shut the door as if he were going to be seen no more in his life, and taking a sheet of paper and uncorking the ink-bottle he began a letter. The dignity of the writer's mind was so powerfully apparent in every line of this effusion that it obscured the logical sequence of facts and intentions to an appreciable degree; and it was not at all clear to a reader whether he there and then left off loving Miss Fancy Day; whether he had never loved her seriously and never meant to; whether he had been dying up to the present moment and now intended to get well again; or whether he had hitherto been in good health and intended to die for her forthwith.

He put this letter in an envelope, sealed it up, directed it in a stern handwriting of straight dashes – easy flourishes

being rigorously excluded. He walked with it in his pocket
down the lane in strides not an inch less than three feet
long. Reaching her gate he put on a resolute expression –
then put it off again, turned back homeward, tore up his
letter, and sat down.

That letter was altogether in a wrong tone – that he
must own. A heartless man-of-the-world tone was what the
juncture required. That he rather wanted her, and rather
did not want her – the latter for choice; but that as a member of society he didn't mind making a query in jaunty
terms, which could only be answered in the same way: did
she mean anything by her bearing towards him, or did she
not?

This letter was considered so satisfactory in every way
that, being put into the hands of a little boy and the order
given that he was to run with it to the school, he was told in
addition not to look behind him if Dick called after him to
bring it back, but to run along with it just the same. Having
taken this precaution against vacillation Dick watched his
messenger down the road, and turned into the house whistling an air in such ghastly jerks and starts that whistling
seemed to be the act the very furthest removed from that
which was instinctive in such a youth.

The letter was left as ordered: the next morning came
and passed – and no answer. The next. The next. Friday
night came. Dick resolved that if no answer or sign were
given by her the next day, on Sunday he would meet her
face to face, and have it all out by word of mouth.

'Dick,' said his father, coming in from the garden at that
moment – in each hand a hive of bees tied in a cloth to
prevent their egress – 'I think you'd better take these two
swarms of bees to Mrs Maybold's tomorrow, instead o' me,
and I'll go wi' Smiler and the wagon.'

It was a relief; for Mrs Maybold, the vicar's mother, who
had just taken into her head a fancy for keeping bees

(pleasantly disguised under the pretence of its being an econ-
omical wish to produce her own honey), lived near the
watering-place[23] of Budmouth Regis, ten miles off, and the
business of transporting the hives thither would occupy the
whole day, and to some extent annihilate the vacant time
between this evening and the coming Sunday. The best
spring-cart was washed throughout, the axles oiled, and the
bees placed therein for the journey.

Part the Third

Summer

1 Driving out of Budmouth

An easy bend of neck and graceful set of head; full and wavy bundles of dark-brown hair; light fall of little feet; pretty devices on the skirt of the dress; clear deep eyes; in short, a bunch of sweets: it was Fancy! Dick's heart went round to her with a rush.

The scene was the corner of Mary Street in Budmouth-Regis, near the King's statue,[1] at which point the white angle of the last house in the row cut perpendicularly an embayed[2] and nearly motionless expanse of salt water projected from the outer ocean – today lit in bright tones of green and opal. Dick and Smart had just emerged from the street, and there on the right, against the brilliant sheet of liquid colour, stood Fancy Day; and she turned and recognized him.

Dick suspended his thoughts of the letter and wonder at how she came there by driving close to the chains of the Esplanade – incontinently[3] displacing two chairmen,[4] who had just come to life for the summer in new clean shirts and revivified clothes, and being almost displaced in turn by a rigid boy rattling along with a baker's cart and looking neither to the right nor the left. He asked if she were going to Mellstock that night.

'Yes, I'm waiting for the carrier,' she replied, seeming, too, to suspend thoughts of the letter.

'Now I can drive you home nicely, and you save half an hour. Will ye come with me?'

As Fancy's power to will anything seemed to have

departed in some mysterious manner at that moment. Dick settled the matter by getting out and assisting her into the vehicle without another word.

The temporary flush upon her cheek changed to a lesser hue which was permanent, and at length their eyes met; there was present between them a certain feeling of embarrassment, which arises at such moments when all the instinctive acts dictated by the position have been performed. Dick, being engaged with the reins, thought less of this awkwardness than did Fancy, who had nothing to do but to feel his presence, and to be more and more conscious of the fact that by accepting the seat beside him in this way, she succumbed to the tone of his note. Smart jogged along, and Dick jogged, and the helpless Fancy necessarily jogged too; and she felt that she was in a measure captured and made a prisoner.

'I am so much obliged to you for your company, Miss Day,' he observed, as they drove past the two semicircular bays of the Old Royal Hotel,[5] where His Majesty King George the Third had many a time attended the balls of the burgesses.[6]

To Miss Day, crediting him with the same consciousness of mastery – a consciousness of which he was perfectly innocent – this remark sounded like a magnanimous intention to soothe her, the captive.

'I didn't come for the pleasure of obliging you with my company,' she said.

The answer had an unexpected manner of incivility in it that must have been rather surprising to young Dewy. At the same time it may be observed that when a young woman returns a rude answer to a young man's civil remark her heart is in a state which argues rather hopefully for his case than otherwise.

There was silence between them till they had left the seafront and passed about twenty of the trees that ornamented the road leading up out of the town towards Casterbridge and Mellstock.

'Though I didn't come for that purpose either, I would have done it,' said Dick at the twenty-first tree.

'Now, Mr Dewy, no flirtation, because it's wrong, and I don't wish it.'

Dick seated himself afresh just as he had been sitting before, arranged his looks very emphatically, and cleared his throat.

'Really, anybody would think you had met me on business and were just going to commence,' said the lady intractably.

'Yes, they would.'

'Why, you never have, to be sure!'

This was a shaky beginning. He chopped round[7] and said cheerily, as a man who had resolved never to spoil his jollity by loving one of womankind –

'Well, how are you getting on, Miss Day, at the present time? Gaily, I don't doubt for a moment.'

'I am not gay, Dick; you know that.'

'Gaily doesn't mean decked in gay dresses.'

'I didn't suppose gaily was gaily dressed. Mighty me, what a scholar you've grown!'

'Lots of things have happened to you this spring, I see.'

'What have you seen?'

'O, nothing; I've heard, I mean!'

'What have you heard?'

'The name of a pretty man with brass studs,[8] and a copper ring, and a tin watch-chain, a little mixed up with your own. That's all.'

'That's a very unkind picture of Mr Shiner, for that's who you mean! The studs are gold as you know, and it's a real silver chain; the ring I can't conscientiously defend, and he only wore it once.'

'He might have worn it a hundred times without showing it half so much.'

'Well, he's nothing to me,' she serenely observed.

'Not any more than I am?'

'Now, Mr Dewy,' said Fancy severely, 'certainly he isn't any more to me than you are!'

'Not so much?'

She looked aside to consider the precise compass of that question. 'That I can't exactly answer,' she replied with soft archness.

As they were going rather slowly another spring-cart, containing a farmer, farmer's wife, and farmer's man, jogged past them; and the farmer's wife and the farmer's man eyed the couple very curiously. The farmer never looked up from the horse's tail.

'Why can't you exactly answer?' said Dick, quickening Smart a little, and jogging on just behind the farmer and farmer's wife and man.

As no answer came, and as their eyes had nothing else to do, they both contemplated the picture presented in front, and noticed how the farmer's wife sat flattened between the two men, who bulged over each end of the seat to give her room till they almost sat upon their respective wheels; and they looked too at the farmer's wife's silk mantle inflating itself between her shoulders like a balloon and sinking flat again at each jog of the horse. The farmer's wife, feeling their eyes sticking into her back, looked over her shoulder. Dick dropped ten yards further behind.

'Fancy, why can't you answer?' he repeated.

'Because how much you are to me depends upon how much I am to you,' said she in low tones.

'Everything,' said Dick, putting his hand towards hers and casting emphatic eyes upon the upper curve of her cheek.

'Now, Richard Dewy, no touching me! I didn't say in

what way your thinking of me affected the question – perhaps inversely, don't you see? No touching, sir! Look; goodness me, don't, Dick!'

The cause of her sudden start was the unpleasant appearance over Dick's right shoulder of an empty timber-wagon and four journeymen-carpenters[9] reclining in lazy postures inside it, their eyes directed upwards at various oblique angles into the surrounding world, the chief object of their existence being apparently to criticize to the very backbone and marrow every animate object that came within the compass of their vision. This difficulty of Dick's was overcome by trotting on till the wagon and carpenters were beginning to look rather misty by reason of a film of dust that accompanied their wagon-wheels and rose around their heads like a fog.

'Say you love me, Fancy.'

'No, Dick, certainly not; 'tisn't time to do that yet.'

'Why, Fancy?'

' "Miss Day" is better at present – don't mind my saying so; and I ought not to have called you Dick.'

'Nonsense! when you know that I would do anything on earth for your love. Why, you make any one think that loving is a thing that can be done and undone, and put on and put off at a mere whim.'

'No, no, I don't,' she said gently; 'but there are things which tell me I ought not to give way to much thinking about you, even if—'

'But you want to, don't you? Yes, say you do; it is best to be truthful. Whatever they may say about a woman's right to conceal where her love lies, and pretend it doesn't exist, and things like that, it is not best; I do know it, Fancy. And an honest woman in that, as well as in all her daily concerns, shines most brightly, and is thought most of in the long run.'

'Well, then, perhaps, Dick, I do love you a little,' she

whispered tenderly; 'but I wish you wouldn't say any more now.'

'I won't say any more now, then, if you don't like it, dear. But you do love me a little, don't you?'

'Now you ought not to want me to keep saying things twice; I can't say any more now, and you must be content with what you have.'

'I may at any rate call you Fancy? There's no harm in that.'

'Yes, you may.'

'And you'll not call me Mr Dewy any more?'

'Very well.'

6 Stinsford Church

7 The church choir, from the *Graphic*, 1891

8   The School, Lower Bockhampton

9   The bridge and riverside walk, Lower Bockhampton

10   Keeper's Cottage, Yellowham Wood

2 Further along the Road

Dick's spirits having risen in the course of these admissions of his sweetheart he now touched Smart with the whip; and on Smart's neck, not far behind his ears. Smart, who had been lost in thought for some time, never dreaming that Dick could reach so far with a whip which, on this particular journey, had never been extended further than his flank, tossed his head and scampered along with exceeding briskness, which was very pleasant to the young couple behind him till, turning a bend in the road, they came instantly upon the farmer, farmer's man, and farmer's wife with the flapping mantle, all jogging on just the same as ever.

'Bother those people! Here we are upon them again.'

'Well, of course. They have as much right to the road as we.'

'Yes, but it is provoking to be overlooked so. I like a road all to myself. Look what a lumbering affair theirs is!' The wheels of the farmer's cart just at that moment jogged into a depression running across the road, giving the cart a twist, whereupon all three nodded to the left, and on coming out of it all three nodded to the right, and went on jerking their backs in and out as usual. 'We'll pass them when the road gets wider.'

When an opportunity seemed to offer itself for carrying this intention into effect they heard light flying wheels behind, and on their quartering[1] there whizzed along past them a brand-new gig,[2] so brightly polished that the spokes of the wheels sent forth a continual quivering light at one point in their circle, and all the panels glared like mirrors in Dick and Fancy's eyes. The driver, and owner as it appeared, was really a handsome man; his companion was Shiner. Both turned round as they passed Dick and Fancy and stared with bold admiration in her face till they were obliged to attend to the operation of passing the farmer. Dick glanced for an instant at Fancy while she was undergoing their scrutiny; then returned to his driving with rather a sad countenance.

'Why are you so silent?' she said after a while, with real concern.

'Nothing.'

'Yes, it is, Dick. I couldn't help those people passing.'

'I know that.'

'You look offended with me. What have I done?'

'I can't tell without offending you.'

'Better out.'

'Well,' said Dick, who seemed longing to tell even at the risk of offending her, 'I was thinking how different you in love are from me in love. Whilst those men were staring you dismissed me from your thoughts altogether and—'

'You can't offend me further now; tell all!'

'And showed upon your face a pleased sense of being attractive to 'em.'

'Don't be silly, Dick! You know very well I didn't.'

Dick shook his head sceptically and smiled.

'Dick, I always believe flattery *if possible* – and it was possible then. Now there's an open confession of weakness. But I showed no consciousness of it.'

Dick, perceiving by her look that she would adhere to her statement, charitably forbore saying anything that could make her prevaricate. The sight of Shiner, too, had recalled another branch of the subject to his mind; that which had been his greatest trouble till her company and words had obscured its probability.

'By the way, Fancy, do you know why our quire is to be dismissed?'

'No: except that it is Mr Maybold's wish for me to play the organ.'

'Do you know how it came to be his wish?'

'That I don't.'

'Mr Shiner, being churchwarden, has persuaded the vicar; who, however, was willing enough before. Shiner, I know, is crazy to see you playing every Sunday; I suppose he'll turn over your music, for the organ will be close to his pew. But – I know you have never encouraged him?'

'Never once!' said Fancy emphatically, and with eyes full of earnest truth. 'I don't like him indeed, and I never heard of his doing this before! I have always felt that I should like to play in a church, but I never wished to turn you and your choir out; and I never even said that I could play till I was asked. You don't think for a moment that I did, surely, do you?'

'I know you didn't, dear.'

'Or that I care the least morsel of a bit for him?'

'I know you don't.'

The distance between Budmouth and Mellstock was ten or eleven miles, and there being a good inn, 'The Ship',[3] four miles out of Budmouth, with a mast and cross-trees[4] in front, Dick's custom in driving thither was to divide his journey into three stages by resting at this inn going and coming, and not troubling the Budmouth stables at all, whenever his visit to the town was a mere call and deposit, as today.

Fancy was ushered into a little tea-room and Dick went to the stables to see to the feeding of Smart. In face of the significant twitches of feature that were visible in the ostler and labouring men idling around, Dick endeavoured to look unconscious of the fact that there was any sentiment between him and Fancy beyond a tranter's desire to carry a passenger home. He presently entered the inn and opened the door of Fancy's room.

'Dick, do you know, it has struck me that it is rather awkward my being here alone with you like this. I don't think you had better come in with me.'

'That's rather unpleasant, dear.'

'Yes, it is, and I wanted you to have some tea as well as myself too, because you must be tired.'

'Well, let me have some with you, then. I was denied once before, if you recollect, Fancy.'

'Yes, yes, never mind! And it seems unfriendly of me now, but I don't know what to do.'

'It shall be as you say, then.' Dick began to retreat with a dissatisfied wrinkling of face, and a farewell glance at the cosy tea-tray.

'But you don't see how it is, Dick, when you speak like that,' she said with more earnestness than she had ever shown before. 'You do know that even if I care very much for you I must remember that I have a difficult position to maintain. The vicar would not like me, as his schoolmistress, to indulge in a *tête-à-tête*[5] anywhere with anybody.'

'But I am not *any* body!' exclaimed Dick.

'No, no, I mean with a young man'; and she added softly, 'unless I were really engaged to be married to him.'

'Is that all? Then, dearest, dearest, why, we'll be engaged at once, to be sure we will, and down I sit! There it is, as easy as a glove!'

'Ah! but suppose I won't! And, goodness me, what have I done!' she faltered, getting very red. 'Positively, it seems as if I meant you to say that!'

'Let's do it! I mean get engaged,' said Dick. 'Now, Fancy, will you be my wife?'

'Do you know, Dick, it was rather unkind of you to say

what you did coming along the road,' she remarked as if she had not heard the latter part of his speech; though an acute observer might have noticed about her breast as the word 'wife' fell from Dick's lips a soft silent escape of breaths, with very short rests between each.

'What did I say?'

'About my trying to look attractive to those men in the gig.'

'You couldn't help looking so, whether you tried or no. And, Fancy, you do care for me?'

'Yes.'

'Very much?'

'Yes.'

'And you'll be my own wife?'

Her heart quickened, adding to and withdrawing from her cheek varying tones of red to match each varying thought. Dick looked expectantly at the ripe tint of her delicate mouth, waiting for what was coming forth.

'Yes – if father will let me.'

Dick drew himself close to her, compressing his lips and pouting them out as if he were about to whistle the softest melody known.

'O no!' said Fancy solemnly.

The modest Dick drew back a little.

'Dick, Dick, kiss me and let me go instantly! – here's somebody coming!' she whisperingly exclaimed.

Half an hour afterwards Dick emerged from the inn, and if Fancy's lips had been real cherries probably Dick's would have appeared deeply stained. The landlord was standing in the yard.

'Heu-heu! hay-hay, Master Dewy? Ho-ho!' he laughed, letting the laugh slip out gently and by degrees that it might make little noise in its exit, and smiting Dick under the fifth rib at the same time. 'This will never do, upon my life,

Master Dewy! calling for tay[6] for a feymel[7] passenger, and then going in and sitting down and having some too, and biding such a fine long time!'

'But surely you know?' said Dick, with great apparent surprise. 'Yes, yes! Ha-ha!' smiting the landlord under the ribs in return.

'Why, what? Yes, yes; ha-ha!'

'You know, of course!'

'Yes, of course! But – that is – I don't.'

'Why, about – between that young lady and me?' nodding to the window of the room that Fancy occupied.

'No; not I!' said the innkeeper, bringing his eyes into circles.

'And you don't!'

'Not a word, I'll take my oath!'

'But you laughed when I laughed.'

'Ay, that was me sympathy; so did you when I laughed!'

'Really, you don't know? Goodness – not knowing that!'

'I'll take my oath I don't!'

'O yes,' said Dick, with frigid rhetoric of pitying astonishment, 'we're engaged to be married, you see, and I naturally look after her.'

'Of course, of course! I didn't know that, and I hope ye'll excuse any little freedom of mine, Mr Dewy. But it is a very odd thing; I was talking to your father very intimate about family matters only last Friday in the world, and who should come in but Keeper Day, and we all then fell a-talking o' family matters; but neither one o' them said a mortal word about it; knowen me too so many years, and I at your father's own wedding. 'Tisn't what I should have expected from an old neighbour!'

'Well, to say the truth, we hadn't told father of the engagement at that time; in fact, 'twasn't settled.'

'Ah! the business was done Sunday. Yes, yes, Sunday's the courting day. Heu-heu!'

'No, 'twasn't done Sunday in particular.'

'After school-hours this week? Well, a very good time, a very proper good time.'

'O no, 'twasn't done then.'

'Coming along the road today then, I suppose?'

'Not at all; I wouldn't think of getting engaged in a dog-cart.'[8]

'Dammy – might as well have said at once the *when* be blowed! Anyhow, 'tis a fine day, and I hope next time you'll come as one.'

Fancy was duly brought out and assisted into the vehicle, and the newly affianced youth and maiden passed up the steep hill to the Ridgeway, and vanished in the direction of Mellstock.

3 A Confession

It was a morning of the latter summer-time; a morning of lingering dews, when the grass is never dry in the shade. Fuchsias and dahlias were laden till eleven o'clock with small drops and dashes of water, changing the colour of their sparkle at every movement of the air; and elsewhere hanging on twigs like small silver fruit. The threads of garden-spiders appeared thick and polished. In the dry and sunny places dozens of long-legged crane-flies[1] whizzed off the grass at every step the passer took.

Fancy Day and her friend Susan Dewy the tranter's daughter were in such a spot as this, pulling down a bough laden with early apples. Three months had elapsed since Dick and Fancy had journeyed together from Budmouth, and the course of their love had run on vigorously during the whole time. There had been just enough difficulty attending its development, and just enough finesse[2] required in keeping it private, to lend the passion an ever-increasing freshness on Fancy's part, whilst, whether from these accessories or not, Dick's heart had been at all times as fond as could be desired. But there was a cloud on Fancy's horizon now.

'She is so well off – better than any of us,' Susan Dewy was saying. 'Her father farms five hundred acres, and she might marry a doctor or curate or anything of that kind if she contrived a little.'

'I don't think Dick ought to have gone to that gipsy-party[3] at all when he knew I couldn't go,' replied Fancy uneasily.

'He didn't know that you would not be there till it was too late to refuse the invitation,' said Susan.

'And what was she like? Tell me.'

'Well, she was rather pretty, I must own.'

'Tell straight on about her, can't you! Come, do, Susan. How many times did you say he danced with her?'

'Once.'

'Twice, I think you said?'

'Indeed I'm sure I didn't.'

'Well, and he wanted to again, I expect.'

'No; I don't think he did. She wanted to dance with him again bad enough, I know. Everybody does with Dick, because he's so handsome and such a clever courter.'

'O, I wish! – How did you say she wore her hair?'

'In long curls, – and her hair is light, and it curls without being put in paper: that's how it is she's so attractive.'

'She's trying to get him away! yes, yes, she is! And through keeping this miserable school I mustn't wear my hair in curls! But I will; I don't care if I leave the school and go home, I will wear my curls! Look, Susan, do! is her hair as soft and long as this?' Fancy pulled from its coil under her hat a twine of her own hair and stretched it down her shoulder to show its length, looking at Susan to catch her opinion from her eyes.

'It is about the same length as that, I think,' said Miss Dewy.

Fancy paused hopelessly. 'I wish mine was lighter, like hers!' she continued mournfully. 'But hers isn't so soft, is it? Tell me, now.'

'I don't know.'

Fancy abstractedly extended her vision to survey a yellow butterfly and a red-and-black butterfly that were flitting along in company, and then became aware that Dick was advancing up the garden.

'Susan, here's Dick coming; I suppose that's because we've been talking about him.'

'Well, then, I shall go indoors now – you won't want me'; and Susan turned practically and walked off.

Enter the single-minded Dick, whose only fault at the gipsying, or picnic, had been that of loving Fancy too exclusively and depriving himself of the innocent pleasure the gathering might have afforded him, by sighing regretfully at her absence, – who had danced with the rival in sheer despair of ever being able to get through that stale, flat, and unprofitable⁴ afternoon in any other way; but this she would not believe.

Fancy had settled her plan of emotion. To reproach Dick? O no, no. 'I am in great trouble,' said she, taking what was intended to be a hopelessly melancholy survey of a few small apples lying under the tree; yet a critical ear might have noticed in her voice a tentative tone as to the effect of the words upon Dick when she uttered them.

'What are you in trouble about? Tell me of it,' said Dick earnestly. 'Darling, I will share it with 'ee and help 'ee.'

'No, no: you can't! Nobody can!'

'Why not! You don't deserve it, whatever it is. Tell me, dear.'

'O, it isn't what you think! It is dreadful: my own sin!'

'Sin, Fancy! as if you could sin! I know it can't be.'

'' 'Tis, 'tis!' said the young lady, in a pretty little frenzy of sorrow. 'I have done wrong, and I don't like to tell it! Nobody will forgive me, nobody! and you above all will not! ... I have allowed myself to – to – fl—'

'What, – not flirt!' he said, controlling his emotion as it were by a sudden pressure inward from his surface. 'And you said only the day before yesterday that you hadn't flirted in your life!'

'Yes, I did; and that was a wicked story! I have let another love me, and—'

'Good G—! Well, I'll forgive you, – yes, if you couldn't help it, – yes, I will!' said the now dismal Dick. 'Did you encourage him?'

'Oh, – I don't know, – yes – no. O, I think so!'

'Who was it?'

A pause.

'Tell me!'

'Mr Shiner.'

After a silence that was only disturbed by the fall of an apple, a long-checked sigh from Dick, and a sob from Fancy, he said with real austerity –

'Tell it all; – every word!'

'He looked at me, and I looked at him, and he said, "Will you let me show you how to catch bullfinches down here by the stream?" And I – wanted to know very much – I did so long to have a bullfinch! I couldn't help that! – and I said, "Yes!" and then he said, "Come here." And I went with him down to the lovely river, and then he said to me, "Look and see how I do it, and then you'll know: I put this bird-lime[5] round this twig, and then I go here," he said, "and hide away under a bush; and presently clever Mister Bird comes and perches upon the twig, and flaps his wings, and you've got him before you can say Jack" – something; O, O, O, I forget what!'

'Jack Sprat,' mournfully suggested Dick through the cloud of his misery.

'No, not Jack Sprat,' she sobbed.

'Then 'twas Jack Robinson!' he said with the emphasis of a man who had resolved to discover every iota of the truth or die.

'Yes, that was it! And then I put my hand upon the rail of the bridge to get across, and – That's all.'

'Well, that isn't much, either,' said Dick critically and more cheerfully. 'Not that I see what business Shiner has to take upon himself to teach you anything. But it seems – it

do seem there must have been more than that to set you up
in such a dreadful taking?'

He looked into Fancy's eyes. Misery of miseries! – guilt
was written there still.

'Now, Fancy, you've not told me all!' said Dick, rather
sternly for a quiet young man.

'O, don't speak so cruelly! I am afraid to tell now! If
you hadn't been harsh I was going on to tell all; now I
can't!'

'Come, dear Fancy, tell: come. I'll forgive; I must, – by
heaven and earth, I must, whether I will or no; I love you
so!'

'Well, when I put my hand on the bridge, he touched
it—'

'A scamp!' said Dick, grinding an imaginary human
frame to powder.

'And then he looked at me, and at last he said, "Are you
in love with Dick Dewy?" And I said, "Perhaps I am!"
and then he said, "I wish you weren't then, for I want to
marry you, with all my soul."'

'There's a villain now! Want to marry you!' And Dick
quivered with the bitterness of satirical laughter. Then suddenly remembering that he might be reckoning without his
host: 'Unless, to be sure, you are willing to have him, –
perhaps you are,' he said, with the wretched indifference of
a castaway.[6]

'No, indeed I am not!' she said, her sobs just beginning
to take a favourable turn towards cure.

'Well, then,' said Dick, coming a little to his senses,
'you've been stretching it very much in giving such a dreadful beginning to such a mere nothing. And I know what
you've done it for, – just because of that gipsy-party!' He
turned away from her and took five paces decisively, as if
he were tired of an ungrateful country, including herself.
'You did it to make me jealous, and I won't stand it!' He

flung the words to her over his shoulder and then stalked on, apparently very anxious to walk to the remotest of the Colonies[7] that very minute.

'O, O, O, Dick – Dick!' she cried, trotting after him like a pet lamb and really seriously alarmed at last, 'you'll kill me! My impulses are bad – miserably wicked, – and I can't help it; forgive me, Dick! And I love you always; and those times when you look silly and don't seem quite good enough for me, – just the same, I do, Dick! And there is something more serious, though not concerning that walk with him.'

'Well, what is it?' said Dick, altering his mind about walking to the Colonies; in fact, passing to the other extreme, and standing so rooted to the road that he was apparently not even going home.

'Why, this,' she said, drying the beginning of a new flood of tears she had been going to shed, 'this is the serious part. Father has told Mr Shiner that he would like him for a son-in-law if he could get me; – that he has his right hearty consent to come courting me!'

4 An Arrangement

'That *is* serious,' said Dick, more intellectually than he had spoken for a long time.

The truth was that Geoffrey knew nothing about his daughter's continued walks and meetings with Dick. When a hint that there were symptoms of an attachment between them had first reached Geoffrey's ears he stated so emphatically that he must think the matter over before any such thing could be allowed that, rather unwisely on Dick's part, whatever it might have been on the lady's, the lovers were careful to be seen together no more in public; and Geoffrey, forgetting the report, did not think over the matter at all. So Mr Shiner resumed his old position in Geoffrey's brain by mere flux of time.[1] Even Shiner began to believe that Dick existed for Fancy no more, – though that remarkably easy-going man had taken no active steps on his own account as yet.

'And father has not only told Mr Shiner that,' continued Fancy, 'but he has written me a letter to say he should wish me to encourage Mr Shiner if 'twas convenient!'

'I must start off and see your father at once!' said Dick, taking two or three vehement steps to the south, recollecting that Mr Day lived to the north, and coming back again.

'I think we had better see him together. Not tell him what you come for, or anything of the kind, until he likes you, and so wins his brain through his heart, which is always the way to manage people. I mean in this way: I am going home on Saturday week to help them in the honey-taking.[2]

You might come there to me, have something to eat and drink, and let him guess what your coming signifies, without saying it in so many words.'

'We'll do it, dearest. But I shall ask him for you, flat and plain; not wait for his guessing.' And the lover then stepped close to her, and attempted to give her one little kiss on the cheek, his lips alighting, however, on an impulse that had caused her to turn her head with a jerk. 'Yes, and I'll put on my second-best suit and a clean shirt and collar, and black my boots as if 'twas a Sunday. 'Twill have a good appearance, you see, and that's a great deal to start with.'

'You won't wear that old waistcoat, will you, Dick?'

'Bless you, no! Why, I—'

'I didn't mean to be personal, dear Dick,' she said, fearing she had hurt his feelings. ' 'Tis a very nice waistcoat, but what I meant was, that though it is an excellent waistcoat for a settled-down man, it is not quite one for' (she waited, and a blush expanded over her face, and then she went on again) – 'for going courting in.'

'No, I'll wear my best winter one, with the leather lining, that mother made. It is a beautiful, handsome waistcoat inside, yes, as ever anybody saw. In fact, only the other day, I unbuttoned it to show a chap that very lining, and he said it was the strongest, handsomest lining you could wish to see on the king's waistcoat himself.'

'*I* don't quite know what to wear,' she said, as if her habitual indifference alone to dress had kept back so important a subject till now.

'Why, that blue frock you wore last week.'

'Doesn't set well round the neck. I couldn't wear that.'

'But I shan't care.'

'No, you won't mind.'

'Well, then it's all right. Because you only care how you look to me, do you, dear? I only dress for you, that's certain.'

'Yes, but you see I couldn't appear in it again very well.'

'Any strange gentleman you mid meet in your journey might notice the set of it, I suppose. Fancy, men in love don't think so much about how they look to other women.' It is difficult to say whether a tone of playful banter or of gentle reproach prevailed in the speech.

'Well then, Dick,' she said, with good-humoured frankness, 'I'll own it. I shouldn't like a stranger to see me dressed badly even though I am in love. 'Tis our nature, I suppose.'

'You perfect woman!'

'Yes; if you lay the stress on "woman",' she murmured, looking at the group of hollyhocks in flowers, round which a crowd of butterflies had gathered like female idlers³ round a bonnet-shop.

'But about the dress. Why not wear the one you wore at our party?'

'That sets well, but a girl of the name of Bet Tallor, who lives near our house, has had one made almost like it (only in pattern, though of miserably cheap stuff), and I couldn't wear it on that account. Dear me, I am afraid I can't go now.'

'O yes, you must; I know you will!' said Dick, with dismay. 'Why not wear what you've got on?'

'What! this old one! After all, I think that by wearing my grey one Saturday, I can make the blue one do for Sunday. Yes, I will. A hat or a bonnet, which shall it be? Which do I look best in?'

'Well, I think the bonnet is nicest, more quiet and matronly.'

'What's the objection to the hat? Does it make me look old?'

'O no; the hat is well enough; but it makes you look rather too – you won't mind me saying it, dear?'

'Not at all, for I shall wear the bonnet.'

'– Rather too coquettish and flirty for an engaged young woman.'

She reflected a minute. 'Yes; yes. Still, after all, the hat would do best; hats *are* best, you see. Yes, I must wear the hat, dear Dicky, because I ought to wear a hat, you know.'

Part the Fourth

Autumn

1 Going Nutting

Dick, dressed in his second-best suit, burst into Fancy's sitting-room with a glow of pleasure on his face.

It was two o'clock on Friday, the day before her contemplated visit to her father, and for some reason connected with cleaning the school the children had been given this Friday afternoon for pastime, in addition to the usual Saturday.

'Fancy! it happens just right that it is a leisure half-day with you. Smart is lame in his near-foot-afore,[1] and so, as I can't do anything, I've made a holiday afternoon of it, and am come for you to go nutting with me!'

She was sitting by the parlour window with a blue frock lying across her lap and scissors in her hand.

'Go nutting! Yes. But I'm afraid I can't go for an hour or so.'

'Why not? 'Tis the only spare afternoon we may both have together for weeks.'

'This dress of mine, that I am going to wear on Sunday at Yalbury; I find it fits so badly that I must alter it a little, after all. I told the dressmaker to make it by a pattern I gave her at the time; instead of that, she did it her own way, and made me look a perfect fright.'

'How long will you be?' he inquired, looking rather disappointed.

'Not long. Do wait and talk to me; come, do, dear.'

Dick sat down. The talking progressed very favourably amid the snipping and sewing till about half-past two, at

which time his conversation began to be varied by a slight
tapping upon his toe with a walking-stick he had cut from
the hedge as he came along. Fancy talked and answered
him, but sometimes the answers were so negligently given
that it was evident her thoughts lay for the greater part in
her lap with the blue dress.

The clock struck three. Dick arose from his seat, walked
round the room with his hands behind him, examined all
the furniture, then sounded a few notes on the harmonium,
then looked inside all the books he could find, then
smoothed Fancy's head with his hand. Still the snipping
and sewing went on.

The clock struck four. Dick fidgeted about, yawned privately; counted the knots in the table, yawned publicly;
counted the flies on the ceiling, yawned horribly; went into
the kitchen and scullery[2] and so thoroughly studied the
principle upon which the pump was constructed that he
could have delivered a lecture on the subject. Stepping back
to Fancy, and finding still that she had not done, he went
into her garden and looked at her cabbages and potatoes,
and reminded himself that they seemed to him to wear a
decidedly feminine aspect; then pulled up several weeds
and came in again. The clock struck five, and still the snipping and sewing went on.

Dick attempted to kill a fly, peeled all the rind off his
walking-stick, then threw the stick into the scullery because
it was spoilt, produced hideous discords from the harmonium, and accidentally overturned a vase of flowers, the
water from which ran in a rill across the table and dribbled
to the floor, where it formed a lake, the shape of which,
after the lapse of a few minutes, he began to modify considerably with his foot till it was like a map of England and
Wales.

'Well, Dick, you needn't have made quite such a mess.'

'Well, I needn't, I suppose.' He walked up to the blue

dress, and looked at it with a rigid gaze. Then an idea seemed to cross his brain.

'Fancy.'

'Yes.'

'I thought you said you were going to wear your grey gown all day tomorrow on your trip to Yalbury, and in the evening too, when I shall be with you, and ask your father for you?'

'So I am.'

'And the blue one only on Sunday?'

'And the blue one Sunday.'

'Well, dear, I shan't be at Yalbury Sunday to see it.'

'No, but I shall walk to Longpuddle church in the afternoon with father, and such lots of people will be looking at me there, you know; and it did set so badly round the neck.'

'I never noticed it, and 'tis like nobody else would.'

'They might.'

'Then why not wear the grey one on Sunday as well? 'Tis as pretty as the blue one.'

'I might make the grey one do, certainly. But it isn't so good; it didn't cost half so much as this one, and besides, it would be the same I wore Saturday.'

'Then wear the striped one, dear.'

'I might.'

'Or the dark one.'

'Yes, I might; but I want to wear a fresh one they haven't seen.'

'I see, I see,' said Dick, in a voice in which the tones of love were decidedly inconvenienced by a considerable emphasis, his thoughts meanwhile running as follows: 'I, the man she loves best in the world, as she says, am to understand that my poor half-holiday is to be lost, because she wants to wear on Sunday a gown there is not the slightest necessity for wearing, simply, in fact, to appear more striking than usual in the eyes of the Longpuddle young men; and I not there, either.'

'Then there are three dresses good enough for my eyes, but neither is good enough for the youths of Longpuddle,' he said.

'No, not that exactly, Dick. Still, you see, I do want – to look pretty to them – there, that's honest! But I shan't be much longer.'

'How much?'

'A quarter of an hour.'

'Very well; I'll come in in a quarter of an hour.'

'Why go away?'

'I mid as well.'

He went out, walked down the road, and sat upon a gate. Here he meditated and meditated, and the more he meditated the more decidedly did he begin to fume, and the more positive was he that his time had been scandalously trifled with by Miss Fancy Day – that, so far from being the simple girl who had never had a sweetheart before, as she had solemnly assured him time after time, she was, if not a flirt, a woman who had had no end of admirers; a girl most certainly too anxious about her frocks; a girl, whose feelings, though warm, were not deep; a girl who cared a great deal too much how she appeared in the eyes of other men. 'What she loves best in the world,' he thought, with an incipient spice of his father's grimness, 'is her hair and complexion. What she loves next best, her gowns and hats; what she loves next best, myself, perhaps!'

Suffering great anguish at this disloyalty in himself and harshness to his darling, yet disposed to persevere in it, a horribly cruel thought crossed his mind. He would not call for her, as he had promised, at the end of a quarter of an hour! Yes, it would be a punishment she well deserved. Although the best part of the afternoon had been wasted he would go nutting as he had intended, and go by himself.

He leaped over the gate, and pushed up the lane for nearly two miles, till a winding path called Snail-Creep sloped up a hill and entered a hazel copse by a hole like a rabbit's burrow. In he plunged, vanished among the bushes, and in a short time there was no sign of his existence upon earth save an occasional rustling of boughs and snapping of twigs in divers points of Grey's Wood.

Never man nutted as Dick nutted that afternoon. He worked like a galley slave. Half-hour after half-hour passed away, and still he gathered without ceasing. At last, when the sun had set, and bunches of nuts could not be distinguished from the leaves which nourished them, he shouldered his bag, containing quite two pecks[3] of the finest produce of the wood, about as much use to him as two pecks of stones from the road, strolled down the woodland track, crossed the highway and entered the homeward lane, whistling as he went.

Probably, Miss Fancy Day never before or after stood so low in Mr Dewy's opinion as on that afternoon. In fact, it is just possible that a few more blue dresses on the Longpuddle young men's account would have clarified Dick's brain entirely, and made him once more a free man.

But Venus[4] planned other developments, at any rate for the present. Cuckoo Lane, the way he pursued, passed over a ridge which rose keenly against the sky about fifty yards in his van.[5] Here, upon the bright after-glow about the horizon, was now visible an irregular shape, which at first he conceived to be a bough standing a little beyond the line of its neighbours. Then it seemed to move, and, as he advanced still further, there was no doubt that it was a living being sitting in the bank, head bowed on hand. The grassy margin entirely prevented his footsteps from being heard, and it was not till he was close that the figure recognized him. Up it sprang, and he was face to face with Fancy.

'Dick, Dick! O, is it you, Dick!'

'Yes, Fancy,' said Dick, in a rather repentant tone, and lowering his nuts.

She ran up to him, flung her parasol on the grass, put her little head against his breast, and then there began a narrative disjointed by such a hysterical weeping as was never surpassed for intensity in the whole history of love.

'O Dick,' she sobbed out, 'where have you been away from me? O, I have suffered agony, and thought you would never come any more! 'Tis cruel, Dick; no 'tisn't, it is justice! I've been walking miles and miles up and down Grey's Wood, trying to find you, till I was wearied and worn out, and I could walk no further, and had come back this far! O Dick, directly you were gone I thought I had offended you and I put down the dress; 'tisn't finished now, and I never will finish it, and I'll wear an old one Sunday! Yes, Dick, I will, because I don't care what I wear when you are not by my side – ha, you think I do, but I don't! – and I ran after you, and I saw you go up Snail-Creep and not look back once, and then you plunged in, and I after you; but I was too far behind. O, I did wish the horrid bushes had been cut down so that I could see your dear shape again! And then I called out to you and nobody answered, and I was afraid to call very loud lest anybody else should hear me. Then I kept wandering and wandering about, and it was dreadful misery, Dick. And then I shut my eyes and fell to picturing you looking at some other woman, very pretty and nice, but with no affection or truth in her at all, and then imagined you saying to yourself, "Ah, she's as good as Fancy, for Fancy told me a story, and was a flirt, and cared for herself more than me, so now I'll have this one for my sweetheart." O, you won't, will you, Dick, for I do love you so!'

It is scarcely necessary to add that Dick renounced his freedom there and then, and kissed her ten times over, and promised that no pretty woman of the kind alluded to

should ever engross his thoughts; in short, that though he
had been vexed with her all such vexation was past, and that
henceforth and for ever it was simply Fancy or death for
him. And then they set about proceeding homewards, very
slowly on account of Fancy's weariness, she leaning upon
his shoulder and in addition receiving support from his arm
round her waist; though she had sufficiently recovered from
her desperate condition to sing to him, 'Why are you
wandering here, I pray?'[6] during the latter part of their
walk. Nor is it necessary to describe in detail how the bag
of nuts was quite forgotten until three days later, when it
was found among the brambles and restored empty to Mrs
Dewy, her initials being marked thereon in red cotton; and
how she puzzled herself till her head ached upon the question of how on earth her meal-bag could have got into
Cuckoo Lane.

2 Honey-taking, and Afterwards

Saturday evening saw Dick Dewy journeying on foot to Yalbury Wood, according to the arrangement with Fancy.

The landscape being concave, at the going down of the sun everything suddenly assumed a uniform robe of shade. The evening advanced from sunset to dusk long before Dick's arrival, and his progress during the latter portion of his walk through the trees was indicated by the flutter of terrified birds that had been roosting over the path. And in crossing the glades, masses of hot dry air that had been formed on the hills during the day greeted his cheeks alternately with clouds of damp night air from the valleys. He reached the keeper-steward's house, where the grass-plot and the garden in front appeared light and pale against the unbroken darkness of the grove from which he had emerged, and paused at the garden gate.

He had scarcely been there a minute when he beheld a sort of procession advancing from the door in his front. It consisted first of Enoch the trapper, carrying a spade on his shoulder and a lantern dangling in his hand; then came Mrs Day, the light of the lantern revealing that she bore in her arms curious objects about a foot long in the form of Latin crosses[1] (made of lath and brown paper dipped in brimstone[2] – called matches by bee-masters); next came Miss Day with a shawl thrown over her head; and behind all, in the gloom, Mr Frederick Shiner.

Dick in his consternation at finding Shiner present was at a loss how to proceed, and retired under a tree to collect his thoughts.

'Here I be, Enoch,' said a voice; and the procession advancing further, the lantern's rays illuminated the figure of Geoffrey awaiting their arrival beside a row of bee-hives in front of the path. Taking the spade from Enoch he proceeded to dig two holes in the earth beside the hives, the others standing round in a circle except Mrs Day, who deposited her matches in the fork of an apple-tree and returned to the house. The party remaining were now lit up in front by the lantern in their midst, their shadows radiating each way upon the garden-plot like the spokes of a wheel. An apparent embarrassment of Fancy at the presence of Shiner caused a silence in the assembly, during which the preliminaries of execution were arranged, the matches fixed, the stake kindled, the two hives placed over the two holes, and the earth stopped round the edges. Geoffrey then stood erect, and rather more, to straighten his backbone after the digging.

'They were a peculiar family,' said Mr Shiner, regarding the hives reflectively.

Geoffrey nodded.

'Those holes will be the grave of thousands!' said Fancy. 'I think 'tis rather a cruel thing to do.'

Her father shook his head. 'No,' he said, tapping the hives to shake the dead bees from their cells, 'if you suffocate 'em this way, they only die once: if you fumigate 'em in the new way, they come to life again, and die o' starvation; so the pangs o' death be twice upon 'em.'

'I incline to Fancy's notion,' said Mr Shiner, laughing lightly.

'The proper way to take honey,[3] so that the bees be neither starved nor murdered, is a puzzling matter,' said the keeper steadily.

'I should like never to take it from them,' said Fancy.

'But 'tis the money,' said Enoch musingly. 'For without money a man is a shadder!'[4]

The lantern-light had disturbed many bees that had

escaped from hives destroyed some days earlier, and, demoralized by affliction, were now getting a living as marauders about the doors of other hives. Several flew round the head and neck of Geoffrey; then darted upon him with an irritated bizz.

Enoch threw down the lantern and ran off and pushed his head into a currant bush; Fancy scudded up the path; and Mr Shiner floundered away helter-skelter among the cabbages. Geoffrey stood his ground, unmoved and firm as a rock. Fancy was the first to return, followed by Enoch picking up the lantern. Mr Shiner still remained invisible.

'Have the craters stung ye?' said Enoch to Geoffrey.

'No, not much – on'y a little here and there,' he said with leisurely solemnity, shaking one bee out of his shirt sleeve, pulling another from among his hair, and two or three more from his neck. The rest looked on during this proceeding with a complacent sense of being out of it, – much as a European nation in a state of internal commotion is watched by its neighbours.

'Are those all of them, father?' said Fancy, when Geoffrey had pulled away five.

'Almost all, – though I feel one or two more sticking into my shoulder and side. Ah! there's another just begun again upon my backbone. You lively young mortals, how did you get inside there? However, they can't sting me many times more, poor things, for they must be getting weak. They mid as well stay in me till bedtime now, I suppose.'

As he himself was the only person affected by this arrangement it seemed satisfactory enough; and after a noise of feet kicking against cabbages in a blundering progress among them the voice of Mr Shiner was heard from the darkness in that direction.

'Is all quite safe again?'

No answer being returned to this query he apparently

assumed that he might venture forth, and gradually drew near the lantern again. The hives were now removed from their position over the holes, one being handed to Enoch to carry indoors, and one being taken by Geoffrey himself.

'Bring hither the lantern, Fancy: the spade can bide.'

Geoffrey and Enoch then went towards the house, leaving Shiner and Fancy standing side by side on the garden-plot.

'Allow me,' said Shiner, stooping for the lantern and seizing it at the same time with Fancy.

'I can carry it,' said Fancy, religiously repressing all inclination to trifle. She had thoroughly considered that subject after the tearful explanation of the bird-catching adventure to Dick, and had decided that it would be dishonest in her as an engaged young woman to trifle with men's eyes and hands any more. Finding that Shiner still retained his hold of the lantern she relinquished it, and he, having found her retaining it, also let go. The lantern fell and was extinguished. Fancy moved on.

'Where is the path?' said Mr Shiner.

'Here,' said Fancy. 'Your eyes will get used to the dark in a minute or two.'

'Till that time will ye lend me your hand?'

Fancy gave him the extreme tips of her fingers and they stepped from the plot into the path.

'You don't accept attentions very freely.'

'It depends upon who offers them.'

'A fellow like me, for instance.'

A dead silence.

'Well, what do you say, Missie?'

'It then depends upon how they are offered.'

'Not wildly, and yet not careless-like; not purposely, and yet not by chance; not too quick nor yet too slow.'

'How then?' said Fancy.

'Coolly and practically,' he said. 'How would that kind of love be taken?'

'Not anxiously, and yet not indifferently; neither blushing nor pale; nor religiously nor yet quite wickedly.'

'Well, how?'

'Not at all.'

Geoffrey Day's storehouse at the back of his dwelling was hung with bunches of dried horehound,[5] mint, and sage; brown-paper bags of thyme and lavender; and long ropes of clean onions. On shelves were spread large red and yellow apples, and choice selections of early potatoes for seed next year; – vulgar crowds of commoner kind lying beneath in heaps. A few empty beehives were clustered around a nail in one corner, under which stood two or three barrels of new cider of the first crop, each bubbling and squirting forth from the yet open bunghole.

Fancy was now kneeling beside the two inverted hives, one of which rested againt her lap for convenience in operating upon the contents. She thrust her sleeves above her elbows, and inserted her small pink hand edgewise between each white lobe[6] of honeycomb, performing the act so adroitly and gently as not to unseal a single cell. Then cracking the piece off at the crown of the hive by a slight backward and forward movement she lifted each portion as it was loosened into a large blue platter placed on a bench at her side.

'Bother these little mortals!' said Geoffrey, who was holding the light to her and giving his back an uneasy twist. 'I really think I may as well go indoors and take 'em out, poor things! for they won't let me alone. There's two a-stinging wi' all their might now. I'm sure I wonder their strength can last so long.'

'All right, friend; I'll hold the candle whilst you are gone,' said Mr Shiner, leisurely taking the light and allowing Geoffrey to depart, which he did with his usual long paces.

He could hardly have gone round to the house-door when other footsteps were heard approaching the outbuilding; the tip of a finger appeared in the hole through which the wood latch was lifted, and Dick Dewy came in, having been all this time walking up and down the wood vainly waiting for Shiner's departure.

Fancy looked up and welcomed him rather confusedly. Shiner grasped the candlestick more firmly, and lest doing this in silence should not imply to Dick with sufficient force that he was quite at home and cool, he sang invincibly –

'"King Arthur he had three sons."'[7]

'Father here?' said Dick.

'Indoors, I think,' said Fancy, looking pleasantly at him.

Dick surveyed the scene and did not seem inclined to hurry off just at that moment. Shiner went on singing –

'"The miller was drown'd in his pond,
    The weaver was hung in his yarn,[8]
    And the d— ran away with the little tail-or,
    With the broadcloth[9] under his arm."'

'That's a terrible crippled rhyme,[10] if that's your rhyme!' said Dick, with a grain of superciliousness in his tone.

'It's no use your complaining to me about the rhyme!' said Mr Shiner. 'You must go to the man that made it.'

Fancy by this time had acquired confidence.

'Taste a bit, Mr Dewy,' she said, holding up to him a small circular piece of honeycomb that had been the last in the row of layers, remaining still on her knees and flinging back her head to look in his face; 'and then I'll taste a bit too.'

'And I, if you please,' said Mr Shiner. Nevertheless the farmer looked superior, as if he could even now hardly join the trifling from very importance of station; and after receiving the honeycomb from Fancy he turned it over in his hand till the cells began to be crushed, and the liquid honey ran down from his fingers in a thin string.

Suddenly a faint cry from Fancy caused them to gaze at her.

'What's the matter, dear?' said Dick.

'It is nothing, but – O-o! – a bee has stung the inside of my lip! He was in one of the cells I was eating!'

'We must keep down the swelling or it may be serious!' said Shiner, stepping up and kneeling beside her. 'Let me see it.'

'No, no!'

'Just let *me* see it,' said Dick kneeling on the other side; and after some hesitation she pressed down her lip with one finger to show the place. 'O, I hope 'twill soon be better! I don't mind a sting in ordinary places, but it is so bad upon your lip,' she added with tears in her eyes, and writhing a little from the pain.

Shiner held the light above his head and pushed his face close to Fancy's, as if the lip had been shown exclusively to himself, upon which Dick pushed closer, as if Shiner were not there at all.

'It is swelling,' said Dick to her right aspect.

'It isn't swelling,' said Shiner to her left aspect.

'Is it dangerous on the lip?' cried Fancy. 'I know it is dangerous on the tongue.'

'O no, not dangerous,' answered Dick.

'Rather dangerous,' had answered Shiner simultaneously.

'I must try to bear it!' said Fancy, turning again to the hives.

'Hartshorn[11]-and-oil is a good thing to put to it, Miss Day,' said Shiner with great concern.

'Sweet-oil-and-hartshorn I've found to be a good thing to cure stings, Miss Day,' said Dick with greater concern.

'We have some mixed indoors; would you kindly run and get it for me?' she said.

Now whether by inadvertence or whether by mischievous intention, the individuality of the *you* was so carelessly denoted that both Dick and Shiner sprang to their feet like twin acrobats, and marched abreast to the door; both seized the latch and lifted it, and continued marching on shoulder to shoulder in the same manner to the dwelling-house. Not only so but, entering the room, they marched as before straight up to Mrs Day's chair, letting the door in the oak partition slam so forcibly that the rows of pewter on the dresser rang like a bell.

'Mrs Day, Fancy has stung her lip and wants you to give me the hartshorn, please,' said Mr Shiner, very close to Mrs Day's face.

'O, Mrs Day, Fancy has asked me to bring out the hartshorn, please, because she has stung her lip!' said Dick, a little closer to Mrs Day's face.

'Well, men alive! that's no reason why you should eat me, I suppose!' said Mrs Day, drawing back.

She searched in the corner-cupboard, produced the bottle and began to dust the cork, the rim, and every other part very carefully, Dick's hand and Shiner's hand waiting side by side.

'Which is head man?' said Mrs Day. 'Now, don't come mumbudgeting so close again. Which is head man?'

Neither spoke; and the bottle was inclined towards Shiner. Shiner, as a high-class man, would not look in the least triumphant, and turned to go off with it as Geoffrey came downstairs after the search in his linen for concealed bees.

'O – that you, Master Dewy?'

Dick assured the keeper that it was; and the young man then determined upon a bold stroke for the attainment of

his end, forgetting that the worst of bold strokes is the dis-
astrous consequences they involve if they fail.

'I've come on purpose to speak to you very particular,
Mr Day,' he said, with a crushing emphasis intended for the
ears of Mr Shiner, who was vanishing round the door-post
at that moment.

'Well, I've been forced to go upstairs and unrind[12] myself, and shake some bees out o' me,' said Geoffrey, walking
slowly towards the open door and standing on the threshold. 'The young rascals got into my shirt and wouldn't be
quiet nohow.'

Dick followed him to the door.

'I've come to speak a word to you,' he repeated, looking
out at the pale mist creeping up from the gloom of the
valley. 'You may perhaps guess what it is about.'

The keeper lowered his hands into the depths of his
pockets, twirled his eyes, balanced himself on his toes,
looked as perpendicularly downward as if his glance were a
plumb-line,[13] then horizontally, collecting together the
cracks that lay about his face till they were all in the neighbourhood of his eyes.

'Maybe I don't know,' he replied.

Dick said nothing; and the stillness was disturbed only
by some small bird that was being killed by an owl in the
adjoining wood, whose cry passed into the silence without
mingling with it.

'I've left my hat up in chammer,'[14] said Geoffrey; 'wait
while I step up and get en.'

'I'll be in the garden,' said Dick.

He went round by a side wicket into the garden, and
Geoffrey went upstairs. It was the custom in Mellstock and
its vicinity to discuss matters of pleasure and ordinary
business inside the house, and to reserve the garden for
very important affairs: a custom which, as is supposed,
originated in the desirability of getting away at such times

from the other members of the family when there was only one room for living in, though it was now quite as frequently practised by those who suffered from no such limitation to the size of their domiciles.

The head-keeper's form appeared in the dusky garden, and Dick walked towards him. The elder paused and leant over the rail of a piggery that stood on the left of the path, upon which Dick did the same; and they both contemplated a whitish shadowy shape that was moving about and grunting among the straw of the interior.

'I've come to ask for Fancy,' said Dick.

'I'd as lief[15] you hadn't.'

'Why should that be, Mr Day?'

'Because it makes me say that you've come to ask what ye be'n't likely to have. Have ye come for anything else?'

'Nothing.'

'Then I'll tell 'ee you've come on a very foolish errand. D'ye know what her mother was?'

'No.'

'A teacher in a landed family's[16] nursery, who was foolish enough to marry the keeper of the same establishment; for I was only a keeper then, though now I've a dozen other irons in the fire[17] as steward here for my lord, what with the timber sales and the yearly fellings, and the gravel and sand sales, and one thing and t'other. However, d'ye think Fancy picked up her good manners, the smooth turn of her tongue, her musical notes, and her knowledge of books, in a homely[18] hole like this?'

'No.'

'D'ye know where?'

'No.'

'Well, when I went a-wandering after her mother's death she lived with her aunt, who kept a boarding-school, till her aunt married Lawyer Green – a man as sharp as a needle – and the school was broke up. Did ye know that then she

went to the training-school, and that her name stood first
among the Queen's scholars[19] of her year?'

'I've heard so.'

'And that when she sat for her certificate as Government
teacher,[20] she had the highest of the first class?'

'Yes.'

'Well, and do ye know what I live in such a miserly way
for when I've got enough to do without it, and why I make
her work as a schoolmistress instead of living here?'

'No.'

'That if any gentleman, who sees her to be his equal in
polish, should want to marry her, and she want to marry
him, he shan't be superior to her in pocket. Now do ye
think after this that you be good enough for her?'

'No.'

'Then goodnight t'ee, Master Dewy.'

'Goodnight, Mr Day.'

Modest Dick's reply had faltered upon his tongue, and he
turned away wondering at his presumption in asking for a
woman whom he had seen from the beginning to be so
superior to him.

3 Fancy in the Rain

The next scene is a tempestuous afternoon in the following month, and Fancy Day is discovered walking from her father's home towards Mellstock.

A single vast grey cloud covered the country, from which the small rain and mist had just begun to blow down in wavy sheets, alternately thick and thin. The trees of the fields and plantations writhed like miserable men as the air wound its way swiftly among them: the lowest portions of their trunks, that had hardly ever been known to move, were visibly rocked by the fiercer gusts, distressing the mind by its painful unwontedness, as when a strong man is seen to shed tears. Low-hanging boughs went up and down; high and erect boughs went to and fro; the blasts being so irregular, and divided into so many cross-currents, that neighbouring branches of the same tree swept the skies in independent motions, crossed each other, or became entangled. Across the open spaces flew flocks of green and yellowish leaves which, after travelling a long distance from their parent trees, reached the ground and lay there with their under-sides upward.

As the rain and wind increased, and Fancy's bonnet-ribbons leapt more and more snappishly against her chin, she paused on entering Mellstock Lane to consider her latitude, and the distance to a place of shelter. The nearest house was Elizabeth Endorfield's[1] in Higher Mellstock, whose cottage and garden stood not far from the junction of that hamlet with the road she followed. Fancy hastened onward, and in five minutes entered a gate which shed upon her toes a flood of water-drops as she opened it.

'Come in, chiel!' a voice exclaimed before Fancy had knocked: a promptness that would have surprised her had she not known that Mrs Endorfield was an exceedingly and exceptionally sharp woman in the use of her eyes and ears.

Fancy went in and sat down. Elizabeth was paring potatoes for her husband's supper.

Scrape, scrape, scrape; then a toss, and splash went a potato into a bucket of water.

Now as Fancy listlessly noted these proceedings of the dame she began to reconsider an old subject that lay uppermost in her heart. Since the interview between her father and Dick the days had been melancholy days for her. Geoffrey's firm opposition to the notion of Dick as a son-in-law was more than she had expected. She had frequently seen her lover since that time, it is true, and had loved him more for the opposition than she would have otherwise dreamt of doing – which was a happiness of a certain kind. Yet, though love is thus an end in itself it must be believed to be the means to another end if it is to assume the rosy hues of an unalloyed pleasure. And such a belief Fancy and Dick were emphatically denied just now.

Elizabeth Endorfield had a repute among women which was in its nature something between distinction and notoriety. It was founded on the following items of character. She was shrewd and penetrating; her house stood in a lonely place; she never went to church; she wore a red cloak; she always retained her bonnet indoors; and she had a pointed chin. Thus far her attributes were distinctly Satanic; and those who looked no further called her, in plain terms, a witch. But she was not gaunt, nor ugly in the upper part of her face, nor particularly strange in manner; so that, when her more intimate acquaintances spoke of her the term was softened, and she became simply a Deep Body, who was as long-headed as she was high. It may be stated that Elizabeth belonged to a class of suspects who were gradually losing their mysterious characteristics under the administration of the young vicar; though during the long reign of Mr Grinham the parish of Mellstock had proved extremely favourable to the growth of witches.

While Fancy was revolving all this in her mind, and putting it to herself whether it was worth while to tell her troubles to Elizabeth, and ask her advice in getting out of them, the witch spoke.

'You be down – proper down,'[2] she said suddenly, dropping another potato into the bucket.

Fancy took no notice.

'About your young man.'

Fancy reddened. Elizabeth seemed to be watching her thoughts. Really one would almost think she must have the powers people ascribed to her.

'Father not in the humour for't, hey?' Another potato was finished and flung in. 'Ah, I know about it. Little birds tell me things that people don't dream of my knowing.'

Fancy was desperate about Dick, and here was a chance – O, such a wicked chance! – of getting help; and what was goodness beside love!

'I wish you'd tell me how to put him in the humour for it?' she said.

'That I could soon do,' said the witch quietly.

'Really? O, do; anyhow – I don't care – so that it is done! How could I do it, Mrs Endorfield?'

'Nothing so mighty wonderful in it.'

'Well, but how?'

'By witchery, of course!' said Elizabeth.

'No!' said Fancy.

''Tis, I assure ye. Didn't you ever hear I was a witch?'

'Well,' hesitated Fancy, 'I have heard you called so.'

'And you believed it?'

'I can't say that I did exactly believe it, for 'tis very horrible and wicked; but, O, how I do wish it was possible for you to be one!'

'So I am. And I'll tell you how to bewitch your father to let you marry Dick Dewy.'

'Will it hurt him, poor thing?'

'Hurt who?'

'Father.'

'No; the charm is worked by common sense, and the spell can only be broke by your acting stupidly.'

Fancy looked rather perplexed, and Elizabeth went on:

> 'This fear of Lizz – whatever 'tis –
> By great and small,
> She makes pretence to common sense,
> And that's all.

You must do it like this.' The witch laid down her knife and potato, and then poured into Fancy's ear a long and detailed list of directions, glancing up from the corner of her eye into Fancy's face with an expression of sinister humour. Fancy's face brightened, clouded, rose and sank, as the narrative proceeded. 'There,' said Elizabeth at length, stooping for the knife and another potato, 'do that, and you'll have him by-long and by-late, my dear.'

'And do it I will!' said Fancy.

She then turned her attention to the external world once more. The rain continued as usual, but the wind had abated considerably during the discourse. Judging that it was now possible to keep an umbrella erect she pulled her hood again over her bonnet, bade the witch goodbye, and went her way.

4 The Spell

Mrs Endorfield's advice was duly followed.

'I be proper sorry that your daughter isn't so well as she might be,' said a Mellstock man to Geoffrey one morning.

'But is there anything in it?' said Geoffrey uneasily, as he shifted his hat to the right. 'I can't understand the report. She didn't complain to me a bit when I saw her.'

'No appetite at all, they say.'

Geoffrey crossed to Mellstock and called at the school that afternoon. Fancy welcomed him as usual, and asked him to stay and take tea with her.

'I be'n't much for tea this time o' day,' he said, but stayed.

During the meal he watched her narrowly. And to his great consternation discovered the following unprecedented change in the healthy girl – that she cut herself only a dia-phanous[1] slice of bread-and-butter, and, laying it on her plate, passed the meal-time in breaking it into pieces, but eating no more than about one-tenth of the slice. Geoffrey hoped she would say something about Dick and finish up by weeping, as she had done after the decision against him a few days subsequent to the interview in the garden. But nothing was said, and in due time Geoffrey departed again for Yalbury Wood.

' 'Tis to be hoped poor Miss Fancy will be able to keep on her school,' said Geoffrey's man Enoch to Geoffrey the following week, as they were shovelling up ant-hills in the wood.

Geoffrey stuck in the shovel, swept seven or eight ants from his sleeve, and killed another that was prowling round his ear, then looked perpendicularly into the earth, as usual, waiting for Enoch to say more. 'Well, why shouldn't she?' said the keeper at last.

'The baker told me yesterday,' continued Enoch, shaking out another emmet[2] that had run merrily up his thigh, 'that the bread he've left at that there school-house this last month would starve any mouse in the three creations;[3] that 'twould so! And afterwards I had a pint o' small[4] down at Morrs's, and there I heard more.'

'What might that ha' been?'

'That she used to have a pound o' the best rolled butter a week, regular as clockwork, from Dairyman Viney's for herself, as well as just so much salted for the helping girl, and the 'ooman she calls in; but now the same quantity d'last her three weeks, and then 'tis thoughted she throws it away sour.'

'Finish doing the emmets, and carry the bag home-along.' The keeper resumed his gun, tucked it under his arm, and went on without whistling to the dogs, who however followed with a bearing meant to imply that they did not expect any such attentions when their master was reflecting.

On Saturday morning a note came from Fancy. He was not to trouble about sending her the couple of rabbits as was intended, because she feared she should not want them. Later in the day Geoffrey went to Casterbridge and called upon the butcher who served Fancy with fresh meat, which was put down to her father's account.

'I've called to pay up our little bill, Neighbour Haylock, and you can gie me the chiel's account at the same time.'

Mr Haylock turned round three-quarters of a circle in the midst of a heap of joints, altered the expression of his face from meat to money, went into a little office consisting only of a door and a window, looked very vigorously into a book which possessed length but no breadth; and then, seizing a piece of paper and scribbling thereupon, handed the bill.

Probably it was the first time in the history of commercial transactions that the quality of shortness in a butcher's bill was a cause of tribulation to the debtor. 'Why, this isn't all she've had in a whole month!' said Geoffrey.

'Every mossel,'[5] said the butcher – '(now, Dan, take that leg and shoulder to Mrs White's, and this eleven pound here to Mr Martin's) – you've been treating her to smaller joints lately, to my thinking, Mr Day?'

'Only two or three little scram rabbits this last week, as I am alive – I wish I had!'

'Well, my wife said to me – (Dan! not too much, not too much on that tray at a time; better go twice) – my wife said to me as she posted up[6] the books: "Haylock," she says, "Miss Day must have been affronted[7] this summer during that hot muggy weather that spoilt so much for us; for depend upon't," she says, "she've been trying John Grimmett unknown to us: see her account else." 'Tis little, of course, at the best of times, being only for one, but now 'tis next kin to nothing.'

'I'll inquire,' said Geoffrey despondingly.

He returned by way of Mellstock, and called upon Fancy in fulfilment of a promise. It being Saturday the children were enjoying a holiday, and on entering the residence Fancy was nowhere to be seen. Nan the charwoman was sweeping the kitchen.

'Where's my da'ter?'[8] said the keeper.

'Well, you see, she was tired, with the week's teaching, and this morning she said, "Nan, I shan't get up till the evening." You see, Mr Day, if people don't eat they can't work; and as she've gie'd up eating she must gie up working.'

'Have ye carried up any dinner to her?'

'No; she don't want any. There, we all know that such

things don't come without good reason – not that I wish to say anything about a broken heart or anything of the kind.'

Geoffrey's own heart felt inconveniently large just then. He went to the staircase and ascended to his daughter's door.

'Fancy!'

'Come in, father.'

To see a person in bed from any cause whatever on a fine afternoon is depressing enough; and here was his only child Fancy not only in bed, but looking very pale. Geoffrey was visibly disturbed.

'Fancy, I didn't expect to see thee here, chiel,' he said. 'What's the matter?'

'I'm not well, father.'

'How's that?'

'Because I think of things.'

'What things can you have to think o' so mortal much?'

'You know, father.'

'You think I've been cruel to thee in saying that that penniless Dick o' thine shan't marry thee, I suppose?'

No answer.

'Well, you know, Fancy, I do it for the best, and he isn't good enough for thee. You know that well enough.' Here he again looked at her as she lay. 'Well, Fancy, I can't let my only chiel die; and if you can't live without en, you must ha' en, I suppose.'

'O, I don't want him like that; all against your will, and everything so disobedient!' sighed the invalid.

'No, no, 'tisn't against my will. My wish is, now I d'see how 'tis hurten thee to live without en, that he shall marry thee as soon as we've considered a little. That's my wish flat and plain, Fancy. There, never cry, my little maid! You ought to have cried afore; no need o' crying now 'tis all over. Well, howsoever, try to step over and see me and mother-law[9] tomorrow, and ha' a bit of dinner wi' us.'

'And – Dick too?'

'Ay, Dick too, 'far's I know.'

'And *when* do you think you'll have considered, father, and he may marry me?' she coaxed.

'Well, there, say next Midsummer;[10] that's not a day too long to wait.'

On leaving the school Geoffrey went to the tranter's. Old William opened the door.

'Is your grandson Dick in 'ithin, William?'

'No, not just now, Mr Day. Though he've been at home a good deal lately.'

'O, how's that?'

'What wi' one thing, and what wi' t'other, he's all in a mope,[11] as might be said. Don't seem the feller he used to. Ay, 'a will sit studding[12] and thinking as if 'a were going to turn chapel-member,[13] and then do nothing but traypse and wamble about.[14] Used to be such a chatty boy, too, Dick did; and now 'a don't speak at all. But won't ye step inside? Reuben will be home soon, 'a b'lieve.'

'No, thank you, I can't stay now. Will ye just ask Dick if he'll do me the kindness to step over to Yalbury tomorrow with my da'ter Fancy, if she's well enough? I don't like her to come by herself, now she's not so terrible topping in health.'

'So I've heard. Ay, sure, I'll tell him without fail.'

5 After gaining her Point

The visit to Geoffrey passed off as delightfully as a visit might have been expected to pass off when it was the first day of smooth experience in a hitherto obstructed love-course. And then came a series of several happy days of the same undisturbed serenity. Dick could court her when he chose; stay away when he chose, – which was never; walk with her by winding streams and waterfalls and autumn scenery till dews and twilight sent them home. And thus they drew near the day of the Harvest Thanksgiving, which was also the time chosen for opening the organ in Mellstock Church.

It chanced that Dick on that very day was called away from Mellstock. A young acquaintance had died of consumption at Charmley, a neighbouring village, on the previous Monday, and Dick in fulfilment of a long-standing promise was to assist in carrying him to the grave. When on Tuesday Dick went towards the school to acquaint Fancy with the fact it is difficult to say whether his own disappointment at being denied the sight of her triumphant _début_[1] as organist, was greater than his vexation that his pet should on this great occasion be deprived of the pleasure of his presence. However, the intelligence was communicated. She bore it as she best could, not without many expressions of regret and convictions that her performance would be nothing to her now.

Just before eleven o'clock on Sunday he set out upon his sad errand. The funeral was to be immediately after the morning service, and as there were four good miles to walk, driving being inconvenient, it became necessary to start comparatively early. Half an hour later would certainly have answered his purpose quite as well, yet at the last moment nothing would content his ardent mind but that he must go a mile out of his way in the direction of the school, in the hope of getting a glimpse of his Love as she started for church.

Striking therefore into the lane towards the school, instead of across the ewelease direct to Charmley, he arrived opposite her door as his goddess emerged.

If ever a woman looked a divinity Fancy Day appeared on that morning as she floated down those school steps, in the form of a nebulous collection of colours inclining to blue. With an audacity unparalleled in the whole history of village-schoolmistresses at this date – partly owing, no doubt, to papa's respectable accumulation of cash, which rendered her profession not altogether one of necessity – she had actually donned a hat and feather and lowered her hitherto plainly looped-up hair, which now fell about her shoulders in a profusion of curls. Poor Dick was astonished: he had never seen her look so distractingly beautiful before save on Christmas Eve, when her hair was in the same luxuriant condition of freedom. But his first burst of delighted surprise was followed by less comfortable feelings as soon as his brain recovered its power to think.

Fancy had blushed; – was it with confusion? She had also involuntarily pressed back her curls. She had not expected him.

'Fancy, you didn't know me for a moment in my funeral clothes, did you?'

'Good morning, Dick – no, really, I didn't know you for an instant in such a sad suit.'

He looked again at the gay tresses and hat. 'You've never dressed so charming before, dearest.'

'I like to hear you praise me in that way, Dick,' she said, smiling archly. 'It is meat and drink to a woman. Do I look nice really?'

'Fie! you know it. Did you remember, – I mean didn't you remember about my going away today?'

'Well, yes, I did, Dick; but, you know, I wanted to look well; – forgive me.'

'Yes, darling; yes, of course, – there's nothing to forgive. No, I was only thinking that when we talked on Tuesday and Wednesday and Thursday and Friday about my absence today, and I was so sorry for it, you said, Fancy, so were you sorry, and almost cried, and said it would be no pleasure to you to be the attraction of the church today since I could not be there.'

'My dear one, neither will it be so much pleasure to me. ... But I do take a little delight in my life, I suppose,' she pouted.

'Apart from mine?'

She looked at him with perplexed eyes. 'I know you are vexed with me, Dick, and it is because the first Sunday I have curls and a hat and feather since I have been here happens to be the very day you are away and won't be with me. Yes, say it is, for that is it! And you think that all this week I ought to have remembered you wouldn't be here today, and not have cared to be better dressed than usual. Yes, you do, Dick, and it is rather unkind!'

'No, no,' said Dick earnestly and simply, 'I didn't think so badly of you as that. I only thought that – if *you* had been going away, I shouldn't have tried new attractions for the eyes of other people. But then of course you and I are different, naturally.'

'Well, perhaps we are.'

'Whatever will the vicar say, Fancy?'

'I don't fear what he says in the least!' she answered

proudly. 'But he won't say anything of the sort you think. No, no.'

'He can hardly have conscience to, indeed.'

'Now come, you say, Dick, that you quite forgive me, for I must go,' she said with sudden gaiety, and skipped backwards into the porch. 'Come here, sir; – say you forgive me, and then you shall kiss me; – you never have yet when I have worn curls, you know. Yes, just where you want to so much, – yes, you may!'

Dick followed her into the inner corner, where he was probably not slow in availing himself of the privilege offered.

'Now that's a treat for you, isn't it?' she continued. 'Goodbye, or I shall be late. Come and see me tomorrow; you'll be tired tonight.'

Thus they parted, and Fancy proceeded to the church. The organ stood on one side of the chancel, close to and under the immediate eye of the vicar when he was in the pulpit and also in full view of the congregation. Here she sat down, for the first time in such a conspicuous position, her seat having previously been in a remote spot in the aisle.

'Good heavens – disgraceful! Curls and a hat and feather!' said the daughters of the small gentry, who had either only curly hair without a hat and feather, or a hat and feather without curly hair. 'A bonnet² for church always!' said sober matrons.

That Mr Maybold was conscious of her presence close beside him during his sermon; that he was not at all angry at her development of costume; that he admired her, she perceived. But she did not see that he loved her during that sermon-time as he had never loved a woman before; that her proximity was a strange delight to him; and that he gloried in her musical success that morning in a spirit quite beyond a mere cleric's glory at the inauguration of a new order of things.

The old choir, with humbled hearts, no longer took their seats in the gallery as heretofore (which was now given up to the schoolchildren who were not singers, and a pupil-teacher), but were scattered about with their wives in different parts of the church. Having nothing to do with conducting the service for almost the first time in their lives they all felt awkward, out of place, abashed, and inconvenienced by their hands. The tranter had proposed that they should stay away today and go nutting, but grandfather William would not hear of such a thing for a moment. 'No,' he replied reproachfully, and quoted a verse: ' "Though this has come upon us let not our hearts be turned back, or our steps go out of the way." '[3]

So they stood and watched the curls of hair trailing down the back of the successful rival, and the waving of her feather as she swayed her head. After a few timid notes and uncertain touches her playing became markedly correct, and towards the end full and free. But, whether from prejudice or unbiased judgment, the venerable body of musicians could not help thinking that the simpler notes they had been wont to bring forth were more in keeping with the simplicity of their old church than the crowded chords and interludes it was her pleasure to produce.

6 Into Temptation

The day was done, and Fancy was again in the school-house. About five o'clock it began to rain, and in rather a dull frame of mind she wandered into the schoolroom for want of something better to do. She was thinking – of her lover Dick Dewy? Not precisely. Of how weary she was of living alone; how unbearable it would be to return to Yalbury under the rule of her strange-tempered step-mother; that it was far better to be married to anybody than do that; that eight or nine long months had yet to be lived through ere the wedding could take place.

At the side of the room were high windows of Ham-hill stone,[1] upon either sill of which she could sit by first mounting a desk and using it as a foot-stool. As the evening advanced here she perched herself, as was her custom on such wet and gloomy occasions, put on a light shawl and bonnet, opened the window, and looked out at the rain.

The window overlooked a field called the Grove, and it was the position from which she used to survey the crown of Dick's passing hat in the early days of their acquaintance and meetings. Not a living soul was now visible anywhere; the rain kept all people indoors who were not forced abroad by necessity, and necessity was less importunate on Sundays than during the week.

Sitting here and thinking again – of her lover, or of the sensation she had created at church that day? – well, it is unknown – thinking and thinking she saw a dark masculine figure arising into distinctness at the further end of the

Grove – a man without an umbrella. Nearer and nearer he came, and she perceived that he was in deep mourning, and then that it was Dick. Yes, in the fondness and foolishness of his young heart, after walking four miles in a drizzling rain without overcoat or umbrella and in face of a remark from his love that he was not to come because he would be tired, he had made it his business to wander this mile out of his way again from sheer wish of spending ten minutes in her presence.

'O Dick, how wet you are!' she said, as he drew up under the window. 'Why, your coat shines as if it had been varnished, and your hat – my goodness, there's a streaming hat!'

'Oh, I don't mind, darling!' said Dick cheerfully. 'Wet never hurts me, though I am rather sorry for my best clothes. However, it couldn't be helped; we lent all the umbrellas to the women. I don't know when I shall get mine back.'

'And look, there's a nasty patch of something just on your shoulder.'

'Ah, that's japanning;[2] it rubbed off the clamps of poor Jack's coffin when we lowered him from our shoulders upon the bier! I don't care about that, for 'twas the last deed I could do for him; and 'tis hard if you can't afford a coat for an old friend.'

Fancy put her hand to her mouth for half a minute. Underneath the palm of that little hand there existed for that half-minute a little yawn.

'Dick, I don't like you to stand there in the wet. And you mustn't sit down. Go home and change your things. Don't stay another minute.'

'One kiss after coming so far,' he pleaded.

'If I can reach, then.'

He looked rather disappointed at not being invited round to the door. She twisted from her seated position and bent herself downwards, but not even by standing on the plinth[3] was it possible for Dick to get his lips into contact with hers as she held them. By great exertion she might have reached a little lower; but then she would have exposed her head to the rain.

'Never mind, Dick; kiss my hand,' she said, flinging it down to him. 'Now, goodbye.'

'Goodbye.'

He walked slowly away, turning and turning again to look at her till he was out of sight. During the retreat she said to herself, almost involuntarily, and still conscious of that morning's triumph –

'I like Dick, and I love him; but how plain and sorry a man looks in the rain, with no umbrella, and wet through!'

As he vanished she made as if to descend from her seat; but glancing in the other direction she saw another form coming along the same track. It was also that of a man. He, too, was in black from top to toe; but he carried an umbrella.

He drew nearer, and the direction of the rain caused him so to slant his umbrella that from her height above the ground his head was invisible, as she was also to him. He passed in due time directly beneath her, and in looking down upon the exterior of his umbrella her feminine eyes perceived it to be superior silk – less common at that date than since – and of elegant make. He reached the entrance to the building, and Fancy suddenly lost sight of him. Instead of pursuing the roadway as Dick had done he had turned sharply round into her own porch.

She jumped to the floor, hastily rung off her shawl and bonnet, smoothed and patted her hair till the curls hung in passable condition, and listened. No knock. Nearly a minute passed, and still there was no knock. Then there arose a soft series of raps no louder than the tapping of a distant woodpecker, and barely distinct enough to reach her ears. She composed herself and flung open the door.

In the porch stood Mr Maybold.

There was a warm flush upon his face and a bright flash in his eyes which made him look handsomer than she had ever seen him before.

'Good evening, Miss Day.'

'Good evening, Mr Maybold,' she said, in a strange state of mind. She had noticed, beyond the ardent hue of his face, that his voice had a singular tremor in it, and that his hand shook like an aspen[4] leaf when he laid his umbrella in the corner of the porch. Without another word being spoken by either he came into the schoolroom, shut the door, and moved close to her. Once inside the expression of his face was no more discernible by reason of the increasing dusk of evening.

'I want to speak to you,' he then said; 'seriously – on a perhaps unexpected subject, but one which is all the world to me – I don't know what it may be to you, Miss Day.'

No reply.

'Fancy, I have come to ask if you will be my wife?'

As a person who has been idly amusing himself with rolling a snowball might start at finding he had set in motion an avalanche, so did Fancy start at these words from the young vicar. And in the dead silence which followed them the breathings of the man and of the woman could be distinctly and separately heard; and there was this difference between them – his respirations gradually grew quieter and less rapid after the enunciation; hers, from having been low and regular, increased in quickness and force till she almost panted.

'I cannot, I cannot, Mr Maybold – I cannot! Don't ask me!' she said.

'Don't answer in a hurry!' he entreated. 'And do listen to me. This is no sudden feeling on my part. I have loved you for more than six months! Perhaps my late interest in teaching the children here has not been so single-minded as it seemed. You will understand my motive – like me better, perhaps, for honestly telling you that I have struggled against my emotion continually, because I have thought that it was not well for me to love you! But I resolved to struggle no longer; I have examined the feeling; and the love I bear you is as genuine as that I could bear any woman! I see your great charm; I respect your natural talents and the refinement they have brought into your nature – they are quite enough, and more than enough for me! They are equal to anything ever required of the mistress of a quiet parsonage-house – the place in which I shall pass my days, wherever it may be situated. O Fancy, I have watched you, criticized you even severely, brought my feelings to the light of judgment, and still have found them rational, and such as any man might have expected to be inspired with by a woman like you! So there is nothing hurried, secret, or untoward in my desire to do this. Fancy, will you marry me?'

No answer was returned.

'Don't refuse; don't,' he implored. 'It would be foolish of you – I mean cruel! Of course we would not live here, Fancy. I have had for a long time the offer of an exchange of livings with a friend in Yorkshire, but I have hitherto refused on account of my mother. There we would go. Your musical powers shall be still further developed; you shall have whatever pianoforte you like; you shall have anything, Fancy, anything to make you happy – pony-carriage, flowers, birds, pleasant society; yes, you have enough in you for any society, after a few months of travel with me! Will you, Fancy, marry me?'

Another pause ensued, varied only by the surging of the rain against the window-panes, and then Fancy spoke, in a faint and broken voice.

'Yes, I will,' she said.

'God bless you, my own!' He advanced quickly, and put his arm out to embrace her. She drew back hastily. 'No no, not now!' she said in an agitated whisper. 'There are things; – but the temptation is, O, too strong, and I can't resist it; I can't tell you now, but I must tell you! Don't, please, don't come near me now! I want to think. I can scarcely get myself used to the idea of what I have promised yet.' The next minute she turned to a desk, buried her face in her hands, and burst into a hysterical fit of weeping. 'O, leave me to myself!' she sobbed, 'leave me! O, leave me!'

'Don't be distressed; don't, dearest!' It was with visible difficulty that he restrained himself from approaching her. 'You shall tell me at your leisure what it is that grieves you so; I am happy – beyond all measure happy – at having your simple promise.'

'And do go and leave me now!'

'But I must not, in justice to you, leave for a minute, until you are yourself again.'

'There then,' she said, controlling her emotion, and standing up; 'I am not disturbed now.'

He reluctantly moved towards the door. 'Goodbye!' he murmured tenderly. 'I'll come tomorrow about this time.'

7   Second Thoughts

The next morning the vicar rose early. The first thing he did was to write a long and careful letter to his friend in Yorkshire. Then, eating a little breakfast, he crossed the meadows in the direction of Casterbridge, bearing his letter in his pocket, that he might post it at the town office, and obviate the loss of one day in its transmission that would have resulted had he left it for the foot-post[1] through the village.

It was a foggy morning, and the trees shed in noisy waterdrops the moisture they had collected from the thick air, an acorn occasionally falling from its cup to the ground in company with the drippings. In the meads[2] sheets of spiders'-web, almost opaque with wet, hung in folds over the fences, and the falling leaves appeared in every variety of brown, green, and yellow hue.

A low and merry whistling was heard on the highway he was approaching, then the light footsteps of a man going in the same direction as himself. On reaching the junction of his path with the road the vicar beheld Dick Dewy's open and cheerful face. Dick lifted his hat, and the vicar came out into the highway that Dick was pursuing.

'Good morning, Dewy. How well you are looking!' said Mr Maybold.

'Yes, sir, I am well – quite well! I am going to Casterbridge now, to get Smart's collar; we left it there Saturday to be repaired.'

'I am going to Casterbridge, so we'll walk together,' the vicar said. Dick gave a hop with one foot to put himself in step with Mr Maybold, who proceeded: 'I fancy I didn't see you at church yesterday, Dewy. Or were you behind the pier?'

'No; I went to Charmley. Poor John Dunford chose me to be one of his bearers a long time before he died, and yesterday was the funeral. Of course I couldn't refuse, though I should have liked particularly to have been at home as 'twas the day of the new music.'

'Yes, you should have been. The musical portion of the service was successful – very successful indeed; and what is more to the purpose no ill-feeling whatever was evinced by any of the members of the old choir. They joined in the singing with the greatest good-will.'

' 'Twas natural enough that I should want to be there, I suppose,' said Dick, smiling a private smile; 'considering who the organ-player was.'

At this the vicar reddened a little, and said, 'Yes, yes,' though not at all comprehending Dick's true meaning, who, as he received no further reply, continued hesitatingly, and with another smile denoting his pride as a lover –

'I suppose you know what I mean, sir? You've heard about me and – Miss Day?'

The red in Maybold's countenance went away: he turned and looked Dick in the face.

'No,' he said constrainedly, 'I've heard nothing whatever about you and Miss Day.'

'Why, she's my sweetheart, and we are going to be married next Midsummer. We are keeping it rather close just at present, because 'tis a good many months to wait; but it is her father's wish that we don't marry before, and of course we must submit. But the time 'ill soon slip along.'

'Yes, the time will soon slip along – Time glides away every day – yes.'

Maybold said these words, but he had no idea of what they were. He was conscious of a cold and sickly thrill throughout him; and all he reasoned was this, that the young creature whose graces had intoxicated him into making the most imprudent resolution of his life was less an angel than a woman.

'You see, sir,' continued the ingenuous Dick, ''twill be better in one sense. I shall by that time be the regular manager of a branch o' father's business which we think of starting elsewhere. It has very much increased lately, and we expect next year to keep a' extra couple of horses. We've already our eye on one – brown as a berry, neck like a rainbow, fifteen hands,[3] and not a grey hair in her – offered us at twenty-five want a crown.[4] And to kip[5] pace with the times I have had some cards prented, and I beg leave to hand you one, sir.'

'Certainly,' said the vicar, mechanically taking the card that Dick offered him.

'I turn in here by Grey's Bridge,'[6] said Dick. 'I suppose you go straight on and up town?'

'Yes.'

'Good morning, sir.'

'Good morning, Dewy.'

Maybold stood still upon the bridge, holding the card as it had been put into his hand, and Dick's footsteps died away towards Durnover Mill. The vicar's voluntary action was to read the card:

DEWY AND SON,
TRANTERS AND HAULIERS,
MELLSTOCK.
N.B. – Furniture, Coals, Potatoes, Live and Dead Stock,
removed to any distance on the shortest notice.

Mr Maybold leant over the parapet of the bridge and looked into the river. He saw – without heeding – how the water came rapidly from beneath the arches, glided down a little steep, then spread itself over a pool in which dace, trout, and minnows[7] sported at ease among the long green locks of weed that lay heaving and sinking with their roots towards the current. At the end of ten minutes spent leaning thus he drew from his pocket the letter to his friend, tore it deliberately into such minute fragments that scarcely two syllables remained in juxtaposition, and sent the whole handful of shreds fluttering into the water. Here he watched them eddy, dart, and turn, as they were carried downwards towards the ocean and gradually disappeared from his view. Finally he moved off, and pursued his way at a rapid pace back again to Mellstock Vicarage.

Nerving himself by a long and intense effort he sat down in his study and wrote as follows:

'DEAR MISS DAY, – The meaning of your words, "the temptation is too strong", of your sadness and your tears, has been brought home to me by an accident. I know today what I did not know yesterday – that you are not a free woman.

'Why did you not tell me – why didn't you? Did you suppose I knew? No. Had I known, my conduct in coming to you as I did would have been reprehensible.

'But I don't chide you! Perhaps no blame attaches to you – I can't tell. Fancy, though my opinion of you is assailed and disturbed in a way which cannot be expressed, I love you still, and my word to you holds good yet. But will you, in justice to an honest man who relies upon your word to him, consider whether, under the circumstances, you can honourably forsake him? – Yours ever sincerely,

'ARTHUR MAYBOLD'

He rang the bell. 'Tell Charles to take these copybooks and this note to the school at once.'

The maid took the parcel and the letter, and in few minutes a boy was seen to leave the vicarage gate with the one under his arm and the other in his hand. The vicar sat with his hand to his brow, watching the lad as he descended

Church Lane and entered the waterside path which intervened between that spot and the school.

Here he was met by another boy, and after a free salutation and pugilistic frisk had passed between the two the second boy came on his way to the vicarage, and the other vanished out of sight.

The boy came to the door, and a note for Mr Maybold was brought in.

He knew the writing. Opening the envelope with an unsteady hand he read the subjoined words:

'DEAR MR MAYBOLD, – I have been thinking seriously and sadly through the whole of the night of the question you put to me last evening; and of my answer. That answer, as an honest woman, I had no right to give.

'It is my nature – perhaps all women's – to love refinement of mind and manners; but even more than this, to be ever fascinated with the idea of surroundings more elegant and pleasing than those which have been customary. And you praised me and praise is life to me. It was alone my sensations at these things which prompted my reply. Ambition and vanity they would be called; perhaps they are so.

'After this explanation I hope you will generously allow me to withdraw the answer I too hastily gave.

'And one more request. To keep the meeting of last night, and all that passed between us there, for ever a secret. Were it to become known it would utterly blight the happiness of a trusting and generous man, whom I love still, and shall love always. – Yours sincerely,

'FANCY DAY'

The last written communication that ever passed from the vicar to Fancy was a note containing these words only:

'Tell him everything; it is best. He will forgive you.'

Part the Fifth

Conclusion

1 'The Knot there's no Untying'[1]

The last day of the story is dated just subsequent to that point in the development of the seasons when country people go to bed among nearly naked trees, are lulled to sleep by a fall of rain, and awake next morning among green ones; when the landscape appears embarrassed with the sudden weight and brilliancy of its leaves; when the night-jar[2] comes and strikes up for the summer his tune of one note; when the apple-trees have bloomed, and the roads and orchard-grass have bloomed, and the roads and orchard-grass become spotted with fallen petals; when the faces of the delicate flowers are darkened and their heads weighed down by the throng of honey-bees, which increase their humming till humming is too mild a term for the all-pervading sound; and when cuckoos, blackbirds, and sparrows, that have hitherto been merry and respectful neighbours, become noisy and persistent intimates.

The exterior of Geoffrey Day's house in Yalbury Wood appeared exactly as was usual at that season, but a frantic barking of the dogs at the back told of unwonted movements somewhere within. Inside the door the eyes beheld a gathering which was a rarity indeed for the dwelling of the solitary wood-steward and keeper.

About the room were sitting and standing, in various gnarled[3] attitudes, our old acquaintance grandfathers James and William, the tranter, Mr Penny, two or three children, including Jimmy and Charley, besides three or four country ladies and gentlemen from a greater distance who do not require any distinction by name. Geoffrey was seen and heard stamping about the outhouse and among the bushes of the garden, attending to details of daily routine before the proper time arrived for their performance, in order that they might be off his hands for the day. He appeared with his shirt-sleeves rolled up; his best new garments, in which he had arrayed himself that morning, being temporarily disguised under a weekday apron whilst these proceedings were in operation. He occasionally glanced at the hives in passing to see if his wife's bees were swarming, ultimately rolling down his shirt-sleeves and going indoors, talking to tranter Dewy whilst buttoning the wristbands, to save time; next going upstairs for his best waistcoat, and coming down again to make another remark whilst buttoning that, during the time looking fixedly in the tranter's face as if he were a looking-glass.

The furniture had undergone attenuation to an alarming extent, every duplicate piece having been removed, including the clock by Thomas Wood; Ezekiel Saunders being at last left sole referee in matters of time.

Fancy was stationary upstairs, receiving her layers of clothes and adornments and answering by short fragments of laughter which had more fidgetiness than mirth in them, remarks that were made from time to time by Mrs Dewy and Mrs Penny, who were assisting her at the toilet, Mrs Day having pleaded a queerness in her head as a reason for shutting herself up in an inner bedroom for the whole morning. Mrs Penny appeared with nine corkscrew curls on each side of her temples, and a back comb stuck upon her crown like a castle on a steep.[4]

The conversation just now going on was concerning the banns,[5] the last publication of which had been on the Sunday previous.

'And how did they sound?' Fancy subtly inquired.

'Very beautiful indeed,' said Mrs Penny. 'I never heard any sound better.'

'But *how*?'

'Oh, *so* natural and elegant, didn't they, Reuben!' she cried through the chinks of the unceiled[6] floor to the tranter downstairs.

'What's that?' said the tranter, looking up inquiringly at the floor above him for an answer.

'Didn't Dick and Fancy sound well when they were called home in church last Sunday?' came downwards again in Mrs Penny's voice.

'Ay, that they did, my sonnies! —especially the first time. There was a terrible whispering piece of work in the congregation, wasn't there, neighbour Penny?' said the tranter, taking up the thread of conversation on his own account and, in order to be heard in the room above, speaking very loud to Mr Penny, who sat at the distance of three feet from him, or rather less.

'I never can mind seeing such a whispering as there was,' said Mr Penny, also loudly, to the room above. 'And such sorrowful envy on the maidens' faces; really, I never did see such envy as there was!'

Fancy's lineaments[7] varied in innumerable little flushes and her heart palpitated innumerable little tremors of pleasure. 'But perhaps,' she said, with assumed indifference, 'it was only because no religion was going on just then?'

'O, no; nothing to do with that. 'Twas because of your high standing in the parish. It was just as if they had one and all caught Dick kissing and coling[8] ye to death, wasn't it, Mrs Dewy?'

'Ay; that 'twas.'

'How people will talk about one's doings!' Fancy exclaimed.

'Well, if you make songs about yourself, my dear, you can't blame other people for singing 'em.'

'Mercy me! how shall I go through it?' said the young lady again, but merely to those in the bedroom, with a breathing of a kind between a sigh and a pant, round shining eyes, and warm face.

'O, you'll get through it well enough, child,' said Mrs Dewy placidly. 'The edge of the performance is took off at the calling home; and when once you get up to the chancel end o' the church you feel as saucy as you please. I'm sure I felt as brave as a sodger[9] all through the deed – though of course I dropped my face and looked modest, as was becoming to a maid. Mind you do that, Fancy.'

'And I walked into the church as quiet as a lamb, I'm sure,' subjoined Mrs Penny. 'There, you see Penny is such a little small man. But certainly I was flurried in the inside o' me. Well, thinks I, 'tis to be, and here goes! And do you do the same: say, " 'Tis to be, and here goes!"'

'Is there such wonderful virtue in " 'Tis to be, and here goes!"?' inquired Fancy.

'Wonderful! 'Twill carry a body through it all from wedding to churching,[10] if you only let it out with spirit enough.'

'Very well, then,' said Fancy, blushing. ' 'Tis to be, and here goes!'

'That's a girl for a husband!' said Mrs Dewy.

'I do hope he'll come in time!' continued the bride-elect, inventing a new cause of affright now that the other was demolished.

' 'Twould be a thousand pities if he didn't come, now you be so brave,' said Mrs Penny.

Grandfather James, having overheard some of these remarks, said downstairs with mischievous loudness –

'I've known some would-be weddings when the men didn't come.'

'They've happened not to come, before now, certainly,' said Mr Penny, cleaning one of the glasses of his spectacles.

'O, do hear what they are saying downstairs,' whispered Fancy. 'Hush, hush!'

She listened.

'They have, haven't they, Geoffrey?' continued grim grandfather James, as Geoffrey entered.

'Have what?' said Geoffrey.

'The men have been known not to come.'

'That they have,' said the keeper.

'Ay; I've knowed times when the wedding had to be put off through his not appearing, being tired of the woman. And another case I knowed was when the man was catched in a man-trap[11] crossing Oaker's Wood, and the three months had run out before he got well, and the banns had to be published over again.'

'How horrible!' said Fancy.

'They only say it on purpose to tease 'ee, my dear,' said Mrs Dewy.

' 'Tis quite sad to think what wretched shifts poor maids have been put to,' came again from downstairs. 'Ye should hear Clerk Wilkins, my brother-law, tell his experiences in marrying couples these last thirty year: sometimes one thing, sometimes another – 'tis quite heart-rending – enough to make your hair stand on end.'

'Those things don't happen very often, I know,' said Fancy with smouldering uneasiness.

'Well, really 'tis time Dick was here,' said the tranter.

'Don't keep on at me so, grandfather James and Mr Dewy, and all you down there!' Fancy broke out, unable to endure any longer. 'I am sure I shall die, or do something, if you do!'

'Never you hearken to these old chaps, Miss Day!' cried Nat Callcome the best man, who had just entered, and threw his voice upward through the chinks of the floor as the others had done. ' 'Tis all right; Dick's coming on like a wild feller; he'll be here in a minute. The hive o' bees his mother gie'd en for his new garden swarmed jist as he was starting, and he said, "I can't afford to lose a stock o' bees; no, that I can't, though I fain would; and Fancy wouldn't wish it on any account." So he jist stopped to ting[12] to 'em and shake 'em.'

'A genuine wise man,' said Geoffrey.

'To be sure what a day's work we had yesterday!' Mr Callcome continued, lowering his voice as if it were not necessary any longer to include those in the room above among his audience, and selecting a remote corner of his best clean handkerchief for wiping his face. 'To be sure!'

'Things so heavy, I suppose,' said Geoffrey, as if reading through the chimney-window from the far end of the vista.

'Ay,' said Nat, looking round the room at points from which furniture had been removed. 'And so awkward to carry, too. 'Twas ath'art and across[13] Dick's garden; in and out Dick's door; up and down Dick's stairs; round and round Dick's chammers till legs were worn to stumps: and Dick is so particular, too. And the stores of victuals and drink that lad has laid in: why, 'tis enough for Noah's ark! I'm sure I never wish to see a choicer half-dozen of hams than he's got there in his chimley; and the cider I tasted was a very pretty drop, indeed; – none could desire a prettier cider.'

'They be for the love and the stalled ox both.[14] Ah, the greedy martels!' said grandfather James.

'Well, may-be they be. "Surely," says I, "that couple between 'em have heaped up so much furniture and victuals that anybody would think they were going to take hold the big end of married life first, and begin wi' a grown-up family." Ah, what a bath of heat we two chaps were in, to be sure, a-getting that furniture in order!'

'I do so wish the room below was ceiled,' said Fancy as the dressing went on; 'we can hear all they say and do down there.'

'Hark! Who's that?' exclaimed a small pupil-teacher,[15] who also assisted this morning to her great delight. She ran half-way down the stairs and peeped round the banister. 'O, you should, you should, you should!' she exclaimed, scrambling up to the room again.

'What?' said Fancy.

'See the bridesmaids! They've just a-come! 'Tis wonderful, really! 'tis wonderful how muslin can be brought to it. There, they don't look a bit like themselves, but like some very rich sisters o' theirs that nobody knew they had!'

'Make them come up to me, make them come up!' cried Fancy ecstatically; and the four damsels appointed, namely, Miss Susan Dewy, Miss Bessie Dewy, Miss Vashti Sniff, and Miss Mercy Onmey[16] surged upstairs and floated along the passage.

'I wish Dick would come!' was again the burden of Fancy.

The same instant a small twig and flower from the creeper outside the door flew in at the open window, and a masculine voice said, 'Ready, Fancy dearest?'

'There he is, he is!' cried Fancy, tittering spasmodically and breathing as it were for the first time that morning.

The bridesmaids crowded to the window and turned their heads in the direction pointed out, at which motion eight earrings all swung as one: – not looking at Dick because they particularly wanted to see him, but with an important sense of their duty as obedient ministers of the will of that apotheosised[17] being – the Bride.

'He looks very taking!' said Miss Vashti Sniff, a young lady who blushed cream-colour and wore yellow bonnet-ribbons.

Dick was advancing to the door in a painfully new coat of shining cloth, primrose-coloured waistcoat, hat of the same painful style of newness, and with an extra quantity of whiskers shaved off his face and hair cut to an unwonted shortness in honour of the occasion.

'Now I'll run down,' said Fancy, looking at herself over her shoulder in the glass, and flitting off.

'O Dick!' she exclaimed, 'I am so glad you are come! I knew you would, of course, but I thought, O, if you shouldn't!'

'Not come, Fancy! Het[18] or wet, blow or snow, here come I today! Why, what's possessing your little soul? You never used to mind such things a bit.'

'Ah, Mr Dick, I hadn't hoisted my colours and committed myself then!' said Fancy.

''Tis a pity I can't marry the whole five of ye!' said Dick, surveying them all round.

'Heh-heh-heh!' laughed the four bridesmaids, and Fancy privately touched Dick and smoothed him down behind his shoulder as if to assure herself that he was there in flesh and blood as her own property.

'Well, whoever would have thought such a thing?' said Dick, taking off his hat, sinking into a chair, and turning to the elder members of the company.

The latter arranged their eyes and lips to signify that in their opinion nobody could have thought such a thing, whatever it was.

'That my bees should ha' swarmed just then, of all times and seasons!' continued Dick, throwing a comprehensive glance like a net over the whole auditory.[19] 'And 'tis a fine swarm, too: I haven't seen such a fine swarm for these ten years.'

'A' excellent sign,'[20] said Mrs Penny, from the depths of experience. 'A' excellent sign.'

'I am glad everything seems so right,' said Fancy with a breath of relief.

'And so am I,' said the four bridesmaids with much sympathy.

'Well, bees can't be put off,' observed the inharmonious grandfather James. 'Marrying a woman is a thing you can do at any moment; but a swarm o' bees won't come for the asking.'

Dick fanned himself with his hat. 'I can't think,' he said thoughtfully, 'whatever 'twas I did to offend Mr Maybold, – a man I like so much, too. He rather took to me when he came first, and used to say he should like to see me married, and that he'd marry me, whether the young woman I chose lived in his parish or no. I just hinted to him of it when I put in the banns, but he didn't seem to take kindly to the notion now, and so I said no more. I wonder how it was.'

'I wonder!' said Fancy, looking into vacancy with those beautiful eyes of hers – too refined and beautiful for a tranter's wife; but, perhaps, not too good.

'Altered his mind, as folks will, I suppose,' said the tranter. 'Well, my sonnies, there'll be a good strong party looking at us today as we go along.'

'And the body of the church,' said Geoffrey, 'will be lined with females, and a row of young fellers' heads, as far down as the eyes, will be noticed just above the sills of the chancel-winders.'

'Ay, you've been through it twice,' said Reuben, 'and well mid know.'

'I can put up with it for once,' said Dick, 'or twice either, or a dozen times.'

'O Dick!' said Fancy reproachfully.

'Why, dear, that's nothing, – only just a bit of a flourish. You be as nervous as a cat today.'

'And then, of course, when 'tis all over,' continued the tranter, 'we shall march two and two round the parish.'[21]

'Yes, sure,' said Mr Penny: 'two and two: every man hitched up to his woman, 'a b'lieve.'

'I never can make a show of myself in that way!' said Fancy, looking at Dick to ascertain if he could.

'I'm agreed to anything you and the company like, my dear!' said Mr Richard Dewy heartily.

'Why, we did when we were married, didn't we, Ann?' said the tranter; 'and so do everybody, my sonnies.'

'And so did we,' said Fancy's father.

'And so did Penny and I,' said Mrs Penny: 'I wore my best Bath clogs,[22] I remember, and Penny was cross because it made me look so tall.'

'And so did father and mother,' said Miss Mercy Onmey.

'And I mean to, come next Christmas!' said Nat the groomsman vigorously, and looking towards the person of Miss Vashti Sniff.

'Respectable people don't nowadays,' said Fancy. 'Still, since poor mother did, I will.'

'Ay,' resumed the tranter, ''twas on a White Tuesday when I committed it. Mellstock Club walked the same day, and we new-married folk went a-gaying round the parish behind 'em. Everybody used to wear something white at Whitsuntide in them days. My sonnies, I've got the very white trousers that I wore, at home in box now. Ha'n't I, Ann?'

'You had till I cut 'em up for Jimmy,' said Mrs Dewy.

'And we ought, by rights, after doing this parish, to go round Higher and Lower Mellstock, and call at Viney's, and so work our way hither again across He'th,'[23] said Mr Penny, recovering scent of the matter in hand. 'Dairyman Viney is a very respectable man, and so is Farmer Kex, and we ought to show ourselves to them.'

'True,' said the tranter, 'we ought to go round Mellstock to do the thing well. We shall form a very striking object walking along in rotation, good-now, neighbours?'

'That we shall: a proper pretty sight for the nation,' said Mrs Penny.

'Hullo!' said the tranter, suddenly catching sight of a singular human figure standing in the doorway, and wearing a long smock-frock of pillow-case cut and of snowy whiteness. 'Why, Leaf! whatever dost thou do here?'

'I've come to know if so be I can come to the wedding – hee-hee!' said Leaf in a voice of timidity.

'Now, Leaf,' said the tranter reproachfully, 'you know we don't want 'ee here today: we've got no room for 'ee, Leaf.'

'Thomas Leaf, Thomas Leaf, fie upon 'ee for prying!' said old William.

'I know I've got no head, but I thought, if I washed and put on a clane shirt and smock-frock, I must just call,' said Leaf, turning away disappointed and trembling.

'Poor feller!' said the tranter, turning to Geoffrey. 'Suppose we must let en come? His looks are rather against en, and he is terribly silly; but 'a have never been in jail, and 'a won't do no harm.'

Leaf looked with gratitude at the tranter for these praises, and then anxiously at Geoffrey, to see what effect they would have in helping his cause.

'Ay, let en come,' said Geoffrey decisively. 'Leaf, th'rt welcome, 'st know'; and Leaf accordingly remained.

They were now all ready for leaving the house, and began to form a procession in the following order: Fancy and her father, Dick and Susan Dewy, Nat Callcome and Vashti Sniff, Ted Waywood and Mercy Onmey, and Jimmy and Bessie Dewy. These formed the executive, and all appeared in strict wedding attire. Then came the tranter and Mrs Dewy, and last of all Mr and Mrs Penny; – the tranter conspicuous by his enormous gloves, size eleven and three-quarters, which appeared at a distance like boxing gloves bleached and sat rather awkwardly upon his brown hands; this hall-mark of respectability having been set upon himself today (by Fancy's special request) for the first time in his life.

'The proper way is for the bridesmaids to walk together,' suggested Fancy.

'What? 'Twas always young man and young woman, arm in crook,[24] in my time!' said Geoffrey, astounded.

'And in mine!' said the tranter.

'And in ours!' said Mr and Mrs Penny.

'Never heard o' such a thing as woman and woman!' said old William; who, with grandfather James and Mrs Day, was to stay at home.

'Whichever way you and the company like, my dear!' said Dick, who, being on the point of securing his right to Fancy, seemed willing to renounce all other rights in the world with the greatest pleasure. The decision was left to Fancy.

'Well, I think I'd rather have it the way mother had it,' she said, and the couples moved along under the trees, every man to his maid.

'Ah!' said grandfather James to grandfather William as they retired, 'I wonder which she thinks most about, Dick or her wedding raiment!'

'Well, 'tis their nature,' said grandfather William. 'Remember the words of the prophet Jeremiah: "Can a maid forget her ornaments, or a bride her attire?" '[25]

Now among dark perpendicular firs, like the shafted columns of a cathedral; now through a hazel copse, matted with primroses and wild hyacinths; now under broad beeches in bright young leaves they threaded their way into the high road over Yalbury Hill, which dipped at that point directly into the village of Geoffrey Day's parish; and in the space of a quarter of an hour Fancy found herself to be Mrs Richard Dewy, though, much to her surprise, feeling no other than Fancy Day still.

On the circuitous return walk through the lanes and fields, amid much chattering and laughter, especially when they came to stiles, Dick discerned a brown spot far up a turnip field.

'Why, 'tis Enoch!' he said to Fancy. 'I thought I missed him at the house this morning. How is it he's left you?'

'He drank too much cider, and it got into his head, and they put him in Weatherbury stocks[26] for it. Father was obliged to get somebody else for a day or two, and Enoch hasn't had anything to do with the woods since.'

'We might ask him to call down tonight. Stocks are nothing for once, considering 'tis our wedding day.' The bridal party was ordered to halt.

'Eno-o-o-o-ch!' cried Dick at the top of his voice.

'Y-a-a-a-a-a-as!' said Enoch from the distance.

'D'ye know who I be-e-e-e-e-e?'

'No-o-o-o-o-o-o!'

'Dick Dew-w-w-w-wy!'

'O-h-h-h-h-h!'

'Just a-ma-a-a-a-a-arried!'

'O-h-h-h-h-h!'

'This is my wife, Fa-a-a-a-a-ancy!' (holding her up to Enoch's view as if she had been a nosegay).

'O-h-h-h-h-h!'

'Will ye come across to the party to-ni-i-i-i-i-ight!'

'Ca-a-a-a-a-an't!'

'Why n-o-o-o-o-ot?'

'Don't work for the family no-o-o-o-ow!'

'Not nice of Master Enoch,' said Dick as they resumed their walk.

'You mustn't blame en,' said Geoffrey; 'the man's not hisself now; he's in his morning frame of mind. When he's had a gallon o' cider or ale, or a pint or two of mead, the man's well enough, and his manners be as good as anybody's in the kingdom.'

2 Under the Greenwood Tree

The point in Yalbury Wood which abutted on the end of Geoffrey Day's premises was closed with an ancient tree, horizontally of enormous extent, though having no great pretensions to height. Many hundreds of birds had been born amidst the boughs of this single tree; tribes of rabbits and hares had nibbled at its bark from year to year; quaint tufts of fungi had sprung from the cavities of its forks; and countless families of moles and earthworms had crept about its roots. Beneath and beyond its shade spread a carefully-tended grass-plot, its purpose being to supply a healthy exercise-ground for young chickens and pheasants: the hens, their mothers, being enclosed in coops placed upon the same green flooring.

All these encumbrances were now removed, and as the afternoon advanced the guests gathered on the spot, where music, dancing, and the singing of songs went forward with great spirit throughout the evening. The propriety of every one was intense, by reason of the influence of Fancy, who, as an additional precaution in this direction had strictly charged her father and the tranter to carefully avoid saying 'thee' and 'thou'[1] in their conversation, on the plea that those ancient words sounded so very humiliating to persons of newer taste; also that they were never to be seen drawing the back of the hand across the mouth after drinking – a local English custom of extraordinary antiquity, but stated by Fancy to be decidedly dying out among the better classes of society.

In addition to the local musicians present a man who had a thorough knowledge of the tambourine[2] was invited from the village of Tantrum Clangley,[3] – a place long celebrated for the skill of its inhabitants as performers on instruments of percussion. These important members of the assembly were relegated to a height of two or three feet from the ground, upon a temporary erection of planks supported by barrels. Whilst the dancing progressed the older persons sat in a group under the trunk of the tree, – the space being allotted to them somewhat grudgingly by the young ones, who were greedy of pirouetting room, – and fortified by a table against the heels of the dancers. Here the gaffers and gammers[4] whose dancing days were over told stories of great impressiveness, and at intervals surveyed the advancing and retiring couples from the same retreat, as people on shore might be supposed to survey a naval engagement in the bay beyond; returning again to their tales when the pause was over. Those of the whirling throng who, during the rests between each figure, turned their eyes in the direction of these seated ones, were only able to discover, on account of the music and bustle, that a very striking circumstance was in course of narration – denoted by an emphatic sweep of the hand, snapping of the fingers, close of the lips, and fixed look into the centre of the listener's eye for the space of a quarter of a minute, which raised in that listener such a reciprocating working of face as to sometimes make the distant dancers half-wish to know what such an interesting tale could refer to.

Fancy caused her looks to wear as much matronly expression as was obtainable out of six hours' experience as a wife, in order that the contrast between her own state of life and that of the unmarried young women present might be duly impressed upon the company: occasionally stealing glances of admiration at her left hand, but this quite privately; for her ostensible bearing concerning the matter

was intended to show that, though she undoubtedly occupied the most wondrous position in the eyes of the world
that had ever been attained, she was almost unconscious of
the circumstance, and that the somewhat prominent position in which that wonderfully-emblazoned left hand was
continually found to be placed when handing cups and
saucers, knives, forks, and glasses, was quite the result of
accident. As to wishing to excite envy in the bosoms of her
maiden companions by the exhibition of the shining ring,
every one was to know it was quite foreign to the dignity of
such an experienced married woman. Dick's imagination in
the meantime was far less capable of drawing so much
wontedness from his new condition. He had been for two or
three hours trying to feel himself merely a newly-married
man, but had been able to get no further in the attempt than
to realize that he was Dick Dewy, the tranter's son, at a
party given by Lord Wessex's head man-in-charge, on the
outlying Yalbury estate, dancing and chatting with Fancy
Day.

Five country dances, including 'Haste to the Wedding',
two reels,[5] and three fragments of hornpipes,[6] brought
them to the time for supper which, on account of the dampness of the grass from the immaturity of the summer
season, was spread indoors. At the conclusion of the
meal Dick went out to put the horse in; and Fancy,
with the elder half of the four bridesmaids, retired upstairs
to dress for the journey to Dick's new cottage near Mellstock.

'How long will you be putting on your bonnet, Fancy?'
Dick inquired at the foot of the staircase. Being now a man
of business and married he was strong on the importance of
time, and doubled the emphasis of his words in conversing,
and added vigour to his nods.

'Only a minute.'

'How long is that?'

'Well dear, five.'

'Ah, sonnies!' said the tranter, as Dick retired, '' 'tis a talent of the female race that low numbers should stand for high, more especially in matters of waiting, matters of age, and matters of money.'

'True, true, upon my body,' said Geoffrey.

'Ye spak with feeling, Geoffrey, seemingly.'

'Anybody that d'know my experience might guess that.'

'What's she doing now, Geoffrey?'

'Claning out all the upstairs drawers and cupboards, and dusting the second-best chainey[7] – a thing that's only done once a year. "If there's work to be done I must do it," says she, "wedding or no." '

' 'Tis my belief she's a very good woman at bottom.'

'She's terrible deep, then.'

Mrs Penny turned round. 'Well, 'tis humps and hollers[8] with the best of us; but still and for all that, Dick and Fancy stand as fair a chance of having a bit of sunsheen[9] as any married pair in the land.'

'Ay, there's no gainsaying it.'

Mrs Dewy came up, talking to one person and looking at another. 'Happy, yes,' she said. '' 'Tis always so when a couple is so exactly in tune with one another as Dick and she.'

'When they be'n't too poor to have time to sing,' said grandfather James.

'I tell ye, neighbours, when the pinch comes,' said the tranter: 'when the oldest daughter's boots be only a size less than her mother's, and the rest o' the flock close behind her. A sharp time for a man that, my sonnies; a very sharp time! Chanticleer's comb is a-cut[10] then, 'a believe.'

'That's about the form o't,' said Mr Penny. 'That'll put the stuns upon a man,[11] when you must measure mother and daughters' lasts to tell 'em apart.'

'You've no cause to complain, Reuben, of such a close-coming flock,' said Mrs Dewy; 'for ours was a straggling lot enough, God knows!'

'I d'know it, I d'know it,' said the tranter. 'You be a well-enough woman, Ann.'

Mrs Dewy put her mouth in the form of a smile and put it back again without smiling.

'And if they come together, they go together,' said Mrs Penny, whose family had been the reverse of the tranter's; 'and a little money will make either fate tolerable. And money can be made by our young couple, I know.'

'Yes, that it can!' said the impulsive voice of Leaf, who had hitherto humbly admired the proceedings from a corner. 'It can be done – all that's wanted is a few pounds to begin with. That's all! I know a story about it!'

'Let's hear thy story, Leaf,' said the tranter. 'I never knew you were clever enough to tell a story. Silence, all of ye! Mr Leaf will tell a story.'

'Tell your story, Thomas Leaf,' said grandfather William in the tone of a schoolmaster.

'Once,' said the delighted Leaf, in an uncertain voice, 'there was a man who lived in a house! Well, this man went thinking and thinking night and day. At last, he said to himself, as I might, "If I had only ten pound, I'd make a fortune." At last by hook or by crook, behold he got ten pounds!'

'Only think of that!' said Nat Callcome satirically.

'Silence!' said the tranter.

'Well, now comes the interesting part of the story! In a little time he made that ten pounds twenty. Then a little time after that he doubled it, and made it forty. Well, he went on, and a good while after that he made it eighty, and on to a hundred. Well, by-and-by he made it two hundred! Well, you'd never believe it, but – he went on and made it four hundred! He went on, and what did he do? Why, he made it eight hundred! Yes, he did,' continued

Leaf in the highest pitch of excitement, bringing down his fist upon his knee with such force that he quivered with the pain; 'yes, and he went on and made it A THOUSAND!'

'Hear, hear!' said the tranter. 'Better than the history of England, my sonnies!'

'Thank you for your story, Thomas Leaf,' said grand-father William; and then Leaf gradually sank into nothing-ness again.

Amid a medley of laughter, old shoes,[12] and elder-wine, Dick and his bride took their departure side by side in the excellent new spring-cart which the young tranter now pos-sessed. The moon was just over the full, rendering any light from lamps or their own beauties quite unnecessary to the pair. They drove slowly along Yalbury Bottom, where the road passed between two copses. Dick was talking to his companion.

'Fancy,' he said, 'why we are so happy is because there is such full confidence between us. Ever since that time you confessed to that little flirtation with Shiner by the river (which was really no flirtation at all), I have thought how artless and good you must be to tell me o' such a trifling thing, and to be so frightened about it as you were. It has won me to tell you my every deed and word since then. We'll have no secrets from each other, darling, will we ever? – no secret at all.'

'None from today,' said Fancy. 'Hark! what's that?'

From a neighbouring thicket was suddenly heard to issue in a loud, musical, and liquid voice –

'Tippiwit! swe-e-et! ki-ki-ki! Come hither, come hither, come hither!'

'O, 'tis the nightingale,'[13] murmured she, and thought of a secret she would never tell.

Key to Wessex Place-names

HARDY'S NAME	REAL NAME
Mellstock	Stinsford and the Bockhamptons
Mellstock Lane	Leading from Lower Bockhampton to the turning to Higher Bockhampton
Mellstock Cross	Bockhampton Cross
Upper Mellstock	Higher Bockhampton
Lower Mellstock	Lower Bockhampton
Lewgate	F. B. Pinion writes in *A Hardy Companion*: 'It was the name often suggested for Hardy's home at Higher Bockhampton during his lifetime but never adopted. "Lew" indicates sheltered, "gate" a road or lane. It was the name used for Upper Mellstock in the early editions of *Under the Greenwood Tree*.'
Ewelease Stile	now a gate into open fields, once a short-cut from Higher Bockhampton to the Dorchester–Tincleton road
Hollow Hill	part of the above road still known by the same name
Longpuddle	Piddlehinton and possibly including Piddletrenthide
Weatherbury	Puddletown
Casterbridge	Dorchester
Bloom's End	a valley running south from that part of Hardy's Egdon known as Duddle Heath, to the River Frome
Yalbury Wood	Yellowham Wood, halfway between Dorchester and Puddletown
Chalk Newton	Maiden Newton, eight miles north-west of Dorchester

the Froom	the River Frome which flows from Evershot through Dorchester to the sea at Wareham
Mellstock Church	Stinsford Church
Budmouth Regis	Weymouth
The Ridgeway	steep hill-road between Weymouth and Dorchester
Snail-Creep	path that leads from Hardy's cottage over the main road up to Grey's Wood
Cuckoo Lane	road between the main Dorchester-to-Puddletown road and the top of the lane to Higher Bockhampton
Charmley	Charminster
Durnover	Fordington, part of Dorchester
Grey's Bridge	on the outskirts of Dorchester on the London road
Oaker's Wood	Hardy uses the real name of a stretch of woodland eight miles east of Stinsford.

Notes

13   [32]   *whipcord* tightly-twisted cord used for making whip lashes

14   [32]   *twine* string of two or more strands of hemp twisted together

15   [33]   *fugues* musical compositions in which a short melodic theme is introduced by one of the parts or instruments and then successively taken up by the others

16   [33]   *intermediate symphonies* opening or closing instrumental passages in the songs

17   [33]   *transcendent* more serious

18   [33]   *extant* still existing

19   [33]   *in verse elsewhere* Among poems mentioning the Mellstock Quire are 'Friends Beyond', 'The Dead Quire', and 'The Paphian Ball'.

Part the First

Chapter 1

1   [37]   *feature* physical appearance

2   [37]   *within living memory* The novel was published in 1872. The author is looking back to his childhood.

3   [37]   *daffodowndilly* daffodil

4   [38]   *fellow-craters* fellow-creatures

5   [38]   *a gentleman in black cardboard* Cut-out silhouette pictures were popular in Victorian times.

6   [39]   *severally* separately

7   [39]   *Etruscan* the name of a vanished race of people who lived in Italy in ancient times and are now known only by their works of art

8   [39]   *lath-like* as thin as a strip of wood

9   [40]   *Ewelease* the old name for an unmown grass field or down stocked with sheep in summer. Here Hardy uses it as the name of a stile.

10   [40]   *'Od rabbit it all'* Od is short for God and the phrase is a harmless and meaningless oath.

11   [40]   *parenthetically* without reference to the remarks of the others

12   [40]   *wicket* small gate

Chapter 2

1   [41]   *hipped* with sloping sides

2   [41]   *dormer* straight projecting windows in a sloping roof

3 [41] *window-shutters* outside wooden panels on hinges, closed at night

4 [41] *box* a small evergreen shrub or bush

5 [41] *laurestinus* evergreen bush with pinkish-white flowers, a type of *viburnum*

6 [41] *codlin-trees* Codlins were cooking apples with long tapering shapes.

7 [41] *espaliers* trees trained on lattice-work or fences

8 [41] *beetle* tool with heavy head and handle for ramming or crushing

9 [41] *wedges* wood or metal tools with sharp-angled edges

10 [41] *scurr* jerk. The sound of the word expresses its meaning.

11 [42] *hogshead* large cask

12 [42] *horsed* raised on legs so that mugs could be placed underneath to catch the liquor

13 [42] *broaching* piercing the cask to draw the liquor

14 [42] *plaits* usually 'pleats' now

15 [43] *settle* a bench with a high back and arms usually beside or inside an ingle-nook fireplace

16 [43] *flitches* salted sides of hog, cured by smoke from the fire

17 [43] *lining the chimney* The cottage had a deep fireplace where the sides of bacon and ham would hang above the fire for smoking.

18 [43] *broiled* cooked, instead of cured

19 [43] *Sansoms* sweet cider apples

20 [43] *Stubbards* early codlin apples

21 [43] *Five-corners* may have been apples with five points round the stalk

22 [43] *you d'mind?* do you remember?

23 [43] *stimmilent* stimulant

24 [44] *Grammer Kaytes's* grammer or grandmother denoted an old lady. Several families of Keates lived in Bockhampton Lane in Hardy's day and he here changes the spelling slightly to avoid too close identification.

25 [44] *fourteens* small candles, fourteen to the pound

26 [44] *smock-frock* overall worn in the old days by agricultural workers, usually white and shirtlike in shape with the upper part closely gathered and sometimes embroidered

27 [44] *multiplication table* a pun on the word 'multiply', indicating that Mrs Brownjohn had many children

28 [45] *squizzling* squirting out

29 [45] *husbird* a term of abuse, a rascal

30 [45] *shillens* shillings
31 [45] *jimcrack* rubbishy, worthless
32 [46] *King's Arms* a hotel in Dorchester, still standing. It is the
         scene of the Mayor's dinner in *The Mayor of Casterbridge.*
33 [46] *oilen* oiling
34 [46] *martel* mortal
35 [47] *Idd it cold inthide te hole?* Is it cold inside the hole?
         Charley had a cold in his head.
36 [47] *chiel* child
37 [47] *bass-viol* a viol da gamba, for playing the bass part in
         older concerted music

Chapter 3

1   [49] *ribstone-pippin* red eating apple
2   [49] *mead* alcoholic drink of fermented honey and water
3   [49] *long-headed* far-seeing, shrewd
4   [49] *half-a-crown* coin worth 12½p
5   [49] *cleaving* splitting
6   [50] *fustian* thick cotton cloth usually dyed dark
7   [50] *buttery* pantry, literally the place where the butter is kept
8   [51] *hard boy-chap* robust boy
9   [51] *mint o' practice* a lot of practice, like 'a mint of money'
10 [51] *linnet* lint, bits of cloth
11 [51] *carrel* carol
12 [51] *thirtinghill* perverse, wrong-headed
13 [51] *last* shoemaker's wooden model on which to shape shoes
14 [52] *bradded* fastened with brads, thin, flat, slightly headed
         nails used in shoemaking
15 [52] *pomace* mass of crushed apples left after cider-making, or
         any pulp
16 [52] *full-butt* right on target, with full force
17 [52] *husband-high* ready for marriage
18 [53] *voot* foot
19 [53] *fantastical* fanciful
20 [54] *un'rayed* undressed
21 [54] *pitch it* find a footing
22 [54] *teaving* form of the verb 'to tave', to throw oneself about
23 [54] *jineral* general
24 [54] *leaf* page, literally a single thickness of folded paper i.e.
         two pages in a book
25 [54] *sommat* something
26 [55] *rot me* let me rot

27 [55]   *upsides with* as good as
28 [55]   *gainsay* deny, criticise

Chapter 4

1 [56]   *horn-lanterns* lanterns with horn panels instead of glass
2 [57]   *counter-boys* bass singers
3 [57]   *Farmer Ledlow* This man is named as one of the people buried in Mellstock churchyard in Hardy's poem, 'Friends Beyond'; 'Farmer Ledlow late at plough'. Hardy often made cross references like this to his other writings, showing how real his fictional world was to him.
4 [57]   *metheglin* spiced kind of mead
5 [57]   *warmer* saucepan
6 [57]   *church-hatch* north gate of churchyard, a hatch being usually the lower half of a divided gate: see p. 72.
7 [58]   *Manor* Kingston Maurward House in the parish of Stinsford where Mrs Martin lived who was helpful to Hardy in his childhood
8 [58]   *panoramas* continuous passing scenes
9 [58]   *things . . . foot* small organs with bellows worked by the feet
10 [58]   *varmits* varmints, here in the sense of objectionable things
11 [58]   *serpents* wind-instruments, wooden tubes with several bends giving a powerful note, now obsolete
12 [59]   *Clar'nets* clarinets, wood-wind instruments with single-reed mouthpiece, holes and keys
13 [59]   *hedger-and-ditcher* farm worker who cut the hedges and cleared the ditches, usually in early spring
14 [59]   *chimley-corner* chimney-corner, ingle-nook
15 [59]   *spet* spit
16 [59]   *span* the maximum distance between the tips of the thumb and the little finger; as a measure it is about 130 millimetres (9 inches).
17 [59]   *the Lard* the Lord
18 [59]   *the Wicked One* the Devil
19 [60]   *rafting* rousing, disturbing
20 [60]   *reed-man* player of reed instruments such as the clarinet
21 [60]   *is a dab at* is adept at
22 [60]   *dumbledores* humble or bumble bees, drones
23 [60]   *to keep upon the grass* so that their footsteps could not be heard
24 [62]   *thirty-nine and forty-three* 1839 and 1843

Chapter 5

1   [63]   *architrave* moulded parts surrounding the window
2   [64]   *rale* real
3   [64]   *sich* such
4   [64]   *woll'ee* will you
5   [65]   *fortissimy* fortissimo, a musical direction meaning very loud
6   [65]   *spaking* speaking
7   [66]   *clinked off home-along* made off homewards
8   [66]   *treble man* one who plays the tune or melody in an orchestra
9   [66]   *counter chap* the player of the bass instrument
10 [67]   *drownded* The rustic speaker gives the word an extra syllable.
11 [67]   *scram* small, puny
12 [67]   *b'st* are you
13 [67]   *snap* a snack
14 [67]   *traypsing* tramping or trudging about
15 [67]   *incumbent* a holder of an office
16 [69]   *zeed* saw

Chapter 6

1   [70]   *gridiron* barred metal utensil for broiling
2   [71]   *blacking* old form of shoe polish
3   [71]   *rencounter* meeting
4   [71]   *flashes in the pan* trifles
5   [72]   *altar-tomb* with flat rectangular block of stone shaped like an altar
6   [72]   *nave* the body of the church from the inner door to the chancel or choir
7   [72]   *gallery folk* They would be out of sight from the nave.
8   [72]   *minims* long notes in music, half a semibreve
9   [72]   *clerk* lay officer of a parish church with various duties
10 [72]   *dust-hole* hole in the floor into which the dust could be swept
11 [73]   *one which chronologically follows it* Churching, the ceremony of a woman going to church to have thanks offered for the delivery of her child, would follow the marriage service in time. See p. 230.
12 [73]   *knot-hole* hole left by the knot in the wood coming out
13 [73]   *exemplars* models
14 [73]   *Pyramus and Thisbe* two legendary lovers who lived in

adjoining houses in Babylon and used to talk to each other through a hole in the wall as their parents would not let them meet. Shakespeare's rustics in *A Midsummer Night's Dream* burlesque the same story.

15 [73] *altos* highest-voiced male singers

16 [73] *supernumeraries* the less important extra members

17 [73] *chancel* the eastern part of the church, usually railed off, reserved for the clergy, choir etc., including on this occasion the 'throng of Sunday-school girls'

18 [74] *capitals of the piers* flat, protruding tops of the pillars

19 [74] *hemming* clearing the throat, saying 'hem'

20 [75] *proclivity* tendency towards action

21 [75] *'ooman* woman

22 [76] *jined* joined

23 [77] *gentle or simple* gentle-folk or simple-folk, the higher classes or the villagers

Chapter 7

1 [78] *stratum* layer

2 [78] *Shear-steel* special quality of steel fit for shears and other cutting tools

3 [79] *nater* nature

4 [80] *chimney-crook* an adjustable iron bar coming down from the chimney on which pots and kettles could be hung over the fire

5 [80] *Cain* Adam's son who killed his brother Abel (see Genesis 4)

6 [80] *sky-folk* angels

7 [81] *zhinerally* generally

8 [82] *two slurs in music* curved marks used in music-writing to show that two or more notes are to be sung to one syllable or played or sung smoothly, without breaks

9 [83] *Jericho* used in slang or colloquial phrases for a place far out of the way

10 [84] *frantic bowing* wild fiddle-playing. Hardy uses this word also in the poem, 'The Self-Unseeing', where he speaks of his father playing the violin in the cottage and 'bowing it higher and higher'.

11 [84] *cast off* country dance movement where partners are exchanged

12 [85] *minutiae* trivial details

13 [85] *hands-across* country dance where the partners clasp hands

Chapter 8

1   [86]   *six-hands-round* Hardy is said to have named this 'The College Hornpipe', a reel where the couples interweave.

2   [86]   *pot-housey* like an ale house, low-class public house

3   [87]   *incandescence* glowing with heat

4   [87]   *cadaverous* corpse-like, deathly pale

5   [87]   *zephyr* west wind, warm breeze

6   [88]   *humming-tops sleep* when they spin so steadily as to appear motionless

7   [88]   *Midsummer-eves* There was an old belief that girls would have a vision of their future lovers if they observed certain rites on this night. Hardy made use of the superstition again in his novel *The Woodlanders.*

8   [89]   *by-long and by-late* in the long run, in the end

9   [89]   *miff* slight quarrel or misunderstanding, a tiff

10 [89]   *go snacks with him* go shares with him, get married

11 [89]   *mid* might

12 [91]   *village sharpener* village schoolmistress, sharpener of wits

13 [91]   *'Dead March'* the March from *Saul*, the oratorio by Handel, frequently played at funerals

14 [91]   *vlock* flock

15 [91]   *last trump* Here he means the last trumpet-note of the Last Post, the bugle-call played at military funerals. Usually the phrase refers to the trumpet to arouse the dead on the Day of Judgement.

16 [91]   *Dree Mariners* The Three Mariners Hotel in High East Street, Dorchester, mentioned in *The Mayor of Caster-bridge.* It was first called 'The King of Prussia', but the building has since been replaced.

17 [91]   *lights* lungs of sheep, pigs, bullocks etc.

18 [91]   *chawing* chewing

19 [92]   *six-eight time* two dotted crotchets or six quavers to the bar

20 [92]   *common time* two or four beats in the bar

21 [93]   *nor shirked the purlieus of the mistletoe* did not avoid the place where the mistletoe was hanging, where she could be kissed

22 [93]   *pro tem* for the time being (Latin *pro tempore*)

23 [94]   *elder wine* usually elderberry wine, made from the fruit of the elder tree

24 [94]   *Nasmyth hammer* steam hammer invented by James Nasmyth in 1839

25 [94] *lime-basket* Lime has to be kept dry to be useful; after combination with water it becomes slaked lime.

26 [94] *draw up the clock* wind the grandfather clock by drawing up the pendulum from the position at the bottom to which it had sunk during the course of the day

Chapter 9

1 [97] *cross-dadder* children's chasing game, Cross Touch

Part the Second

Chapter 1

1 [101] *elixir* liquid believed in ancient times to turn all metals into gold or prolong life; anything that gives health or vigour

Chapter 2

1 [102] *nebulous* cloudy, indistinct

2 [102] *Moroni* sixteenth-century Italian portrait painter, with an easy, natural style

3 [102] *awl* a shoemaker's small tool for pricking holes

4 [103] *Wellington-boot* originally a leather military boot covering the knee in front and cut away at the back

5 [103] *mercantile* commercial

6 [103] *gawk-hammer* a gaping fool, one who stares vacantly

7 [103] *Old Eccl'iastes* Ecclesiastes the preacher, pen-name of the writer of the Book of that name in the Bible.

8 [103] *spouter* one who talks in a declamatory way, an orator

9 [103] *penneth* pennyworth

10 [104] *at the extension of arms* as he stretched out his arms

11 [104] *Herculean* Hercules was a hero of great strength in Greek and Roman myth who performed twelve immense labours.

12 [104] *neck and crop* bodily, headlong. The crop is the gullet or throat of a chicken.

13 [104] *Tory* The Tories and Whigs were the two great political rivals in the old days. The Tory Party accepted the established order in Church and State, opposed the Reform Bill in 1832, and has been succeeded by the modern Conservative Party, the name *Tory* being used now chiefly in a colloquial or hostile way.

14 [104] *Whiggism* After the revolution of 1688 the Whigs tried to subordinate the power of the Crown to that of Parliament, passed the Reform Bill, and were succeeded in the nineteenth century by the Liberal Party.

15 [105] *coalesced with* came together with

16 [105] *come mumbudgeting* come unexpectedly, unannounced

17 [105] *pitch-halfpenny* a game played with copper coins or other round discs, the object being to pitch them into a hole in the ground from a certain point

18 [106] *jinerous* generous

19 [106] *on-end for* looking forward to

20 [106] *vinger* finger

21 [106] *borus-snorus* William Barnes in his *Grammar and Glossary of the Dorset Dialect* gives this as *boris-noris*, meaning going on blindly, without any thought of risk or decency; here the meaning is probably without worrying about other people's opinions.

22 [107] *Titanic* colossal. The Titans were Greek mythological characters of a gigantic race.

23 [107] *clane* clean

24 [107] *drong* narrow passage or lane between two walls or hedges

25 [107] *full-buff* face to face

26 [107] *strent* rent, slit

27 [107] *brimbles* brambles

Chapter 3

1 [109] *'tmay* it may

2 [109] *down-along* along down

3 [109] *spar* here, the split stick pointed at each end and doubled and twisted in the middle, still used for fastening down thatch to roofs. Marty South in *The Woodlanders* makes them when her father is ill.

4 [111] *... died very young* Hardy's humour frequently has serious undertones.

5 [111] *pot-sick winder-flower* a window plant that has become sickly because its roots have grown too large for the flower pot

6 [111] *trate* treat

7 [112] *man-jack* individual

8 [112] *het* gulp down

Chapter 4

1 [113] *arrant* errand
2 [114] *dilating like circles in a pond* when a stone is thrown into it
3 [114] *neither to the right hand nor to the left* biblical phrase that a vicar's servant might be expected to use, possibly from Joshua 23:6
4 [115] *reedy* high and shaky like reed music
5 [115] *chips* straws
6 [116] *your holiness* more appropriate form of address to a pope
7 [116] *good-now* interjection adding weight to the statement it follows
8 [116] *ghastly* here ghostly
9 [118] *cabinet-organ* harmonium
10 [119] *Laodicean* lukewarm, especially in politics and religion. Saint John found the church at Laodicea 'neither cold nor hot' in spirit. One of Hardy's novels is called *A Laodicean.*
11 [121] *quat* squat
12 [122] *member* limb, part of the body
13 [123] *Michaelmas* feast day of St Michael and all Angels, 29 September

Chapter 5

1 [124] *thik gr't* that great
2 [124] *mischty* mischief
3 [125] *woll* will
4 [125] *stud* study, quandary
5 [125] *zot* sat
6 [125] *spring bottoms* a new type of chair then with springs in the seats
7 [126] *can't onriddle her* can't make her out
8 [126] *a twister* someone hard to understand
9 [126] *ink-bottle chaps* men who work in city offices
10 [126] *driblets* small quantities

Chapter 6

1 [128] *spring-cart* a cart mounted on springs for comfort
2 [128] *Wessex* Hardy brought back into the language the name of the old Saxon kingdom of Wessex and used it for the country of his novels. It covers an area made up chiefly of Dorset and adjoining parts of Hampshire, Wiltshire,

and Somerset, but in *Jude the Obscure* it extends as far north as Berkshire and Oxfordshire and in *A Pair of Blue Eyes* to Cornwall.

3 [129] *riser* vertical part of the step

4 [129] *knotty glass* bottle glass, popular in Victorian times

5 [129] *Noah* the animals in his ark were all in pairs (Genesis 7)

6 [130] *Italian flourishes* ornamental curves in Italian handwriting

7 [130] *dumb-waiters* upright construction with revolving shelves so that a waiter was not needed to hand things round

8 [130] *warming-pans* flat, closed, long-handled vessels, usually of brass, holding live coals for warming beds before they were occupied

9 [130] *mantel* mantelpiece

10 [131] *poaching fray* fight with poachers

11 [132] *stap-mother* step-mother

12 [132] *pot-luck* take the meal already in the pot, not one specially prepared

13 [133] *rum* odd, strange

14 [133] *kick up Bob's-a-dying* make a great fuss

15 [135] *A young woman's face will turn the north wind* will change the direction of the wind or of a man's course in life. See Dick's remarks further on about 'the power of maiden faces in settling your courses'.

16 [135] *raw-mil' cheese* cheese made from 'raw' (unskimmed) milk and therefore very rich

17 [137] *union beggars* The union was formerly the name for the workhouse, the place provided by the parish for destitute people.

18 [137] *damask-linen* twilled table linen with woven designs shown by the reflection of light

19 [137] *horn-handled knives* knives with handles made from animal horns

20 [138] *delf* glazed earthenware originally made at Delft (earlier Delf) in Holland

21 [138] *gossipest, poachest, jailest* most given to gossiping and poaching and most familiar with the insides of jails. These are superlatives made up by Hardy.

Chapter 7

1 [139] *charwoman* woman hired by the hour to do the chores i.e. the housework

2 [139] *fire-irons* tongs, poker, and shovel
3 [140] *making shift* getting along somehow
4 [141] *Her hands . . . water* Hardy seemed to find something romantic about woman's hands under water, as in the poem, 'Under the Waterfall' and in the love scene between Tess and Angel during the cheese-making at Talbothays.
5 [142] *muslin* delicately woven cotton fabric

Chapter 8

1 [144] *handpost* signpost
2 [144] *th'st* thou hast
3 [145] *flourishes* Hardy is here using an architectural image to make the point that women are all basically alike and only differ in the 'flourishes' i.e. the ornamentation of education, wealth etc.
4 [145] *nation* damnation
5 [146] *hollering* shouting
6 [146] *making a husband in her pocket* becoming self-supporting
7 [146] *chick nor chiel* both words mean child
8 [146] *poverty-stric'* poverty-stricken
9 [146] *Dang it* harmless form of 'damn it'
10 [146] *mien* air, appearance
11 [146] *Turk* an expression of surprise. William Barnes defines 'a Turk of a thing' as being a big or formidable one of its kind.
12 [146] *in a taking* upset
13 [147] *hatch* a small gate
14 [147] *flittering* fluttering
15 [147] *Woot hae me?* Wilt thou have, i.e. marry, me?
16 [147] *White Tuesday* two days after Whit Sunday or White Sunday, so-called because christenings, and therefore white robes, were common on that day
17 [147] *Mellstock Club* the local benefit club that held a yearly walk at Whitsun
18 [148] *white lyvered* cowardly. The liver was once thought to be the seat of the emotions.
19 [148] *cappel-faced* white-faced with patches of red
20 [148] *pretty kettle o' fish* awkward state of affairs
21 [148] *bitter weed* mischief-maker
22 [148] *rum-strumming* phrase that makes Fancy's playing sound amateurish

23 [151]   *watering-place* originally a spa where invalids drank medicinal waters and here a seaside place where holiday-makers and invalids go

Part the Third

Chapter 1

1 [155]   *the King's statue* the statue of George III, still on the esplanade at Weymouth, the town he made famous during the latter part of his reign by going there for sea-bathing

2 [155]   *embayed* enclosed in a bay

3 [155]   *incontinently* immediately

4 [155]   *chairmen* attendants who pushed the invalid chairs

5 [156]   *Old Royal Hotel* now the Gloucester Hotel

6 [156]   *burgesses* citizens

7 [157]   *chopped round* reversed his direction suddenly, doubled round

8 [157]   *brass studs* two-headed buttons for fastening collars

9 [159]   *journeymen-carpenters* those who worked for a boss and were hired by the day (from *journée*, French for 'day')

Chapter 2

1 [161]   *quartering* pulling to the side, taking up a new position

2 [161]   *gig* light, two-wheeled, one-horse carriage

3 [163]   *The Ship* An inn of the same name still stands at the junction of the old Ridgeway road, along which Dick and Fancy would have driven, and the new, more winding road leading out of Weymouth towards Dorchester.

4 [163]   *cross-trees* two horizontal cross-timbers bolted to the head of the lower mast to support the mast above

5 [164]   *tête-à-tête* French: a private conversation

6 [166]   *tay* tea

7 [166]   *feymel* female

8 [167]   *dog-cart* open two-wheeled vehicle with back-to-back seats, originally carrying sporting dogs under the seats

Chapter 3

1 [168]   *crane flies* insects better known as daddy-long-legs

2 [168]   *finesse* cunning, artfulness

3 [168]   *gipsy-party* picnic party

4 [170]   *stale, flat and unprofitable* quotation from Shakespeare's

Hamlet (I.2.133–4) 'How weary, stale, flat and unprofitable Seem to me all the uses of this world . . .'

5 [171]   *bird-lime* sticky substance made from holly bark for
catching small birds; bullfinches were kept as cage-birds
6 [172]   *castaway* shipwrecked person
7 [173]   *the Colonies* Many of Hardy's relatives emigrated to the
colonies in the nineteenth century.

Chapter 4

1 [174]   *flux of time* passing of time
2 [174]   *honey-taking* collecting honey from the bees
3 [176]   *like female idlers* Hardy uses a very appropriate image here.

Part the Fourth

Chapter 1

1 [181]   *near-foot-afore* left forefoot
2 [182]   *scullery* back kitchen where dishes were washed, vegetables prepared, etc.
3 [185]   *two pecks* This equals about eighteen litres, a peck being
a measure of capacity for dry goods.
4 [185]   *Venus* the Goddess of Love in Roman mythology
5 [185]   *in his van* ahead of him
6 [187]   *'Why are you wandering here, I pray?'* In *The Life of
Thomas Hardy* by F. E. Hardy (p. 14) this is said to have
been one of Hardy's mother's favourite tunes.

Chapter 2

1 [188]   *Latin crosses* crosses with horizontal cross-beam two-
thirds of the vertical beam
2 [188]   *brimstone* old name for sulphur
3 [189]   *proper way . . . honey* The old method of getting honey
from the bees meant that many were destroyed and only
a few small colonies kept Hardy seems to hear romantic
undertones in bee-keeping: compare the symbolism of
the scene describing the hiving of the bees by Bathsheba
and Troy in *Far from the Madding Crowd* (chapter 27).
4 [189]   *shadder* shadow
5 [192]   *horehound* herb with bitter aromatic juice used for coughs
or as a tonic
6 [192]   *lobe* round and flattish projecting or pendulous part,
forming the honeycomb

7 [193]   *'King Arthur . . . sons'* an old ballad

8 [193]   *yarn* spun thread

9 [193]   *broadcloth* fine, plain-wove, double width, dressed black cloth

10 [193]   *crippled rhyme* 'yarn' and 'arm'

11 [194]   *hartshorn* substance got from the antlers of deer and formerly the chief source of ammonia

12 [196]   *unrind* strip, undress

13 [196]   *plumb-line* length of string with a ball of lead attached, used by masons for testing perpendicularity of walls, etc.

14 [196]   *chammer* chamber

15 [197]   *I'd as lief* I'd rather

16 [197]   *landed family* owners and holders of land

17 [197]   *irons in the fire* undertakings

18 [197]   *homely* here plain, primitive

19 [198]   *Queen's scholars* Queen's scholarships were awarded to poor pupils to help them to go to a training college for teachers.

20 [198]   *Government teacher* one who had a certificate after completing the course at a training college. Both Hardy's sisters, Mary and Kate, and one of his cousins, Tryphena Sparks, were trained as teachers.

Chapter 3

1 [199]   *Endorfield* Hardy incorporates the idea of the Biblical Witch of Endor (1 Samuel 28) into the name of the woman suspected of being a witch in this story.

2 [201]   *proper down* really depressed

Chapter 4

1 [203]   *diaphanous* transparent, very thin

2 [204]   *emmet* ant

3 [204]   *the three creations* the creation of fowl and fishes, the beasts and man (Genesis 1)

4 [204]   *pint o' small* pint of light ale or beer

5 [205]   *mossel* morsel

6 [205]   *posted up* made up, entries transferred from day-book to ledger

7 [205]   *affronted* offended, by being sold bad meat

8 [205]   *da'ter* daughter

9 [206]   *mother-law* he means stepmother

10 [207]   *Midsummer* 24 June

11 [207] *in a mope* listless, depressed
12 [207] *studding* literally, studying, in a daydream
13 [207] *chapel-member* member of the Free Church, a dissenter
14 [207] *wamble* wander to and fro

Chapter 5

1 [208] *début* first appearance
2 [211] *a bonnet* was more old-fashioned than a hat
3 [212] *quoted a verse* a very free version of Psalm 44:17–18

Chapter 6

1 [213] *Ham-hill stone* from a hill-quarry near Yeovil in Somerset from which Hardy's stonemason father got a lot of his stone
2 [214] *japanning* a covering of hard varnish, originally brought from Japan
3 [215] *plinth* projecting part of wall immediately above the ground
4 [216] *aspen* a kind of poplar tree with tremulous leaves

Chapter 7

1 [219] *foot-post* a postman on foot who collected the letters
2 [219] *meads* meadows
3 [221] *hands* the measurement of horses' heights. A hand is just over 100 mm (4 inches)
4 [221] *twenty-five want a crown* £25, minus 5 shillings or 25p; £24·75
5 [221] *kip* keep
6 [221] *I turn . . . Grey's Bridge* Dick takes the path Hardy took for many years when going to and from Dorchester to school.
7 [222] *dace . . . and minnows* small freshwater fish

Part the Fifth

Chapter 1

1 [227] *'The Knot There's no Untying'* A quotation from a song by Thomas Campbell. See Introduction.
2 [227] *night-jar* a bird that frequents heathland with scattered trees and sings mostly at dusk or in the night from May onwards, its song being a distinctive churring trill
3 [227] *gnarled* twisted, an adjective usually applied to trees

4 [228] *steep* slope, precipice

5 [228] *banns* notice in church of intended marriage, read on three different Sundays to give opportunity of objection. This is what Mrs Penny means when later she talks about Dick and Fancy being 'called home in church'.

6 [229] *unceiled* the ceiling below not being plastered

7 [229] *lineaments* features

8 [229] *coling* embracing

9 [230] *sodger* soldier

10 [230] *churching* see note 11, p. 73

11 [231] *man-trap* iron spring-traps for trespassers and poachers, abolished by law in 1827

12 [232] *ting* Bee-keepers used to make a ringing sound to encourage their swarming bees.

13 [232] *ath'art and across* up and down; 'ath'art' literally means obliquely across

14 [232] *love . . . ox both* James is referring to Proverbs 15:17: 'Better is a dinner of herbs where love is, than a stalled ox and hatred therewith', and meaning that Dick and Fancy will have *both* true love and material benefits in their marriage. A stalled ox is one that is brought into its stall for fattening before being killed.

15 [233] *pupil-teacher* an older pupil who stayed on to help younger ones and continue her education as well

16 [233] *Vashti Sniff . . . Mercy Onmey* Hardy's sense of humour is shown even in his choice of proper names.

17 [233] *apotheosised* idealised

18 [234] *Het* hot

19 [234] *whole auditory* all the people present or all the listeners

20 [342] *'A' excellent sign'* The swarming of bees is a sign of the reproduction of the colony, so this could be a good omen for Dick and Fancy's fruitful marriage.

21 [235] *march two and two round the parish* an old local custom after weddings

22 [236] *Bath clogs* shoes with wooden soles made in Bath

23 [236] *He'th* Egdon Heath

24 [238] *arm in crook* in crook of elbow, arm in arm

25 [238] *Can a maid . . . attire* See Jeremiah 2:32.

26 [239] *Weatherbury stocks* a wooden frame with holes, in which wrongdoers were locked for periods of punishment, usually in some public place as here in Weatherbury or Puddletown

Chapter 2

1 [240] *avoid . . . 'thee' and 'thou'* Hardy's ironical treatment of the subject of Fancy's snobbery is shown in this passage. He did not approve of the decline of ancient dialects and ways of behaviour.

2 [241] *tambourine* small drum with metal discs attached

3 [241] *Tantrum Clangley* an imaginary village whose name suggests a lot of noise

4 [241] *gaffers and gammers* old men and women, literally grandfathers and grandmothers

5 [242] *reels* lively dances, usually of two couples in line, performing circular figures

6 [242] *hornpipes* dance usually connected with sailors

7 [243] *chainey* china

8 [243] *humps and hollers* ups and downs

9 [243] *sunsheen* sunshine

10 [243] *Chanticleer's comb is a-cut* Things are less showy. Canticleer is the traditional name for the farmyard cock with its red comb or crest.

11 [243] *put the stuns upon* check, hamper

12 [245] *old shoes* used to be tied to the newly-married pair's carriage to bring good luck

13 [245] *the nightingale* Much of Hardy's symbolism is connected with birds and here the nightingale's song is at one level an expression of human happiness, but Hardy may also have been thinking of the Greek Legend of Philomela, who was ravished by her brother-in-law and then had her tongue cut out so that she could tell no one what had happened to her. Philomela was eventually turned into a nightingale.

Also published by Macmillan

Thomas Hardy
The Making of Poetry

Edited by James Gibson

This audio-visual teaching programme explores an intriguing aspect of Thomas Hardy's world through a selection of his finest love poems.

Designed mainly for sixth formers, it consists of one 12 inch LP record, a 62 frame film strip, and a full set of teachers' notes, packed in a strong, attractive cardboard box.

It offers a well-integrated audio-visual study of the love poems, discussing their evolution from both an inspirational and constructional point of view. Photographs of the original manuscripts and subsequent revisions reveal the 'artist at work', and with the help of the biographical notes and readings on the record the imagery and craftmanship of the poems is investigated in such a way that the student is given a valuable insight into Hardy's literary talent.